About the Author

Gianna Schorno was born and raised in Zurich, Switzerland, where she completed her school and study years.

Her family origin is Italian among others, and she had always been a bit of a nomad.

She decided at a very early age to leave Switzerland, to travel, to work abroad and to explore the globe.

Her knowledge of various languages, her love for nature and her keen interest in getting to know different cultures, religions and life-styles, has taken her on many travels around the world.

She has lived in various countries, including Canada, Turkey, Dubai (UAE), Ecuador and Peru.

She developed her passion for writing during her time living in the Peruvian Amazon.

Her stories are based on real life experiences and also include many travel adventures and cultural aspects of the countries where she has lived and worked. She currently resides in the United Kingdom.

Dedication

To my beautiful friend Bilquees Hussain who I share many lovely memories with from our travel in Morocco.

And to my friend, the real Şenay, who I met during my time living in Turkey in 1992, and who was my inspiration for this novel.

Gianna Schorno

HAPPY MOON

An oriental tale of love, loss, deceit and family secrets

AUSTIN MACAULEY PUBLISHERS™
LONDON * CAMBRIDGE * NEW YORK * SHARJAH

Copyright © Gianna Schorno 2021

The right of Gianna Schorno to be identified as author of this work has been asserted by the author in accordance with section 77 and 78 of the Copyright, Designs and Patents Act 1988.

All rights reserved. No part of this publication may be reproduced, stored in a retrieval system, or transmitted in any form or by any means, electronic, mechanical, photocopying, recording, or otherwise, without the prior permission of the publishers.

Any person who commits any unauthorised act in relation to this publication may be liable to criminal prosecution and civil claims for damages.

This is a work of fiction. Names, characters, businesses, places, events, locales, and incidents are either the products of the author's imagination or used in a fictitious manner. Any resemblance to actual persons, living or dead, or actual events is purely coincidental.

A CIP catalogue record for this title is available from the British Library.

ISBN 9781398449763 (Paperback)
ISBN 9781398449770 (ePub e-book)

www.austinmacauley.com

First Published 2021
Austin Macauley Publishers Ltd®
1 Canada Square
Canary Wharf
London
E14 5AA

Acknowledgements

I would like to express a thank you to the friendliness and kindness of the Turkish people, and my friends who I met during my time of working in Turkey in the summer of 1992, and for introducing their culture and language to me. A big thank you also goes to the people of Morocco I have met during my travels in their country and for introducing their rich and amazing culture to me.

A big thank you goes also to my friend Jamie Sheppard for his input to the story and who was my inspiration for Yasmin's friend Albert.

A great thank you also goes to my lovely friend Bilquees Hussain, who was my inspiration for Yasmin's friend Naila, and who I shared many happy moments with during our travels in Morocco.

And a tremendous thank you goes to my friend Aman Soufi, who took her time to design the beautiful book cover for me. Aman is a young artist from Syria living in the UK, who does various paint work, including bookmarks, coasters, wooden boxes, among others, using her own designs. Her work can be found and bought on Etsy (www.etsy.com).

A great appreciation and thank you goes my dear friend Suzie Chaperlin for supporting me with my project and for proof-reading my novel to a professional standard.

And finally, a huge thank you to all my good friends for always encouraging me to continue writing, and to use my many travel experiences in my stories. The majority of this novel was written during the first lockdown that was introduced due to the outbreak of the worldwide Covid-19 virus (Coronavirus) crisis which occurred in the year 2020, and therefore, it was especially challenging to keep the motivation with the ongoing work and not to give up.

Table of Contents

Prologue	13
London, UK	14
Kusadasi, Turkey	18
A Trip to Manisa	27
Kusadasi, Turkey	39
The Deceit	43
Izmir, Turkey	48
Marrakesh, Morocco	56
Marrakesh, Morocco	68
Amel and Kareem	75
Marrakesh, Morocco	86
Marrakesh, Morocco	103
Marrakesh, Morocco April 2013	119
Unravelling the Truth	134
Metin's Fate	140
Yasmin's Fate	144
The Last Battle	149
Marrakesh, April 2013	160
A Clandestine Operation	163
Tahiri and Yasmin	172
Şenay – A Reunion April 2013	178
Epilogue	188
Glossary Expressions from Turkey and Morocco	193
Information	195

*An oriental tale of
betrayal, loss, love and family secrets*

Prologue

It was a clear night and a bright, silver moon was rising up in the night sky. It was June and already hot; the heat was a little unusual for the time of year and she was bathed in sweat. Her hospital gown was sticking to her body and her skin itched. She had woken up a few minutes ago, her head ached unbearably and her legs felt very weak. She was not sure how long she had been sleeping or if she had been sleeping at all.

She did hear her baby cry. She knew, just knew. No, she did not imagine it. She definitely had heard it. *Her baby*. Or was it only a vision in her delirium? Had she been dreaming it all? Did her mind play tricks? Was she going mad? No, no, no! She knew, her instincts told her, she had not been dreaming, and the bright silver moon she saw shining through the window in the night sky had been her witness.

A heavy sob rose in her throat and she felt as if her heart was being ripped apart. She bit into her hand so that she would not scream. What had happened to her? She knew with certainty that they had been lying to her. She was exhausted from the long labour and after she had been given the anaesthetics for the childbirth, she could not remember anything at all.

Where was her baby? It was as she had never given birth, never been pregnant. When she looked around her, she realised with a shock that she had been moved to another room. She realised she was no longer in the maternity ward and there were no other women in the room. She was alone.

She felt hot tears falling down her cheek. Where was her love? He had promised to be there for the birth. They had big plans. They had planned to return to Europe to start a new life after the baby was born. It had all been arranged. He had promised her. She had believed him. She knew he had never lied to her. He loved her. She knew she could trust him. But where was her husband? And where was her beautiful baby?

What had happened to her baby?

London, UK
June 1991

Yasmin was looking out of her tiny bedroom's window, of her student flat, to the traffic humming below in the busy street in Ealing, a Borough in West London, that had been her home for the past three years. When she reflected on her study years, she knew they had been the best years of her life. She loved this city that was never sleeping. London, always bustling with its constant noise of traffic, sirens and tourists from all over the world rushing around and all over, had become part of her. There was never a time when London slowed down. It was so unlike the small town in the county of Dorset in the West Country where she had grown up. It was lovely there, beautiful countryside, coastal walks and it was a nice seaside town, but here in London, she felt the taste of the big world, the opportunities, and the international vibe. It was preparing her to venture out and explore other countries and cultures through her work in the future.

It was a bright and sunny spring day in late June 1991, and Yasmin felt on top of the world. When the postman delivered her an envelope early that morning, she knew in an instant what it contained. As soon as she had heard him pushing it through the letterbox, she had rushed down the stairs to pick it up. Feeling so excited, she almost fell down the stairs. Nothing could stop her now! She was ready to conquer the world!

Back in her room, she clutched her university exam results in Tourism, Hotel and Catering business in her hand and jumped high in the air.

"I've done it! Yes, yes, yes!" she shouted happily at her reflection in the large mirror of her wardrobe.

She did not mind if her flatmates saw or heard her. No, she thought, she had made it through the tough university years and now she was officially a graduate. She would receive her diploma soon at the graduation ceremony that was taking place in July.

"Are you all right, Yaz? Got some good news?"

The blonde head of her friend and flatmate of the past two years, Albert, appeared in the doorframe of her room. He took one look at her happy face and knew at once that she had received her results that she was waiting for and that they were positive.

He grinned, feeling proud of his friend. "Don't say. I can see it! It's written all over your face! You got the results back?"

"Yes! Albert, I've made it! I've made it! I'm so happy and I want to celebrate! The stress is finally over! Look!" she exclaimed and held her diploma under his nose.

Albert, also in his final year, training to be a Chef, and busy himself with the approaching final exams was excited for his friend. He knew how much hard work she had put into her degree. He stepped into the room and hugged her tight.

"Congrats and well done! I'm so proud of you, girl! I never doubted you would pass. You were so dedicated and really burnt the midnight oil. You're an inspiration for others, I can tell you! It's a great birthday present for you too!"

"Yes, it's my best birthday gift ever! And it'll make my parents happy too. I can't wait to tell them! They'll be looking forward to coming to London for my graduation. And now it's your turn. Hope your exams go well too," Yasmin said encouragingly to her friend.

"Oh, I know, and believe me, I'll be soooo glad when it's over! Now, tell me, what's your first step? Are you going to look for a job right away? Where are you going to look for a job? I remember you saying a cruise ship contract would be your first choice to get some experience under your belt, right?"

"Oh, definitely, yes. I've decided that I'm going to look at either a cruise ship company that cruises the Mediterranean or perhaps the Caribbean, whatever is available really and depending on who will take me on. It'll give me the experience I need because I want to be a Food and Beverage Manager in the future."

"I love your ambition! You'll be successful, I'm totally sure of it. The world is open to you now," Albert said.

"I hope so, yes. But I think I'll only do one or two contracts on the cruise ship. After that, I'm going to look for a new challenge in one of the major hotel chains in Asia or maybe in South America, again depending on where they have some vacancies. It's been my dream forever. But first, I'm going to have a little, well-earned holiday!" She laughed, her pretty green eyes sparkling like diamonds.

"Good for you girl! Let me know when you head off for your first job, and we're going to give you a good sending off. Nothing better than a good leaving party, mate!"

"We will; the hard work will definitely have to be celebrated. When I leave please stay in touch, maybe we can work together sometime, somewhere in the world. That would be so cool," Yasmin smiled at her friend.

"Of course! That goes without saying. One day, I promise you, I'm going to be a celebrity Chef and have my own business. Then you can be my Food and Beverage Manager! Sorry, got to rush, my shift is starting soon. Bye, Yaz, see you later!"

Laughing and happy for his friend, Albert left her room and disappeared down the hall. She heard the door slam shut as he left for his shift.

"Yes, nothing would stop me! See you soon and have a good day!" Yasmin called after him and sat down on her bed, still smiling.

Albert was right. It was her birthday in July and she would now have two reasons to celebrate. Firstly, she was turning 21, a big birthday in the UK because this was when you officially came of age, and the second reason was that her graduation ceremony would take place just a week before her birthday. It was perfect timing.

She stared at her reflection in the long mirror in her room and liked what she saw. *Yes, girl,* she said to herself, *after a little and well-earned holiday to recover from my stressful studies, I will concentrate on finding my first proper job as a professional. And it will definitely be on a cruise ship.*

She knew that it would give her sufficient experience to move on to her dream job in one of the major hotels in the world as a Food and Beverage Manager. She would decide later whether she was going to continue to work on the ship for another six months, once she was more familiar with her work. Now was not the time to worry about this. There was something very important she needed to do first.

She got up and fetched her handbag from her desk. She fished some coins out of her purse to call her parents from the downstairs payphone to give them the good news. They had been patiently waiting for their only daughter's success in her graduation, knowing very well the passion and dedication Yasmin had shown for her chosen profession. She could not wait for her parents to see her in the black gown on her graduation day and to throw the hat in the air like she had seen people do at many graduations before her. They would be very proud of their daughter for this achievement. Both her mother and her father, as well as her grandparents, came from humble Italian backgrounds and neither of them was an academic. Their daughter's success and the fact that she attended university, was even more special to them. She was the first in her family who had gone to university.

Downstairs, Yasmin inserted the coins into the payphone and dialled her parents' number and waited for the dialling tone. It was answered after only a couple of rings as if her parents had been sitting next to the phone waiting for it to ring. She could barely speak because of her excitement.

"Mamma, Papá, guess what! I've done it! I've just received the good news! I've passed my exams and I'm a graduate!"

Kusadasi, Turkey
April 1992
A New Chapter Begins

Yasmin woke with a start. Groaning, she cast a glance over to the clock on her nightstand. It told her it was 5 am. When would she get used to this? From the loudspeaker of the 'Kaleiçi Cami', the little mosque situated next door to the house where she lived in the narrow street, 'Bahar Sokak', the Muezzin was calling the faithful to the morning prayer, the 'Fajr'. She loved the sound of the 'Adhan', the Islamic call to prayer five times a day. It always sounded mystical to her.

But it was so very loud when you lived right next to the loudspeakers of a mosque. Due to the heat, she was always sleeping with the window open. Despite only being late April on the west coast of Turkey and being near the sea, the temperature had risen and it felt like the summer's heat already. Her long, silk nightdress was clinging to her body.

Yasmin sighed, sat up and swung her legs out of the narrow bed. There was no point in trying to get back to sleep. She longed for a strong, Turkish coffee and a 'simit' (A round Turkish bread) before she would get ready for work.

She loved her new job at the 'Grand Hotel Ephesus', a big, luxury hotel overlooking the bay of Kusadasi with its pigeon island, the 'Güvercinada', next to the jetty where the big cruise ships moored. The hotel where she worked hosted three restaurants, a lovely, large garden lined with exotic plants and trees, a 'Hammam' (Turkish bath) and a large, kidney-shaped swimming pool that also the staff were allowed to use in their spare time. Yasmin loved swimming and it was her first morning activity before work. It made her feel alive and fit and besides, it was a good start to the day. However, the best of all, it was Metin, her fiancé, who joined her on her daily morning swim. How she loved this precious hour together!

She buttered her 'simit' and rummaged around her side of the cupboard to find the honey to go with it. The aroma of the coffee pleasantly filled her nose. She filled her coffee mug with the strong Turkish coffee she loved so much, grabbed it and sat down at the small wooden table in the kitchen of the tiny flat she shared with three of her colleagues from the hotel.

While she sipped her coffee, her thoughts travelled back to the cruise ship where she had worked right after her graduation. The events that unfolded just before her contract had ended happened so quickly and since then, she had barely had any time to catch her breath.

Shortly after her graduation ceremony in July, which her parents had attended, and after an extensive job search, she had received a seven-month contract for the job she had applied for to work on a cruise ship. The ship was set to tour the Mediterranean Sea, via Italy, Croatia, some of the Greek islands and even venture as far as the Turkish west coast. They were due to set sail as early as August. How lucky she was, she thought, to be given this opportunity and to start her career in such a special way!

On a hot summer's morning in August 1991, feeling excited and clutching her two suitcases, Yasmin boarded the large cruise-liner 'New Millennium' that was docked at the port of Southampton in Hampshire.

Wow, she thought when she looked up to this huge vessel from the pier; *this massive 7-storey cruise liner is going to be my 'home' for the next seven months.*

As part of her contract and introduction pack, the recruitment company had given her instructions and the entry code to her room on the ship and she was all set for her new job that started the following day. She pulled her suitcases through the long and steep gangway that let up to the cruise liner but just as she wanted to step off the gangway, she tripped and lost the handle of one of her suitcases and nearly fell headlong onto the deck.

"Whoa, watch out, Miss, steady! Please let me help you." She heard a male voice say behind her and a hand grabbed her arm at once to stop her from falling.

Astonished and a bit shaken, she looked up and straight into the face of a handsome young man with wavy, black hair and keen, friendly, dark-brown eyes. He was of slim build but muscular, and only a little taller than her. She noticed that he had darker skin than someone who might be European and guessed that he must have a Mediterranean origin. He was dressed in beige trousers and a blue short-sleeved shirt. The colour of his shirt looked very attractive against his skin. She stood up and stretched her back.

"Oh, I'm ever so sorry! Thank you every so much for catching me, I nearly fell! So embarrassing and I haven't even started working yet! But my suitcases are a little heavy," She laughed and gathered her bags.

"No problem, Miss. I'm happy to help. By the way, I'm Metin. I'm working on this cruise liner as an Assistant Restaurant Manager," he introduced himself in excellent English.

"And I'm Yasmin, nice to meet you too! I'm also coming to work on this ship and today is my first day, well, I start work tomorrow really but today I'm just checking in. Hence the confusion as I'm trying to find my way around the ship and to my cabin."

"Let me help you then with your luggage and to find your cabin, Yasmin. I know my way around by now as I have been working here for a few months. It's a bit daunting when you first come onto the ship, I know. Just follow me," He smiled and grabbed the handle of the larger one of her suitcases.

"Thank you very much, you're ever so kind. They are a little heavy, to be honest. I feel I've packed bricks!"

As they made their way through the maze of the aisles on the floor where the cabins of the staff were located, she was curious to know more about his handsome guy and plucked up her courage to make conversation with him.

"I hope you don't mind me asking. Where are you from? Are you Italian or perhaps Spanish? I noticed you have a Mediterranean look about you," she ventured.

"No, not at all. I don't mind you asking. Well, I am Mediterranean, you could say. I'm originally from Turkey, from a city near Izmir which is located on the west coast of the country," he educated her.

"Oh lovely, so I guess almost correctly," she said.

"Do you know Turkey by any chance? Have you ever been to my country?"

"No, I've never been to Turkey. Or not yet, I should say. But I'm good at geography which is rather important in my job, and therefore, I know where Izmir is located. It must be really nice there. It's right by the sea, isn't it?"

"Yes, it is a pretty place and it has a large international port as well," Metin confirmed. He was looking at her and instantly felt a rush of attraction flow through his body.

"Forgive me for asking you, I don't want to appear rude but are you English? It is just that you don't look very English to me, so I was wondering."

Metin had stopped and observed her, wondering about her exotic look with her long black hair and deep green eyes. She definitely did not have the look of an English rose.

Yasmin smiled, being used to this type of comment. "No, you're totally right. I am actually of Italian origin. My parents are Italian, from the north of the country but I was brought up here in England, in a small town on the west coast by the sea, in the county of Dorset in fact. But I went to university in London and also graduated there."

Metin nodded and smiled, revealing a set of immaculately white teeth. "Oh, I see, so I guessed right, too."

True to his word, Metin helped her to find her cabin in no time. It said in her contract that she was to share her small cabin with another girl and was hoping she would be nice and they would become friends.

"So, here we are," Metin announced and put down her suitcase in front of the room. "I hope you'll enjoy your job here. It's a great and amazing experience but also very hard work. We don't get much free time either. But it's actually a very cosmopolitan environment. You'll meet people from all over the world. I like it for this reason."

Yasmin nodded. "Yes, I know it must be hard work. But it is my first job after university and I've just had a couple of weeks off after my graduation, so I'm prepared. I'm going to work as an Assistant Food and Beverage Manager and I'm using this job opportunity to gain experience during these coming months."

"How long are you planning to work on the cruise ship, do you think?" Metin was interested.

"I haven't actually thought it quite through yet but I think I'm just going to do just this one contract. I'll see how it goes but it might be enough to give me the experience."

"Have you already got any ideas yet about your plans for later?"

"Oh yes, after this contract, I want to find a job as a Food and Beverage Manager in a big hotel somewhere in the world. I haven't decided on a country though, that depends on the vacancies obviously. But believe it or not, it has been my dream since I was a child and I have studied hard for it!"

Metin was truly impressed by this young ambitious lady and her big plans. "That's brilliant and very impressive."

"And what about you? What are your plans?" Yasmin asked Metin.

"Well, it's a little bit like yours, actually. You see, my parents own a restaurant in Turkey, not far from Izmir, and eventually, I'll be taking over their business. That's why I'm also gaining experience on this ship because it's a very international environment and it will help me later on to cope with all the tourists we get in Turkey, as well as gaining managerial experience. It's already my second contract on the cruise liner, you see."

"Wow! That's brilliant and big plans for your future. I hope it'll go well for you," Yasmin said.

She started feeling a little bit exhausted with all the excitement and wanted to unpack and freshen up. Then she planned to get her bearings on the ship and find the restaurant where she was going to be placed at in order to introduce herself to her new boss.

"Right, sorry to cut our conversation a little short but I'd better get on with it, as I have all my unpacking to do and then have a shower. I already feel so hot! Or maybe it's just the excitement. I just hope I'll find my way to the restaurant and then back to my cabin! It's all a little overwhelming right now," She laughed.

"Don't worry, you'll be all right. All you have to remember is which floor your cabin is on and whether it's at the beginning or the end of the aisle, and you should be able to find it. See, we are right at the back of the first aisle, coming from the middle lift and the big staircase. By the way, I live on the same floor, just on the other side. If you want a tour of the ship and maybe have a coffee sometime, just come and knock on my cabin door, it is number 512. I'd love to show you around. It takes a while getting used to this kind of working environment."

He smiled at Yasmin and his face lit up. He looked even more handsome. Then, almost shyly as if he was not quite sure if it was welcomed, he extended his hand to her. Without hesitation, she shook his hand, then turned around and went on his way to his own cabin.

This encounter with Metin on her first day on board the cruise liner had been the beginning of a beautiful friendship. No, it was much than that and she would never have dreamed that she would meet the man of her dreams on the first day of her first job. It was more than she could have dreamed of.

The restaurant where she was going to work was called 'Crystal Palace' and it was situated on the top deck. It served mainly Mediterranean cuisine. She had to take an elevator to reach it. Although she was mainly in the office, which was situated just across from the restaurant, she was expected to help out during busy lunch and dinner times, as well as behind the bar, which would help her gain more experience in the business.

A few days after Yasmin had started her new job, it was her first day off. She considered herself lucky because normally you didn't get any time off. But because she had just graduated, they had asked her to look through some cocktail recipes and learn how to make them. For the rest of the day, she was free.

After she had revised the lecture, it was already early afternoon and Metin turned up at her cabin and offered to give her the promised tour of the ocean liner. When they were exploring, Yasmin was amazed that this cruise ship was almost like a city of its own. It was seven stories high and there were elevators at the back and front of the ship to take you to each area.

There was a large swimming pool on the top deck with slides for the children and a decking area for sunbathing, as well as two hot tubs. When they explored the other areas, she came across two casinos, plenty of shops of all kinds including jewellery shops, three hairdressers, ten restaurants with different types of cuisines ranging from Indian to Sushi, from Chinese and Mediterranean to Mexican among others and even a wine tasting venue, six bars, a theatre offering various shows, as well as several cafes and chill out areas. The wellness area consisted of two large gyms with spas, tanning studios and saunas. There were also two cinemas and even a library. It all looked more like a huge shopping centre than a ship.

"That's absolutely incredible! I never would have imagined the scale of it. You could live here for quite some time and never have to leave the ship," Yasmin said in awe when they had sat down in one of the many cafes to enjoy a cappuccino and a cake.

"See, I've told you! It's a real experience and when I first arrived, I reacted just like you."

"You must think I'm like a child," Yasmin laughed. "But it's just very overwhelming."

"No, don't worry, it's normal. I sometimes think it's a miracle that such a vessel can actually cruise the seas. I thought it gives you a better idea of the place and where to find things when you walk around a bit. At first, it's a bit of a maze but you'll get used to it quickly," Metin said.

After this initial tour, there had been many more and they had also enjoyed some walks on the top deck which gave an amazing view of the vast ocean. It was on one of those walks that they also discovered their common interest of swimming. And when Metin asked her if she would like to go swimming before work, she had readily agreed. So, they had started their daily ritual of swimming before their shift, if they happened to have similar work schedules.

Yasmin's roommate, Carol, had joined her only a day after she had arrived. She was a pleasant English girl, a year older than her, and great fun. They had become good friends after a short time. Carol was also a graduate but as a chef, and she had told Yasmin it was her first job too.

Yasmin was happy to have found a friend, especially of her own age group, with who she could share a lot of stories from their university days. Before leaving the cruise ship after seven months, both of them off to new adventures in other parts of the world, they felt sad that their experience and time together had already ended. When they had hugged on their last day before leaving the cruise liner, they promised each other to stay in touch.

Yasmin snapped out of her daydreaming state and took another sip of her coffee. She reflected on her life. In less than one year, she had come far. She had graduated in her home country, worked on a cruise ship for seven months, then moved from her first job on the ship to a new role as a Food and Beverage Manager in a different country, and the best part of it was that she was now engaged! She smiled to herself. She considered herself a very lucky girl.

It was only a couple of weeks after she had started working on the ship that she and Metin had started dating and when both their contracts had come to an end in February the following year, he had suggested to move together to his home country, Turkey. He told her about his childhood friend Kasun, who was one of the Managers working in a big hotel in the western coastal town of Kusadasi which was a busy and thriving tourist spot.

"You know, Kasun is very professional, extremely experienced, and he will be able to help you with a job as a Food and Beverage Manager. We've known each other for a long time. He is trustworthy and it will be a great career move for you, trust me," Metin had told her; it didn't take long to convince her to make the decision to move with Metin to Turkey.

Before they left, another special event had been waiting for Yasmin. It was on their last night on the ocean liner when she had experienced the biggest surprise of all; Metin had proposed to her! They were standing on the upper deck looking out to the vast ocean, under a bright full moonlit night on the Mediterranean Sea. As if by magic, he had produced a ring and asked her to become his wife. Yasmin had quite literally been over the moon.

"Yes, Metin, I accept! I would really love to become your wife. But is it not a bit early to get married?" she had asked him.

She was a little concerned to move too fast because she was still very young. She was four years younger than Metin and had only turned 21 a few months before.

"We've only known each other for a few months, Metin. We haven't even lived together. And I want to work for a while too, before starting a family."

She cupped his face into her hands and added gently, "And I want to introduce you to my parents too as soon as we dock and get off the cruise ship in the UK. I have told them so much about you. They are curious to meet you and obviously, they want to see me happy."

Metin took her into his arms and held her tight. He felt so much love for her. He waited for a moment and his body savoured the experience to smell her hair and her smooth skin before he spoke again.

"Of course, that's important, sweetheart, and of course, I want to meet them too. But don't worry, Yasmin, we don't have to get married straight away. We can get to know each other better, that's not a problem."

Yasmin looked up to him. "Thank you, my love, it means a lot to me."

"The only thing is, you see, in my culture, as you know I'm Muslim, we will have to get married in order to live together. We don't have the freedom you have in your culture and we cannot just move in together as you do in your part of the world. Our faith does not accept that. We'll have to marry the woman so that she is protected, especially if we live in my country."

Yasmin nodded. "Yes, I do understand, my love, but just let me get used to my new life a little, the new environment and the job. Also, I want to learn more about your religion and the Turkish language, so that I can communicate. If you could teach me and introduce me to your customs, that would help me so much. Would you do this for me?"

"Don't worry, Yaz, I will. Seni seviyorum, I love you. Once we are both working and you're used to your new environment and my country, I will take you to my hometown Manisa and introduce you to my parents. We will make it official then. Just a little warning, they can be a bit old-fashioned but don't worry. It is me you are getting married to, not them. For now, we are engaged and that's already a big step in the right direction. I'll always protect you and love you. I want to make you the happiest woman in the world."

He had kissed her gently and Yasmin had accepted Metin's proposal. She was in an emotional whirlpool and never in her young life had she felt happier. She loved Metin and he treated her well. They were planning to set the date for their wedding for the following year so that they would have enough time to organise their big day.

Organised by Metin's friend, Kasun, Yasmin had been offered her dream job. She had started her new job as a Food and Beverage Manager at the 'Grand Hotel Ephesus' in Kusadasi the following month after they had left the cruise ship, and taken a week off to visit her parents in Dorset to introduce her fiancé before they moved to Turkey together.

Her parents were kind people and sensed immediately that Metin was a genuine and caring man and wanted to make their daughter happy. They had taken to him the straight way. Giovanni and Paola knew their daughter Yasmin well and that her work meant the world to her. Ever since she was a little girl, she had always been talking about wanting to explore the globe. Now, her profession would give her the opportunity to do so. Her parents would not stand in her way to work abroad, even if that meant they would not see their only daughter for quite some time.

A Trip to Manisa

Yasmin drained her coffee and looked at the clock. Oh dear, it's time to get dressed and then off to work, she realised. *No more daydreaming now*, she scolded herself back to reality. She walked over to the sink and quickly washed her cup. The sun was shining brightly through the window, promising a hot day, despite only being early April.

It was still early morning when she left the house, and the shops in the bazaar she usually passed on her way were closed; they opened around 9 am, some of them a little later. As she passed the Caravansary hotel on the main square, she noticed that a few simit sellers were on their way through, pushing their little trolleys through town. She knew some of them and as they smiled at her, she greeted them with the Turkish hello 'Merhaba'. However, the early mornings were nothing like the hustle and bustle of the evenings when all the shops, restaurants, bars, nightclubs and streets were packed with tourists and you could hardly find your way through.

Yasmin always enjoyed her walk to work in the morning. It gave her the opportunity to see the town that had become her new home in a different light. She was still getting used to the different smells, the exotic birds, the fresh sea air, and the new language she didn't yet understand, so different from hers. She loved the old streets, the colourful Mediterranean flowers and plants, the esplanade, the ancient buildings like the 'hammam', the Turkish bath she started using in town, and the small mosques with their shady, cool courtyards. Even the sunsets were different here. They were pink and purple and red. She had never seen anything like it. Often, she wondered what this town had been like before it became such a popular tourist hotspot. Probably a small, quiet fishing village, she assumed.

There were many beaches out of town as well for the tourists to enjoy. One street was even called the 'Bar Street' with, as the name suggests, many bars and pubs, even English and Irish ones that were frequented not only by tourists but also by the locals. Plenty of leather stores were selling their produce at very reasonable prices and it was good quality. Turkish food was, as she had already learnt, among the best in the world. She tried a different dish every day and the fish dishes had become her favourites. Turkish people seemed to be great linguists too. Many spoke several foreign languages, such as German, French, Spanish and Italian. She had never encountered any Turkish person with who she was unable to communicate since she also was multilingual.

When she was turning into the street that took her along the harbour and in direction to the hotel where she worked, the 'Grand Hotel Ephesus', she saw there was a cruise ship on the dock. A radiant smile crossed her lovely face when she looked over to the big ship. She paused for a moment and felt a rush of nostalgia and excitement flow through her body, remembering her own experience on a cruise ship when they had also docked here. In a year's time, she would be married to the love of her life. When she had applied for that first job on the cruise liner after her graduation, which seemed a lifetime ago, she would never have dreamed that this decision would change her life so completely.

Smiling to herself, she adjusted her sunglasses and carried on to her workplace. After a few more minutes, she arrived at the steps that led up to the front of the hotel, quickly climbed up to the entrance, and then crossed the lobby to the rear entrance where the swimming pool was located. She saw that Metin was already in the pool.

"There you are, love! Sorry, I started swimming already because I came quite early," Metin shouted and waved to her from the pool and swam with large strokes to the edge and climbed out of the water. He attempted to embrace her.

Yasmin laughed and stepped back, trying to keep the distance from his dripping body. "Oh no, no! Don't even think about it! I won't touch you right now. I can't get my dress wet. I'll be with you in a minute." And she rushed off to change into her swimming suit.

Metin smiled mischievously and leapt back into the water. Yasmin joined him a few minutes later. She was always looking forward to their morning ritual. It kept them both fit and healthy. After a while when they had finished their exercise, Metin waited for her at the edge of the pool. She swam up to him and joined him.

"I have some news for us, love," he announced, shaking the water out of his hair.

"Oh, really, have you? I hope it's good news. What is it?"

"Yes, I do. Remember when I said I would like to take you to my hometown to introduce you to my parents? Do you remember what my hometown is called?"

"Erm, let me see… Oh yes, I do remember actually! It's Manisa, isn't it?"

"Well done, it is Manisa. I'm impressed. Love, I have made arrangements for us to go in May to introduce you to my parents and to tell them about our engagement. It's not so far from here, so we can go for a long weekend and I'll rent a car. This way we'll be much quicker than catching a bus. By the way, I have already spoken to Fűgen, so don't worry about getting the time off. It's all been arranged with her."

He looked at her expectantly. Yasmin studied her fiancé. She saw in his face that he was genuinely pleased about having it all already arranged. *It must be his culture,* she thought. But she was surprised that it would happen so soon. Fűgen was Yasmin's direct boss, a fair supervisor and a very kind woman. Of course, she would not stand in her way of happiness if it was to meet her parents-in-law and to get her wedding preparations rolling.

"You have already spoken with Fűgen? Why didn't you ask me before?"

"Well, I thought you would be pleased if I'd arrange it," Metin said, taken a little bit aback and a sad expression was creeping into his handsome face.

Yasmin smiled and kissed him on the cheek. "Oh, don't worry, I didn't mean to upset you, my love, it's all right. I just thought I'd ask Fűgen myself because I thought it better came from me regarding having some time off. After all, I haven't been working here so long, that's all."

"So, it's okay then?" Metin looked at her with a hopeful expression.

"Yes, of course, it is. Don't worry. I just need to prepare myself a little to meet my parents-in-law. Okay then, Manisa, here we come!"

They left the swimming pool together and started their busy working day. However, Yasmin could not shake off a nagging feeling that started to creep into her heart. It was a strange sensation that something in their lives would soon change. She could not put her finger on it but being an intuitive person, she knew deep in her heart that something was not quite as it should be. Yet there was nothing she could do about it, so she let her fear go.

A few weeks later, Yasmin and Metin were sitting in a rental car on their way to the small town of Manisa. Yasmin did her best to conceal her feeling of anxiety and tried to look forward to the trip, their first outing together. She had not been to any other place than Kusadasi since they had arrived in Turkey to start their jobs.

"How far is it to Manisa?" She wanted to know when they had left Kusadasi behind.

"Well, I'd say, it's approx. 120 miles from Kusadasi. The drive will take us through Izmir. We can stop there if you like to check it out? It's quite an attractive town actually and we could go on a harbour cruise."

"Maybe on the way back?" suggested Yasmin, "I think we should go to Manisa first, if you don't mind? Your parents might be expecting us soon, I assume."

"Okay, no worries, that's fine with me. We'll have a bit of time when we return if we leave early on Monday morning," Metin agreed.

For the rest of the journey, Yasmin enjoyed watching the interesting landscape of her fiancé's beautiful country. For a while, they were driving along the Aegean coast before their route would take them inland and away from the coast for a while up to Izmir. The sea was deep blue, shimmering brightly in the sunlight and there was not a single cloud in the sky; it was a gorgeous sight. She noticed a few small fishing boats and yachts out on the sea, bobbing on the waves. The view was very peaceful. Before coming to this country, she had never imagined that Turkey was so beautiful.

It was already early afternoon when they arrived in the small town of Manisa. During their trip, Metin had filled her in with a bit of history.

"Manisa is an old establishment, you know, which was founded 3,500 years ago. It was one of the oldest historical cities in Turkey," he told her. She had also learnt that the surroundings of the city embraced a richly forested area, including some hot springs that provided great opportunities for camping.

Metin's parents lived in a two-storey house on the outskirts of the town near another big park. It was a quiet area, although it was only a short drive into the busy town centre, the main mosque and the markets.

"Here we are, love, my parent's house," he announced suddenly, stopping the car in front of the entrance door next to a large, black SUV. It must be his father's car, Yasmin assumed, given the size of it.

It was a typical Turkish-style detached house, painted white and on the top floor, there was an attractive round balcony with wrought-iron railings, overlooking the driveway. There were red flowers hanging from the balcony.

The place looked almost too quiet. Metin pulled into the short driveway and switched off the engine.

"So, this is where you grew up?" Yasmin took in the sight. It looked pleasant enough and certainly upper-middle-class for this country. She remembered that Metin told her his father owned a restaurant in the town centre. They were certainly not poor. The car looked like a fairly recent model too.

"Yes, this is where I have spent my childhood and some of my study years. We moved here when I was a small boy. See that balcony on the top floor? The room next to it on the right-hand side? That was my room when I was still in school. I could always check from the window who was coming. It was brilliant," He laughed. "But later, they gave me the larger room with the balcony. It was nice to study outside when it wasn't cold."

They climbed out of the car and Metin unloaded their carry-on suitcases from the boot. Just as they stepped up to the front door, it opened, and a tall, slim man stood in the doorway. He had dark hair like Metin but shorter and with some streaks of white in it, and a short beard. He looked like a man with authority. Behind him, a woman appeared. Metin's mother was a bit shorter than her husband and she looked in her mid-forties. She was wearing light coloured blue jeans, a dark red blouse and matching the blouse, a red hijab, a headscarf. This surprised Yasmin because in Kusadasi, where they were working, none of the women there were wearing hijabs.

She wondered why Metin had never mentioned that her parents were very traditional. She also knew that in Islam wearing a hijab or niqab was more of a tradition, not an obligation, and many modern women chose not to wear one, especially if they lived in larger cities. A worrying thought crossed her mind. Did they perhaps expect her to wear a headscarf too? Or did they expect her to convert to Islam? She was not quite ready for this change yet, and she would not wear a hijab, no matter what.

Yasmin smiled at both of them. So, these were her future parents-in-law, Hassan and Selda Özgűr. Metin's mother rushed to Metin and took him into her arms. "Merhaba, my son! I'm so happy to see you! Come on in!" she exclaimed.

Yasmin was left standing in the driveway with her suitcase and didn't know how to react. *Why did they not greet her? Were they not happy to meet their son's fiancé? Was she perhaps improperly dressed?* She had taken great care in the morning before they left to choose her dress and made sure it was not revealing too much of her body. She had decided on a long summer dress, bright yellow with large flowers printed on it. She was wearing open sandals that she had purchased just the week before.

Metin embraced his father too, then turned around and faced her. "Please Yasmin, meet my parents."

"Baba, Anne, mum, dad, this is my fiancé, Yasmin, who I have told you so much about."

"Merhaba, Mrs and Mr Özgűr," Yasmin said politely and stretched out her hand.

Both his father and mother shook her hand but the dismissive look they gave her taking in her western outfit made Yasmin feel very uncomfortable. They both said, "Hello, pleased to meet you. Come in. I will show you to your room."

Although, she knew that in Muslim countries you were not allowed to sleep in the same room with your partner, if you were not married, it still took her a bit by surprise. They were officially engaged and she had expected to be in the same room with him. But this was his house, not hers, so she had to follow their rules. She looked at Metin and he nodded.

"It's okay. Please make yourself comfortable and freshen up, if you like, sweetheart. The room has an en-suite. I'll come up to see you shortly. You can unpack later, there is no rush. We will have tea soon. Your favourite 'elma chai'."

Yasmin forced a smile and nodded, and then she followed his mother up the steps that led up to the first floor and was shown into a large, pleasant-looking guest room with a double-bed. At the far end of the room, there was a wide window. She put her suitcase down. "Thank you very much, Mrs Özgűr," she managed.

"There is a towel on the bed for you to use when you have a bath. And drinking water is on the table over there by the window. I'll see you later for tea in the lounge," said Mrs Özgűr and then she was gone.

Yasmin suddenly felt very alone. She closed the bedroom door, then took her suitcase over to the bed and slowly began to unpack. She had a nagging feeling in her stomach that this visit was not going to go well. She had hoped so much that her fiancé's parents would accept her. Metin had told her that his parents could be a little old-fashioned but she didn't expect hostility. She had even been looking forward to meeting them and had bought 'Locum', Turkish Delight, as a present for them that they could share for dessert.

She could not understand what the issue was. After all, Metin's parents knew how they had met and that they were engaged to be married. Were they insulted because they had got engaged without involving them? They did not want a big ceremony and therefore had only invited two friends as witnesses to their engagement.

A tear rolled down her cheek. She brushed it away. No, she thought fiercely, she would not be defeated and she would marry Metin, no matter what. He loved her. She knew that with absolute certainty. And she loved him. That's what mattered. She would fight for her rights. It was hot in the room, so she stepped over her suitcase and went over to the window to let some air in. She opened it wide and a pleasantly warm afternoon breeze greeted her.

The room was at the back of the house and she realised that it was overlooking the big park they skirted around when they approached Metin's parents' house earlier on. Tall trees at the borders of the park were swaying in the breeze and it soothed her to look at them.

Suddenly, she was aware of a noise but she could not place where it came from. She heard what seemed raised voices. She was wondering where the voices came from. She stepped closer to the window, stood quietly and listened carefully.

She became aware that her room must be right above the lounge and that it was Metin and his parents who were shouting at each other. But as they were speaking rapidly in Turkish and her basic knowledge of the language did not give her enough understanding of what the subject was, she could not follow the conversation.

Then for some strange reason Metin suddenly switched to English and yelled, "No, I have told you that I'm going to marry Yasmin! I love her and I have told you many times that I have my own life! I have lived and worked in the western world! Things are changing and you just have to get used to this!"

"This woman is not a Muslim! And she is from Europe. She is not from our culture! Europeans have no sense of decency. And look the way she is dressed!"

"So what? There is nothing wrong with her outfit, it's perfectly decent. I'm allowed to make my own decisions! It's my own judgement and MY feelings. Things are changing, father, we don't live in the Ottoman Empire anymore."

Then Yasmin heard Mr Özgür shouting again. Yasmin had not even known that he spoke such perfect English.

"She will NOT be my daughter-in-law and you will NOT marry this woman, son! We have found you a nice, educated Turkish Muslim woman. She is from an affluent family, good friends of mine, and you will do well with her. It will help our business too. You will marry this woman as you are told. You are my only son and you are to take over my restaurant. We have planned this for you for a long time."

"No, father, I will not marry this other woman, no matter who she is or how rich she is. I don't care. I love Yasmin. She is the one for me. Religion does not matter. Religion is a personal matter. I cannot force her to become Muslim. If she wants to, it'll be her choice and I will support her. But I will not force her to do anything. She is a good person, even if she is a Christian. Her parents are good, decent people, and she is well-educated with a university degree and speaks several languages."

"That's not the point, son. Is this how you repay us for our sacrifices? Is this how you thank us for all we have done for you?"

"Oh yes, it is the point. I'm old enough to make my own deci…," Metin shouted back but could not finish his sentence, his father cut him off.

"Then we will disinherit you. We will have no choice. You will never own my restaurant. I will not allow it. You will not get any money. This is my final word," Mr Özgűr shouted.

Yasmin still stood by the window, frozen and unable to move. She was totally dumbfounded. So, this was what it was all about, because she was not a Muslim and of European origin. In fact, his parents had already chosen a Turkish woman for Metin and arranged a marriage for him, without even telling him. Or did they? Maybe he had known about this all along. But then why did he never say anything to her? At least he could have warned her. She would probably not have agreed to come to Manisa to meet his parents.

She crossed the room, sat down on the bed and burst into tears. She could not have imagined that falling in love with Metin would result in all these problems. And now he would not even be able to take over his father's restaurant. This was what he had studied for and gained work experience in a foreign country and now his whole career was basically over before it had even started. And worse, it all seemed to be her fault.

She jumped when suddenly the bedroom door burst open and Metin stood in the room. His face was red and he looked very angry. She had never seen him like this. He closed the door behind him and sat down on the bed next to her. Yasmin's face looked ashen and she felt it hard to breathe. She leaned against Metin's shoulder and cried. He took her hand into his and tried to soothe her.

"So, you have heard the row?" he asked after a while when she calmed down a little.

"Yes, no, well, yes. Obviously, I only understood the part when you spoke English. But I realised very well that they don't want you to marry me and they've found you a Turkish girl they want to be your wife. I didn't know you still had arranged marriages here."

"Yes, unfortunately, it still exists, especially in the more rural areas and in smaller towns as well as in the eastern part of Turkey, the more agricultural areas. Some of my friends have already got married and theirs were arranged."

"Oh, my God, I cannot even imagine. This is so old-fashioned and so foreign to us from the western world," Yasmin was stunned to hear this.

"I'm so sorry, my love that you had to witness this row. That was the last thing I wanted to happen. I spoke in English because I thought maybe you would catch some of it. I have told you before that my parents can be rather old-fashioned but I would never ever have imagined they would do this to me! I truly thought they would respect my choices. I have my own life! I love you and I want to be with you. You're my fiancé and we will get married, no matter what. That's never going to change. Please believe me."

"But they'll disinherit you! And it makes me feel bad because after all, they have paid for your studies. I don't want to be the reason for all these problems. And you won't take over your father's restaurant either as planned. Metin, this is what you have studied and worked for. It's your career. I don't want to stand in your way!"

"You don't. And you know what? I could not care less. If they hadn't paid for my education, I would simply have gone out and done it myself. I'm 26 years old, an adult, and I have a right to make my own decisions. I would never agree to an arranged marriage, no matter how rich the woman is. It's not their life! Besides, I have made my choice a long time ago. We don't live in the Middle Ages anymore and I want to lead my own life with the choices I have made for myself. We can even go back to Europe to make a new beginning there if you like. Whatever. I'm done here."

Yasmin raised her head and looked at Metin in surprise, her eyes still full of tears. He had spoken quite fiercely and with such sincerity and this impressed her. She had never doubted his love for her but it saddened her that he would have to choose between his parents and her. Was he really serious when he said they could go back to Europe and make a new start there?

"Now, what shall we do? Do you want to stay here today and return to Kusadasi tomorrow or shall we leave right away? If we stay here tonight, we would have to have dinner with my parents, we cannot avoid it, unfortunately," Metin asked her gently.

Yasmin really didn't feel like staying for one minute longer but she felt a strong headache coming on and she was also beginning to feel sick.

"I'm not feeling too well, Metin. I can feel a migraine coming on. It might be better to stay tonight and maybe we can drive back early tomorrow morning? I find it quite stressful what has happened and I need to lie down for a bit if you don't mind. I will make an effort to eat with them tonight and perhaps they will change their mind about me when they know me a little," she said, a hopeful tone in her voice.

Metin knew that would not happen. He knew his parents too well. Once they had made up their mind, there was no going back. But he kept quiet and agreed to stay because he knew Yasmin was going to be sick if she didn't rest and he was worried about her.

"Okay, if you want, then that's fine with me. I'll tell them we will stay for dinner but we'll be leaving tomorrow morning. Now please rest and I'll see you later in the lounge for dinner. I hope you are comfortable in this room despite everything. For what it's worth, I'm very sorry about all this," he said and kissed her on her cheek, then left the guestroom quietly.

The dinner was a quiet affair and despite Yasmin trying to be polite and making conversation with Metin's parents, they did not communicate much and gave her some hostile stares. After a while, she gave up and sat quietly finishing her dinner, chewing the meat with effort. Her appetite had completely eluded her. She did not even enjoy the Elma chai and the locum she had brought as a gift for them.

Yasmin and Metin left early the next morning, her heart heavy and she was tired because she had slept badly. They drove in silence. What had started as a promising mini-break and with the excitement to meet Metin's family had turned out to be a complete nightmare. She felt very sad.

Right now, she could not imagine what their future would look like. Her mind was completely blank. *What a pity,* she thought, it could have been so nice, living in this lovely, quiet place and with Metin having a secure future with the restaurant, once they started a family. For sure, the city would grow in the years to come and would attract more tourists because of its close location to Izmir and the Mediterranean and the opportunities for outdoor sports. Metin had even talked about opening another branch in Kusadasi or Izmir, the areas currently better known and frequented by tourists.

How could she even tell her parents? It was too embarrassing. During her last phone call, the previous month she had mentioned the trip to Manisa with Metin to them and that she was going to meet her parents-in-law and remembered mentioning that she hoped they would like and accept her, due to her different heritage and culture.

Her parents would be wondering why she would not talk about the visit. How could she explain to them that she was not accepted and they would not want him to marry their son? Nor would they ever meet her parents, and that was clear now. It took her all her strength not to burst into tears again as she was conscious that it would upset Metin. She decided to close her eyes and try to sleep for the rest of the journey.

If her boss Fűgen was surprised to see her back at work two days earlier than anticipated, she didn't show it. Being Turkish and knowing her own culture, she was only too well aware of some of the issues that couples could face when they met their partner's parents when they learnt that they were from a different culture, especially if they were traditional. She felt genuine concern and compassion for Yasmin, who didn't seem to be the same bright bubbly person she had been before they had left for Manisa. She was hoping for her friend that they were not getting into more serious difficulties.

"I'm so very sorry, Yaz," Metin said when they were back in Kusadasi, "I would never have thought it would turn out this way. They've always known we were going to get married."

"It's not your fault, love. It's just sad that my parents will never meet your parents. I don't really know how to tell them," Yasmin commented.

"Thank you. You'll tell your parents when you are ready. For now, all we can do is concentrate on ourselves and plan our future in Europe. I will distance myself from my parents and hopefully, one day they will get over it and accept it."

"Do you think so?"

"No, to be honest, I don't. But that's not my problem anymore. My life is with you, not with them. You are my family, and you and our children will be our future, sevgilim."

For the months following their trip, Yasmin threw herself into work to take her mind off the other problems. There was no change in how Metin treated her; in fact, he showed her his love even more as if he wanted to apologize for the incident at his parents' house. She knew their love would survive the problems and she felt more confident.

Kusadasi, Turkey
October 1992

The rest of the summer turned out to be very busy with thousands of tourists flocking to Kusadasi. The streets, restaurants and bazaars were packed and bustling with life. The 'Grand Hotel Ephesus' had been completely full the whole season and both Yasmin and Metin had been up to their eyeballs in work, putting in a lot of overtime due to the high demand of tourists. It was a great experience for Yasmin in her new role.

The nearby 'Ladies beach' was a very popular tourists spot and one of the places Yasmin and Metin also frequented in their spare time. When the hot summer reluctantly gave way to autumn, it was still pleasant and warm in this part of the country. Some tourists preferred this time of year for a holiday when there were no children about and the town was a lot quieter. It was a good time to enjoy this place, just before the season ended.

It was one day in October when Yasmin and Metin were sitting together on their towels on the 'Ladies beach' overlooking the Mediterranean. The sea was quiet and gentle, waves lapping onto the beach. Yasmin was resting her head on Metin's shoulder enjoying their intimate moment.

By now, most tourists had left and it was getting slightly cooler and windier. In a month's time, all tourist businesses would be closed, as well as most restaurants and bars, the owners having returned to their home towns for the winter months, and Kusadasi would once more belong to the locals. It was early afternoon and sunny but quite cool. Not having been able to spend much quality time together during the summer due to their overwhelming schedule, they valued their time in each other's company even more.

"Yaz, I've been thinking about our wedding. It's important to get married and since the summer season is nearly over, we'll have more time starting to make plans. Also, we need to think about our future and where we are going to live next year. This hotel was a great start for our career but I feel we need something a bit more stable," Metin began.

They had not touched that subject anymore since the disaster with Metin's parents in Manisa back in May. They had put off their wedding plans for a while and wanted things to cool down.

Yasmin nodded. "Yes, you are right, I totally agree. But love, first there is something I need to tell you."

Metin looked at her in astonishment and encouraged her. "Oh? What it is? I hope you haven't changed your mind?"

She laughed heartily. "Oh no! Of course not, sevgilim, my darling! Erm, what I want to tell you is… Well, you see, I'm pregnant!"

Metin looked at her in awe. "Oh, wow, Yaz, that's quite some news! Are you sure?"

"Oh, yes, absolutely! There is no doubt!"

To her surprise, Metin was overjoyed. He took her into his arms and kissed her gently. The beach was deserted and so nobody would see them or would mind.

"Sevgilim, that's amazing, wow, I'm going to be a father! How long have you known? When is the baby due?"

"Well, I've only found out a couple of weeks ago, and so I think sometime in June next year. Or it could be at the end of May but only if the baby decides to arrive early," Yasmin smiled and rubbed her stomach.

"I can't get over it. That's indeed very good news. Well, in this case, we should indeed get married as soon as possible, love."

"Yes, I totally feel the same. But what about your parents and the rest of your family?"

"Don't worry, we'll just have to get married here and we'll only have a small party just with our friends and we can invite some of our work colleagues too. My parents won't join as they will never approve of our marriage. I have not forgotten the incident in Manisa, you know. It's just not going to happen."

"Okay, I would also like to invite Hülya as she has been a good friend and colleague so far. She has been so helpful with everything when I have first arrived here in this town, and her husband, of course. But what about your uncle, you know the one you told me is a policeman? And what about your cousins? Is nobody going to come then?"

"You mean uncle Bekim? No, he certainly won't join. He is not a good person and corrupt. I never liked him. And my cousins won't join either because of him. I have long distanced myself from that family. My other cousins live far away and a couple of them even live in the US. They won't be able to come over either. We'll just have to rely on our friends."

"Oh, I'm so sorry, sevgilim. When do you think we should arrange it for? Where shall we have the function? Do you have a good venue in mind?"

"Well, I thought we could rent the restaurant on the 'Güvercinada' on the birds' island. You know where we had dinner a couple of weeks ago and you had that amazing fish dish? It's such a nice place, right by the sea with great views and quite romantic for the occasion. They cater for weddings and other functions there. People have even been using the disco after the wedding ceremony, believe it or not!"

"That's a splendid idea, yes, let's do that. I'm so looking forward to it," Yasmin was excited and clapped her hands.

"Brilliant, so let's pick a date then. It would be nice to organise it in early April when the weather is better and everybody can join. And with regards to returning to Europe, I would suggest to wait until after the baby is born before we make the move. What do you think?"

Yasmin considered Metin's idea. "Yes, that makes sense. I wouldn't be of much help to you in the move with such a large stomach! Where do you want to go in Europe? Have you thought of a country where you'd like to work? Due to the EU, there will be new opportunities, you know."

"Well, I would say it makes sense to go to the UK since you are a British citizen, don't you think? I can easily find a job in London, I'm sure of it. There are plenty of hotels and many 5-star ones where I would like to pursue my career. If we can make a bit of money, I could open my own Turkish restaurant sometime in the future too, obviously when we have saved up enough money."

Yasmin was over the moon to hear that Metin would make this sacrifice for her. She could not begin to imagine what it must mean for him to leave his family and his culture behind. As soon as the baby was a little older, she would return to work and help Metin fulfil his dream. They could even have a wedding ceremony in the UK with her friends there and her parents. The thought made her happy.

"Oh, yes, I'm sure you'll find a job in no time. And it's a great idea to open your own Turkish restaurant in the UK. There is a great demand for it, I can assure you, especially in London but also in other places. The UK is a melting pot of cultures and I do think you'll have more opportunities there. We can stay with my parents in Dorset for a start until you find a job in London. I'll ask them and I'm sure they will help us get started and they'll be happy to spend some time with their first grandchild anyway."

"Have you told them the good news yet?" Metin asked.

"Not yet, no, I wanted to be absolutely sure before I put up their hopes, you know. In the first three months of pregnancy, anything can happen, so I didn't want to jump the gun. But I'll tell them very soon."

For the remaining months of the year, the hotel was used for some functions as well as conferences but it was manageable by a smaller team as many other team members and temporary staff went back home for the winter months. There was not much demand for the whole team to remain there during the colder season. Their friend Hűlya was still working as she was the Human Resources Manager of the hotel and her job was busy all year round. She was overjoyed when she heard Yasmin and Metin were going to have a baby and happily accepted their wedding invitation.

The Deceit

When winter with its windy and rainy climate gave way to spring, they were ready for their big day that was set for the beginning of April 1993. The time was perfect, already warm but not too hot and the masses of tourists had not yet arrived. Only a small number of businesses had already opened. The restaurant for the wedding was booked and the invitations had gone out. Surprisingly, they had forty guests confirmed, despite the absence of Metin's whole family. However, this was still a very small number for a Turkish wedding.

The day had been perfect and Yasmin was admired in her white silk wedding gown, despite her being pregnant, and her olive skin looked flawless and her raven hair shone in the sunlight. 'Cok güzel' which meant 'very beautiful' was the expression she heard spoken by every one of their guests during the whole day.

Metin had felt he was the luckiest man in the world and he was very proud of his bride. It had been the happiest day in Yasmin's life too. She was now a married woman and soon they would be a proper family!

But soon fate intervened. It was one day in May, not long after their wedding, that their luck seemed to turn. She had just come out of a meeting in one of their conference rooms at the hotel and was making her way back to her office which lay behind the reception area. Just before she was turning to the corridor to where her office was located, she saw a couple standing at the reception desk at the hotel. She stopped dead in her tracks. *Oh no*, she thought, shocked. In an instant, she recognised the couple, who were none other than Metin's parents. She knew she could not be seen here. She slowly retraced her steps to the corridor where she had come from in order to take another route to her office.

"You look as if you've just seen a ghost," said a voice behind her.

She jumped and spun around. Then she saw that it was Metin, who was just returning from unloading some deliveries for the evening meal preparation at the restaurant.

"Oh, please don't do that, love; you'll give me a heart attack! And I do feel as if I've seen a ghost. Your parents are at the front desk, Metin."

"What??"

"Yes, they are. I've just seen them. That's why I wanted to go around the back to my office. I obviously don't want them to see me. Why are they here? I thought you haven't spoken to them for a long time?"

"I haven't, I swear, please believe me. I really don't know what they are doing here. Please don't worry about anything. I'll talk to them and I will send them away, they have no business here. Just go to your office and don't come out until I'll tell you the coast is clear. Just get on with your work and I'll come and find you later, okay?"

He took her into his arms and held her tight for a brief moment and soothed her, then made his way in the direction of the lobby, wondering what his parents' visit was all about. He had not spoken to them for several months and they were certainly not aware that he had got married or that Yasmin was pregnant.

Yasmin's heart was racing and when she returned to her office, she had to sit down to catch her breath. She was hoping that this incident would not affect her baby who was due in two months' time. Her stomach was big now and she was not as agile as before.

A couple of hours later, which seemed like an eternity, her office door opened. It was Metin. Yasmin looked at him with questioning eyes. She was worried.

"And? What did your parents want? Why did they come here? Did you tell them about our marriage and that we're soon going to be a family?"

Metin pulled one of the spare chairs from the other table and sat down. He didn't speak for a while and then sighed before he began.

"Actually yes, I did tell them. I didn't want them to know anything at first and I told them to leave. But then they said they wanted me to come back to Manisa with them for a few days because my mother is unwell and has a cancer scare. She'll have to go into hospital for a few days for some tests. Then they insisted again that I would have to marry this other woman. That's why I had to tell them about us, I'm so sorry. They were absolutely furious with me and they didn't even believe me at first. They thought I was making it up. But then they saw my wedding ring, and they knew I was not lying."

Yasmin's face went pale. This was not going well at all. "What are you going to do? Have they left now?"

"No, they are still here. They wanted to come to my place but I said that's not possible anymore because we don't have any space for more people, and anyway, we both live together now, obviously. They were furious and said that I went behind their back."

Yasmin's heart sank. "But that's not true! It's ridiculous! They knew all along that we were going to get married! It was hardly a secret and it's their fault that they didn't want to accept it. They could have joined the wedding!"

"Yes, I know. But that's just the way they are, I'm afraid. They will never change."

"I can't have these issues; it will affect the baby, my love. I really don't want a miscarriage because of this. So, when are they going to leave?"

"Well, that's the thing," Metin began to explain slowly, "they are going to stay at the hotel until tomorrow. Then they want me to go to Manisa with them for a couple of days until my mother is sorted out with her hospital tests and with her medication she will have to take. But it would only be for a short time. I'll come back straight away."

"And you believe them?" she asked incredulously.

"What can I do? Despite everything, she is still my mother. I promise I won't stay longer than three, maximum four days. After all, I have my job here too, and I can't just rush off somewhere at any time. We're going to get really busy soon. They'll have to understand this. And I want to be present at the birth of my baby and welcome our child together!"

Yasmin felt a knot in her stomach. Her intuition told her that his parents were lying and they were trying to take him away from her. She was convinced it was just an excuse to lure him away from Kusadasi. But what else were they up to?

"I can't hinder you from going with them, sevgilim, I know," she said sadly, "I just have a really bad feeling about all of this and I'm sure they haven't told you the whole truth. I'm convinced they are up to something. Promise you won't leave me alone and you will come back soon? Will you call me every day? Please?"

"Of course, sweetheart, that goes without saying. But I will give you a phone number as well for an emergency. If anything goes wrong, whatever it is, please call this number and you will get help. It is just in case and no matter what time of day it is, you can call. I do hope everything will be all right but one can never know. Please keep this number safe and have it with you all the time."

He leaned over her desk and picked up a pen, then jotted down a phone number with a name next to it on the notepad on Yasmin's desk.

"Esma," she read on the paper. The name meant nothing to her. "Who is she?"

"Esma is the only person I can truly trust from my family. She is my auntie and lives in Izmir. She is quite a bit younger than my mother and they have a different father. The two of them don't get on at all. She has not been in contact with my mother literally for decades. Also, she is married to an American. She has spent some years living in America with her husband due to his profession. She speaks perfect English."

"Oh, I see. I understand. And of course, that was not accepted by your family, her being married to a foreigner and a non-Muslim. It does explain a lot."

"Exactly. So, you see what I mean. I have always been in contact with her and she has been good to me all these years. She also supported me with my choice of going abroad."

"But why didn't she come to our wedding? Didn't you tell her we were getting married?"

"I did invite them to our wedding but they could not attend because they were away again in the US at the time for a long stretch due to her husband's job. But she obviously knows we are now married. She is also aware that if anything goes wrong on my part, you will contact her for help."

Metin stood up and took her into his arms. He held her tight as if it was the last time for him that he would feel his wife. He didn't know how right his intuition was.

"Don't worry, everything will be all right. I'll be back soon. Please don't do too much housework in your condition; I'll help you as soon as I get back. I'll stay here at the hotel with my parents tonight and we'll leave tomorrow morning. As soon as I can I'll give you a ring, sevgilim. I love you so much."

Yasmin nodded, totally numb, unable to move. She took his face into her hands and kissed him gently. Then she placed his hands on her stomach so that he could feel his baby. Despite his assurance that he would be back soon, the nagging feeling in her heart persisted. She sent a silent prayer to God that Metin would indeed come back within three days and that nothing bad would befall him when he was away.

"I have to go sevgilim, I'm so sorry. I have to supervise and help with tonight's preparation for dinner. We have a large group booking and we'll be very busy. Please look after yourself and the little one, and I'll see you in a few days. I love you," Metin assured her.

Metin crossed her office, let himself out and silently pulled the door shut. Yasmin stared after him, her heart heavy and with tears in her eyes, her hands resting on her already large stomach. And that was the last Yasmin saw or heard of her husband.

Izmir, Turkey
June 1993 Yasmin

"You'll have to go to the hospital! You can't wait any longer! I'll organise you a taxi, right away. Stay calm, please, Yaz," Hűlya said to Yasmin in a panicky voice. She felt sorry for her friend, who had gone through so much already in the past couple of months.

"Breathe, Yaz, breathe, the taxi will be here shortly. We'll go to the hospital in Izmir and I'll come with you. You're not the first woman having a baby. Everything will be all right."

It was mid-June and Yasmin was at home, lying alone in her bed that she had shared with her husband. She followed Hűlya's advice, the contractions had started but were still far apart, and she was sweating profusely. Yasmin was longing to give birth and finally have it over and done with. She was looking forward to holding her baby in her arms.

Hűlya had been asleep in her house she shared with her husband when the phone rang. It was past midnight. It had taken Hűlya a few minutes to realise who was calling, it was Yasmin. She had sounded frightened. Hűlya was suddenly very alert and jumped out of bed at once, worried about her friend.

"Hűlya, sorry, so sorry to trouble you but I think the baby is coming. Please help me!"

"Relax, Yaz, please, I'm coming over straight away. Keep breathing, and don't do anything until I arrive. I'll be there in 10 minutes."

Hűlya and her husband's house was only a short walk away from Yasmin's place. She glanced at her reflection in the mirror and ran her hand through her dark-brown curls. No time for grooming, she thought. She left a note for her husband to tell him where she had gone, grabbed the dress she had worn the day before from the chair next to the window and pulled it on, then rushed off. When she arrived at Yasmin's place, she called a taxi immediately, then picked up a few items for her friend to take to the hospital and threw them into a holdall bag.

They needed to leave straight away when the taxi arrived. Luckily, it was only ten minutes when their transport pulled up in front of the house. Hűlya helped her friend into the back seat of the car, threw the bag into the boot, and then got into the car next to her.

"To Izmir hospital, please, the maternity yard, as quickly as possible," Hűlya instructed the taxi driver.

He probably had not considered going on such a long drive in the middle of the night as he did not look too pleased. Izmir was a long way to drive but it was money and since he didn't want Yasmin to give birth in his car, he did as he was told.

"I'm so sorry to trouble you, Hűlya," Yasmin said weakly and closed her eyes.

"It's okay, please do not worry. It's important that you are safe. The midwives will know what to do. Just close your eyes and relax until we arrive. Keep breathing."

Upon arrival, a midwife ushered them straight to the maternity yard. She had addressed her as 'Mrs Özgűr' and told Yasmin to follow her. Yasmin nodded and was shown to a bed that stood beside the window. It was much later that Yasmin realised it was very strange that somebody knew her surname straight away without seeing her name at the check-in. When she told the midwife how often the contractions came, she was assured that it would probably be several more hours until the baby would come since the water had not broken yet. Yasmin took off her clothes and put on her hospital gown, then lay down on the bed. She took Hűlya's hand.

"Hűlya, please go back home, I'll be fine now. Thank you so very much for all your help and I'll call you once the baby has arrived."

"Are you sure you're all right? I don't feel good leaving you here all by yourself. I'm really worried about you."

Yasmin nodded. "Yes, I'm sure, I'm fine now. You'll have to work tomorrow and you need to get some more sleep."

Realising that nothing more could be done, Hűlya hugged her friend and made her way out of the hospital. She had told the taxi driver to wait for her to take her back home. Since there were hardly any cars in the parking lot, it was not difficult to find her taxi. She knocked on the window and had to wake up the driver as he had fallen asleep.

Meanwhile, Yasmin settled into her bed but her mind was racing. The contractions came quicker now and she missed Metin so much. She would have needed him here. He had promised that he would be there for the birth of his first child who she knew from the scans would be a boy. She knew that she needed to be strong for her baby and pull through.

She stared into space, her heart heavy. What had happened to her husband, the love of her life? Her mind wandered back to the events on that afternoon in May in her office at the hotel when she last spoke to Metin and when he had told her that he had to accompany his parents to Manisa because his mother was to be admitted to hospital. Even then her intuition had told her that something was wrong. She was sure now that he was lured back to their place under false pretences. She had waited for his call every day but he had not called, nor did he return after the three or four days he had promised he would be back. Nor could she reach him and she was very distressed.

After not hearing from Metin at all, she had subsequently told her boss what was bothering her. Fűgen was worried too. She didn't appreciate her employees just disappearing without a trace.

"And you have no idea where he could be?" Fűgen had asked Yasmin.

"Metin promised even to me he would only be away for a couple of days and then he'd be back. Otherwise, I would not have given him permission. I need him here. We cannot cope without him. We're going into high season now. Is there no way we can contact him?"

Fűgen had noticed her friend's distress mounting every day, especially with her pregnancy. Her baby was due any day now and she was going on maternity leave soon and was not able to work for a while either.

"I have called his parent's house many times but nobody ever picked up. And anyway, they hate me. I'm sure they would not tell me anything anyway. I'm not even sure if he is still alive," Yasmin told her in tears.

"Oh, I'm sure he is. There must be a way of finding out what happened. Do you have any other contact number perhaps? One of his relatives or a friend?"

It was then when Yasmin remembered the note Metin had given her with the name and phone number of his aunt.

"Oh, wait a minute," Yasmin grabbed her handbag and rummaged around.

"I remember something now. Metin gave me his aunt's phone number just before he left. She lives in Izmir and he said I could contact her if anything happened to him, no matter what. I totally forgot about it due to the stress and my tiredness because of the pregnancy. Let me find it and I will try to contact her and see if she knows anything and if she could possibly help somehow. I'm just so frightened that his parents might have done something awful to him."

A terrifying thought crossed her mind. She had heard of honour killings, usually committed by a male member of the family, and suddenly she felt sick. What if his parents had done something very bad to him just because they thought he dishonoured the family by marrying her? It usually happened to a girl but it could also happen to a boy given the circumstances, she was sure.

The note was not in her handbag. It turned out she had it safely tucked away at home and once she found it, she contacted Esma right away.

Esma sounded very pleasant on the phone and sympathetic about her situation. She had known all along about the issues Metin and Yasmin had with his parents and in fact, had almost expected a phone call from her. She was horrified that Yasmin had been left on her own and in the late stage of her pregnancy and she promised to make enquiries on behalf of Yasmin without mentioning her name.

"Let me deal with it, love," Esma had assured her on the phone, "I have a lot of contacts through my husband's work and they will help me. I'll twist an arm or two, and will find out what has happened. I'm so glad you called. Please don't worry, it's not good for you or the baby. We'll find him one way or another. Give me a couple of days and I will call you back once I have found out more."

Suddenly, a contraction ripped through Yasmin's body and brought her back to the present. She screamed. Where was the midwife? After a few minutes, she lay still again, feeling already exhausted. She closed her eyes and her thoughts wandered back again to the conversation she had with Esma following the first phone call with her that day three weeks before.

Yasmin had never found out what strings Esma had pulled to find out where Metin was but a week later she had called Yasmin back with some rather distressing news.

"Yasmin?"

"Yes, speaking," Yasmin answered.

"Merhaba Yasmin, it's Esma. Well, I have made some enquiries since we last spoke and I've found out something. I'm so sorry to tell you that Metin is still at his parent's place in Manisa."

"What? You mean he is still alive?" A spark of hope ignited in Yasmin's heart. Maybe not everything was lost. Her baby needed a father and she needed her husband back.

"Yes, it seems that he is alive. That's the good news. However, it's just that they don't let him leave the house or let him return to his job in Kusadasi and to you. He must be beside himself and worried about you and the baby."

"Yes, I'm sure about that. But why are they doing this? They know he has a busy job! But you know I had a strange feeling something like that would happen. Maybe his father somehow hindered him from leaving as soon as his mother was in the hospital for her treatment," Yasmin cried.

"Hospital? What do you mean?" Esma sounded alert.

"His mother is ill apparently, with cancer," she explained, "that's why they persuaded him to go with them to Manisa to help with her treatment."

"Oh, I see, and they told Metin that his mother had to go to the hospital just to lure him back? What a complete and utter lie! She was never even ill! Oh my God, what a horror to put you through this. I'm so sorry to give you such bad news. But I have an idea. Listen, this is what we are going to do."

And so, they had agreed to go to Manisa together and find Metin. There they would somehow try to kidnap him out of his situation and take him back to his home and his family but only once she had given birth.

The baby was due any minute now and there was nothing they could arrange before. No matter how hard it was that action would have to wait for a couple more weeks.

A new contraction took Yasmin out of her daydreaming state, away from the conversation and plan she had hatched with Esma, and again she screamed. The time between the contractions was a lot shorter and her water had now broken. When the midwife returned, she told her there were some minor complications and therefore, she would need a caesarean section. It was not the birth Yasmin had imagined but she was too tired and exhausted to argue and she agreed to it and soon she was oblivious to the world, not knowing when exactly her son had first seen the light of the world.

It was several hours later, when Yasmin awoke from the anaesthetic. The night was clear and a bright silver moon was rising in the night sky. It was already quite hot despite being only June and Yasmin was bathed in sweat. Her hospital gown was sticking to her body and her skin itched. She had woken up a few minutes ago and her head ached unbearably. Her legs felt very weak. She was not sure how long she had been sleeping or if she had been sleeping at all. She tried to open her eyes, her eyelids feeling heavy.

Where was she? Nothing in the room felt familiar. It was not her home. She blinked and tried to focus. Then, suddenly she remembered something.

She was in hospital because she had given birth! And then she heard her baby cry. Yes, she knew, just knew. No, she did not imagine it. She definitely had heard it. It was her baby. Or was it only a vision in her delirium? Had she been dreaming it all? Did her mind play tricks? Was she going mad? No, no, no!

She knew, her instincts told her, she had not been dreaming, and the bright silver moon she saw shining through the window in the clear night sky had been her witness. And suddenly she knew what had happened. She had been taken to the maternity ward yesterday to give birth to her baby. They would normally give the baby to the mother when it was born. But her baby had not been given to her. And she had been sleeping.

She was trying to remember how she had got to the hospital but her mind drew a blank. A heavy sob rose in her throat and she felt as if her heart was being ripped apart. She bit into her hand so that she would not scream. What had happened to her? She knew with certainty now that they had been lying to her about the caesarean section. She had been exhausted from the long labour and after she had been given the anaesthetics for the childbirth, of course, she could not remember anything at all. And now, when she awoke again, she was on her own.

Where was her baby? It was as she had never given birth, never been pregnant. But on her stomach she could feel the stitches from the caesarean operation that must have been done in a hurry, and it hurt. When she looked around her, she realised with a shock that she had been moved to another room. She was no longer in the maternity ward and there were no other women, no other mothers in the room. She was completely alone.

She felt hot tears falling down her cheek. But where was her husband? He had promised to be there for the birth. They had big plans. They had planned to return to Europe to start a new life after the baby was born. It had all been arranged. He had promised her. She had believed him. She knew he had never lied to her. He loved her. She knew she could trust him. Where was he? And what had happened to her baby?

Then, slowly, as she came out of the haze due to the anaesthetics she began to remember. It was her friend Hűlya who had taken her to hospital yesterday. Yes, that was it. But why Hűlya? Why not Metin? Metin…

She tried to focus and remember. Then an incident came to her mind. Oh my God, she thought! Metin was in Manisa. That was it! Esma had told her. He had been lured there by his parents the month before and he had not returned! She tried to sit up and focus. She must find a nurse and ask where her baby was. Surely, they bring the child back to the mother when she has recovered from childbirth to nurse?

Slowly, she got out of bed and awkwardly took a few steps towards the door and opened it. The corridor was quiet and lay in darkness. She was very weak and the stitches hurt. Was this just the effect of the anaesthetics? Or was there something else? Did they perhaps drug her so that she would not remember anything? In the corridor, she decided to try and find an office of a night nurse or somewhere where they would give her some information. But before she could go any further, a nurse suddenly appeared out of nowhere and took her arm. Yasmin was desperate and spoke quickly to the nurse.

"Please, nurse, do you speak English? I gave birth a few hours ago but my baby is not there. Please can you take me to my baby? I know I had a son. Where is he? My name is Yasmin Özgűr-Bonerti."

"I do speak English, yes. Mrs Özgűr, please listen to me. My name is Gül and I'm the night nurse. Please, you must go back to bed now. You are too weak to wander around the hospital and besides, it's the middle of the night. I'll take you back to your room."

Too weak to object, Yasmin let the night nurse guide her back to the hospital room. But she would not give up before she knew where her son was. A mother's instinct was always right and she needed to see her baby and know he was okay.

"Please tell me, Gül, where is my baby? I've given birth to a son, and my husband and I agreed a long time ago to name him Şenay. Where is my son, please? Why am I not in the maternity ward anymore?"

"Erm, Mrs Özgűr, there is no easy way to say this," the young nurse began to explain and looked at her with compassion. She seemed genuinely concerned and a kind person.

"What? What happened to my baby? Tell me!" Yasmin grew hysterical and her face was ashen and she grabbed the nurse's hand.

"Your son has died, Mrs Özgűr. He died right after you gave birth. There is nothing we could have done. He didn't breathe. I'm ever so sorry to give you this bad news," the nurse Gül told her.

"Nooooo! Nooo! I know my baby is alive! I heard him cry! I heard him! I didn't imagine it! He is somewhere! You are lying to me! I don't believe you!" Yasmin screamed.

"I'm so sorry but no. He died. I truly wish I could give you better news. Please go to sleep now. I'll give you a sedative so you can relax and sleep better."

"I don't want to sleep! I want my baby! Tell me where my baby is!"

"Please madam, you'll have to calm down now. Trust me, you will soon feel better. You can go back home in a day or two."

With these words, nurse Gül quickly pushed a needle into Yasmin's arm giving her the sedative, then gently covered her with the duvet and left the room. Outside in the corridor, she paused, feeling sad and very sorry for this young, distressed woman, who was obviously a foreigner. She understood very well why she was making such a scene. She had witnessed a distressing event earlier that same night, involving one of her colleagues, a midwife called Zeynep. Maybe she could help Mrs Özgűr with some information before she left the hospital? Where was her husband? She had said she was a 'Mrs' and this indicated that she must be married. But then, why did her husband not come to visit her?

Only a few minutes after she had been given the injection with the sedative, Yasmin's world succumbed into blackness once more. She didn't care anymore whether she would ever wake up again or die. Without her baby and Metin, her life was over.

Marrakesh, Morocco
June 2005
An Interesting Revelation

"Hurry up Şenay! Your breakfast is ready! You don't want to be late on your first day to help your father in the restaurant. He is counting on you!" Amel called out from the kitchen to her son where she was preparing their breakfast. She was an attractive woman in her late thirties with a long mane of shiny ebony hair, and large, kind brown eyes.

"Yes, yes, mum, I'm coming!" the boy shouted back.

It was early morning on a hot Saturday in late June. There was no school today. Yet it was a special day for Şenay and he could not help but feel proud and excited. The day before, his father took him into his home office and announced to him some very good news. Şenay could start helping him in the restaurant he owned from today, doing little chores for him, mainly in the kitchen but later also with serving customers! And going forward, he would help him every weekend as well as on the days when there was no school. For a long time, Şenay had been pestering his father to allow him to go to the restaurant and help him with his work and today was the day. He was going to work.

"I'm giving you a responsibility, Şenay, and this way you will learn the trade slowly. I will teach you. If you like it, perhaps you will choose this to be your profession in the future and you may take over my restaurant one day," Kareem had discussed with his son.

"Thank you, dad," Şenay hugged his father. He had never felt so important in his life.

He was a big boy now, already 12 years old, almost a young man, and tall for his age, making him look slightly older than his friends of the same age group. He was smartly dressed and was well-spoken. The week before, his parents, his uncle Tahiri, his auntie Fatima and all his cousins had celebrated his 12th birthday. It had also been the day when his father promised him a surprise which turned out to be helping him in his restaurant 'Al- Kareem'. He had taken it over from his predecessor five years ago after he had retired and made a great success of it by refurbishing it to a modern standard and with the help of a well-known chef, Kareem even prepared many specialities himself.

"Go on Şenay, enjoy your day and make your father proud," his mother said and looked at him gently when she waved him off.

He nodded and rushed out of the house, running the short distance to the restaurant which was located in the Medina. He was wearing a traditional white Moroccan kaftan, which had been one of his birthday presents from his father especially for the occasion.

Amel smiled to herself. She was very proud of her only son, the happy, three-month-old boy Şenay they had adopted back in 1993 from Turkey. Both she and her husband had soon realised that he was a very bright and responsible child, who liked to learn and easily made new friends. They always had some of his friends in the house, him being very popular at school, as well as with his two cousins, Tahiri's children. Nobody would ever suspect that he was not Moroccan but from another country because he blended in very well into their culture. However, lately, she was often wondering if she and Kareem would ever tell Şenay that he had been adopted, especially as he was getting older.

Ah, well, she said to herself, staring into space, *perhaps when the right time comes, we will tell him, there is no rush,* and she went back to finishing her housework before setting off to the market to buy her groceries.

One afternoon a week later, Şenay lay on the bed in his cousin Tariq's room in the house that belonged to his uncle Tahiri, telling his cousin all about his great new adventure at his father's restaurant. Tariq's home, only a few houses down the alleyway from where he was living with his parents, was like his second home and often he came for a sleepover. Not having any siblings, he bonded especially well with his cousin, who was only one year senior. The two boys had become inseparable from a very early age and had developed a unique friendship that went far beyond just being cousins. Suddenly, Tariq jumped up almost throwing Şenay off the bed.

"Hey, I've got it! You know what we could do? But don't tell Ayesha!" he said excitedly.

"No, tell me! Come on! Don't keep me in suspense! You're always doing this! And why not telling Ayesha? She will be sad when she cannot join us," Şenay urged his cousin.

Tariq's younger sister by three years, Ayesha, liked being with her big brother and she also adored her cousin Şenay because he seemed a little different to her from the other kids she knew. Somehow, he seemed more mature to her, even more than her own brother. He looked a little different too, she thought. Not like the typical Moroccan boys she knew from her school. She also liked his name and often wondered why it was different from the common names in her country. Once she had taken the courage and asked her uncle, Şenay's father about it and he had told her that it was actually a Turkish name and that it was homage to a Turkish friend of his that he named his son after. Often the trio went out together to the Medina or the park to play with other children. But for some reason today Tariq didn't want Ayesha involved.

"Because she might be jealous, that's why, and it might not be so much fun then," he answered.

"Why? What are you planning to do?" Şenay looked at his cousin, not understanding.

"Guess! You know, it's my birthday next week…?"

"Oh no, you won't!" It slowly dawned on Şenay what mischief his cousin was up to.

"Oh yes, I will! I know where my parents hide my presents!" Tariq explained.

"But then it's not a surprise for you, is it? Remember, last year, when we found one of Ayesha's presents. It was no surprise for her and she was a bit sad and disappointed. She even said herself that she should not have been snooping around," Şenay reasoned with his cousin.

"True but then she was also a lot younger. Oh, come on! Let's have a look in the room anyway. Dad keeps all sorts of things in there," Tariq didn't give up.

Şenay sighed and stood up to follow him to his father's secret room. It was their term to call it 'secret' because it was Tariq's father's official office and he didn't want his children disrupting anything of his paperwork, so he simply forbade them to enter the room. Tahiri, Tariq's father, owned a small hotel in town and kept all his important papers and documents in his home office where he had more space.

Both his parents were at work and being alone in the house, they knew they would not be disturbed in their mischief. Tariq opened the door which creaked a little, and they found themselves standing in a large, bright room. There was a wardrobe on one side, next to a window, and a tall filing cabinet standing on the opposite wall, behind a desk. Next to the filing cabinet, stood a bookshelf that held many books related to his uncle's work but there were others like history books and language study books in Arabic, English and French. There was even a language book with a CD ROM for learning German. Şenay had always been a keen reader and interested in languages himself and seeing this bookshelf full, he was fascinated. Due to his uncle's profession in the tourist business, he knew he had to be able to speak several languages.

"Let's have a look over there, that's most likely the place where he could hide some parcels," Tariq pointed to the large, wardrobe-like piece of furniture and walked over. He turned the knob and when the door opened, it squeaked slightly.

"I'm not so sure about this," Şenay said unconvinced, still standing by the door, "please don't disrupt anything, otherwise your dad will be angry like hell when he finds out."

"Don't worry, I won't touch any of his documents. I know his work is important," Tariq assured him.

Şenay closed the study door and walked over to join his cousin, who was kneeling on the floor looking through the bottom of the wardrobe.

"And, is there any sign of a parcel, a present? What do you expect from him anyway? Anything special?" Şenay inquired.

"Not really, no. I can't see anything here. Maybe he has hidden them somewhere else," Tariq announced, clearly disappointed.

"Or maybe he just hasn't bought you anything yet, dude."

"True, well, it was worth a try, anyway," Tariq was about to close the wardrobe's door when one of its inside drawers that was not quite shut grabbed his attention. A large brown envelope was stuck inside the drawer and prevented it from closing properly.

"Wait, what is this?" he said, almost to himself, fiddling with the drawer.

"What's that? Did you find anything?"

"No, but there seems to be an envelope stuck in one of the drawers, look here," Tariq said, trying to get the drawer open, totally forgotten all about his birthday presents.

Şenay took a few steps forward and looked over his cousin's shoulder to see what he was talking about. Tariq started to pull on the thick envelope trying to free it from the drawer and finally, it all gave way. But as he pulled it out, the top opened and all the documents inside fell out and scattered all over the floor.

"Oh, no, what a mess! My dad really will kill me!" Tariq exclaimed.

Şenay bent down to help Tariq to gather up the documents and to put them back into the envelope when something caught his eye. Apart from a letter and other papers, there was one that looked like a certificate of some sort. Curious, he picked it up to take a closer look.

"Look, how strange, this looks like a certificate. And the script on these documents? The writing seems to be in another language. How odd, I wonder what this is."

Tariq, now interested himself, about what secret they might have come across, took the certificate and the letter from his cousin to see what he was talking about.

"Yes, I think you're right. Which language is it? It's definitely not French, I can see that. Is it maybe English? Have another look, you know some English, don't you?"

Şenay took the documents from him again and studied them closely. Then he suddenly paled and shocked by what he saw and the realisation about what the document revealed, his whole world he had known came crashing down on him. Even from the little knowledge he had of the English language, which his father always insisted he learned; he understood what these documents told him. Despite his young age, he understood the significance and enormity of it. He stared at the paper.

The document he was holding was his birth certificate. The date and year of his birthday was correct, and his birth name was indeed noted as Şenay. However, his mother and father were listed as a 'Mrs Yasmin Özgűr-Bonerti' and a 'Mr Metin Özgűr'. Next to their names, their birth dates were also listed, July 1970 and February 1966 respectively.

But his family name was Ahmed, and he knew his mother's name was Amel and his father was Kareem! Their birth dates did not match the dates on the certificate. His parents had been lying to him all these years! Why had his gentle mother and kind father never told him that he was adopted? At once, he knew that those names on the birth certificate could not possibly be Moroccan. Which country did they come from?

"Şenay, are you okay? What happened? Say something!" Tariq urged him, worried about how pale his cousin looked.

It took Şenay a while to compose himself until he could speak again. "Yes, it's in English. This is my original birth certificate. And the letter here says that I'm adopted. I'm not even Moroccan, Tariq, I'm from another country!"

"What??" Tariq stared at him, not understanding.

"Yes, it's true, look here," He showed him the letter and the birth certificate and pointed at the names of his parents. "These are the names of my real parents and their birth dates. And these are not Moroccan names, are they, nor is my name?"

Tariq looked at him as if had gone mad or as if he was speaking a completely foreign language. He looked again at the letter and saw for himself that Şenay was right.

"Oh, my God, that's gross! I can't believe it! You're adopted! And that means, we're not even cousins," he said slowly, disappointed about this discovery.

Şenay glanced through the letter again, trying to make sense of it, when he noticed there was an address written on the top. It was an address in a city called Izmir in a country called Turkey.

"I'm Turkish it says here, not Moroccan. The letter is from Turkey, wherever that is," he murmured.

Tariq was as shocked as his cousin, and even more about the realisation that his 'cousin' was not really his cousin at all, nor Ayesha's. They were not even part of the same family.

"Turkey is a country on the Asian continent, on the other side of the Mediterranean Sea. It's in the area also called the Middle East. It's far away from here. You have to take a plane to get there. But how on earth did you come from Turkey to Morocco?"

"I think that's something only my parents can explain. And all the other papers here must be my adoption documents. I'm so mad, you know, why did they lie to me all this time?" Şenay was beginning to get angry as the depth of the deceit became clearer to him.

"Well, I'm sure there must be a good explanation. And maybe they just waited for a good time to tell you and would have done so at some point. But you know what confuses me?"

"No, what is it?"

"Why are these documents hidden in my father's office? These are your adoption papers, so why are they not in your house? Why are they in our house?" Tariq pointed out.

"I don't understand it either, none of it. Did your parents have something to do with my adoption, maybe?" Şenay shook his head. Nothing about this made any sense. All he felt at the moment was betrayal.

"You know what we are going to do? We're going to your home and we will ask your dad and mother about his. Only they can really explain what happened. And I feel you do need to get an explanation from them. We will take all these documents with us and show them," Tariq suggested.

"But what about your dad? He will know at once that we've been snooping around in his office and he would be mad at you," Şenay said.

"Well, I really don't care about this now, I have to admit it anyway that we have been here in his office and why, when we show them the documents. He'll be mad at me anyway. So, do you know when is your dad coming back from work today?"

"I think he is coming back around 4 pm today for his break and goes out again at 8 pm for the dinner shift. That's his usual work pattern."

"Okay, listen, let's go to your house by 4 pm then and find out all about the story around your adoption and why these papers are in my dad's office, shall we?"

Şenay nodded and knew Tariq was right. He had to get to the bottom of this. His parents had some explaining to do. He gathered all documents together and shoved them back into the envelope. Tariq closed the wardrobe, and then they left his father's office and went back to Tariq's room. A little while later, they heard the front door slam and Ayesha's voice calling out to them.

"Tariq? Şenay? Hello! I'm back from school. Are you there?"

"Yes, in my room," Tariq shouted back.

A moment later, Ayesha walked into the room, smiling and in good spirits as always but she stopped dead when she looked at the stern faces of the two boys. Despite being only 10 years old, she noticed something was not quite right. What had happened to them?

"Tariq, what is it? Şenay? Is anything wrong?" she asked in a small voice.

"Something has happened. But don't worry, Ayesha. I'm going to Şenay's house later and we have to talk to his parents. It's something very important," came Tariq's reply.

"Why? Have you done something wrong? I wanted to ask you to come to the park with me to play," Ayesha looked at him hopeful.

"Not now, Ayesha, please understand. Be a good girl and go to your friend's house today, okay? We will go together tomorrow," promised Tariq.

He cared deeply for his baby sister but there were things that she was too young yet to understand. And he didn't want to upset her with what they had just learnt.

"Okay, bye then, see you later," she reluctantly replied, disappointed and not understanding what had happened that they reacted in such a strange way.

She had noticed that even her cousin Şenay had a different look on his face as if he was angry about something. It was a look she did not understand. She had never seen him like this. She shrugged, turned around and left the room. A few minutes later, they heard the front door slam again.

When he was sure his cousin had gone, Şenay sat up on the bed and asked Tariq what was troubling him. "What do you think, will this situation change us?"

"How do you mean?" Tariq frowned.

"Well, us, our family, the way we are, and our friendship? All these years we thought we were family but now we know we are not."

"We are family, Şenay, okay! We are also friends and we are close. We have grown up together, we have always been together. Whether you are adopted or not or even if you came from the moon, that has nothing to do with us or how we feel about each other. We have always been close and that is not going to change," Tariq said with great compassion and leaned over to hug him.

"Thank you, Tariq. It means a lot to me." Şenay answered, moved by his cousin's reply.

Şenay, given his gentle nature, was close to tears but he would not show any weakness. After all, he was almost a man and he had to be strong. He felt, however, a tense sensation building up in his heart knowing it had something to with his parents and he was struggling with the anger against them. The unfamiliar feeling scared him.

It was later in the afternoon when the two boys left Tariq's house, Şenay clutching the important envelope in his hands as if his life depended on it, and made their way up to his parents' place. When they entered, they immediately saw that both parents were home, standing in the kitchen, busy with preparing tea. It was his father's break and it was his habit to always drink tea and eat some homemade sweets during his afternoon break.

Amel looked up in surprise when she saw her nephew entering with Şenay.

"Oh, hello Tariq, how nice to see you! How are you? We're just making mint tea with some sweets, would you like a cup? Yes?"

"I'm fine, thank you, and yes, please, auntie, I would like some tea," Tariq replied politely with a smile. He liked his auntie, who always had a nice word for him and always something to eat whenever he visited them at their house. He was very much a part of their family, too.

"Lovely. Go into the salon boys, and we will be joining you shortly for a chat. It's nice to have you over, Tariq," Kareem told the boys.

When he looked at his son, he became aware of a large brown envelope his son was holding, which somehow seemed familiar to him but he could not place it. Where had he seen this envelope before? When the boys disappeared into the living room, he stared after him for a while until Amel told him to prepare the cups for the tea.

Shaking his head, he placed the cups on the silver plate, put one more for his nephew, then selected some Moroccan sweets from the cupboard and placed them on another plate. Then he took it all into the living room, followed by his wife. They were met by silence.

Kareem frowned. Something was not quite right here. The boys, usually busy with chatting excitedly were up to something, he just knew. He looked over at Amel, who had sat down opposite him. Their eyes met and at once a flicker of recognition crossed their faces, like a mutual understanding. Without speaking a word, they knew that the time of the truth had come. Amel nodded at her husband in encouragement and leaned over to pour the tea.

Seeing his wife's reaction, Kareem suddenly realised what the envelope his son was holding contained. Of course! That was it! How could he ever forget?

What he didn't know was how Şenay had come into possession of it. It must have completely slipped his mind that those documents were still at his brother's house where they had stored all their important documents during the refurbishment of their house a few years ago. Although, he was sure he had taken all the boxes back, he must have just overlooked it. How embarrassing. It was all his fault. His son's silence showed that he must be mad at him, with good reason. He never wanted him to find out the truth in this way. How he even found those documents, he wondered.

Şenay sat stone-faced in his chair. He didn't say a word nor did Tariq. But before either of them could speak, Kareem broke the silence.

"You are very quiet. Is there something you would like to tell me boys?" he asked gently, looking at his son.

They both looked up at once, startled, not expecting that Şenay's father would get straight to the point. Tariq mouthed a "go on" at Şenay, encouraging him to speak. It was after all his family in question, his parents, and his adoption. He didn't want to intrude. He had only come along to support his cousin.

"Mum, Dad, why am I adopted? And why have you never told me about it? Why did you lie to me all these years?" Şenay's voice had a coldness about him that his parents had never heard before.

Kareem cleared his throat, took a sip of his mint tea and carefully placed the cup back on the tray before he began to speak.

"I'm so very sorry about this, Şenay. It was not meant to happen this way and we certainly didn't want you to find out the way you obviously did. I don't even want to know how you found these documents. Anyway, let's just leave that for a moment. We'll come back to that later. We wanted to tell you many times about your adoption but for some reason, we never found the right moment. Then the years passed. Perhaps, now is the right time to tell you and that you understand as you are also older."

"And we never wanted you to think we didn't love you because we do," his mother added.

"But I'm not your son!" Şenay almost shouted.

"Now, let me ask you something. Please listen to me carefully, Şenay and reply to my questions with the truth. Now, have you ever been hungry in your life and felt we didn't give you enough to eat?"

"No, never."

"Have you ever felt that we didn't treat you fairly?"

"No."

"Have you ever had any problems with your mother and me or the way we have treated you? I mean, have we ever treated you badly or disrespectfully or abused you even?"

"No."

"Have you ever been short of books and other materials for school? Did you ever have to beg to go to school and get an education? Even to get additional lessons to learn English?"

"No."

"Have you ever felt during all these years you were not loved?"

"No, I haven't," came the slow reply.

"Have you ever had to beg for clothes or to be dressed in respectable clothes and shoes?"

"No, Dad."

"And finally, have you ever had to complain about anybody in your family, about your cousins, your uncle Tahiri and auntie Fatima, and about anybody in our extended family?"

"No," Şenay whispered, casting a quick glance at Tariq.

"Thank you, Şenay for being honest. So, in other words, there is nothing you could say we didn't do for you or that made you less loved, less comfortable, and you would not be able to talk about it if there were any issues in your life you needed help with?"

"Erm, no, there isn't, abee. I'm so sorry," was Şenay's slow reply, his eyes now wet with tears. He was looking straight at his father, who had studied him closely. All he could see was love in his father's eyes. He glanced over to his mother and he saw the same expression in her eyes that now also glistened with tears.

"Well, then. That's very good. What I wanted to achieve with this little exercise is, that it doesn't matter whether or not you are adopted or who your biological parents are. All that matters is that you are loved, cared for and be treated in a respectful way. We want to provide you with good education and to have a chance in your life, to study and to be anything you want to be when you grow up."

"I think your father is right, Şenay," Tariq chipped in, "it certainly doesn't make a difference to me, who you are or where you came from. Just like I told you earlier, remember? You are my cousin and my best friend too. Besides, you could have biological parents and they might not care about you. They might treat you a lot worse than adoptive parents."

His mother Amel nodded. "Yes, this is certainly true. All we ever wanted is to love you and for you to have a chance in life and happiness. I hope you understand this."

Şenay's voice was small when he replied, "I'm so sorry Mum and Dad. I do appreciate you and I do love you so much. You're my family. Thank you. Please forgive me that I've reacted in this way but I was so angry when I saw these documents and realised that I'm adopted and not even Moroccan. It was such a shock."

Kareem smiled. "No, you're not Moroccan but don't worry, you truly blend in very well here. And as you can see, we didn't change the name that was given to you when you were born. We liked your name and decided not to change it. It's also part of your origin. We were told it means 'Happy Moon' in Turkish."

"Oh, that's a nice name and I like it. Thank you for keeping it. But, erm… Do you know what happened to my birth parents and why they gave me away?" Şenay asked timidly.

"No, unfortunately not. We don't have any information at all regarding your birth parents, and therefore we cannot pass anything on to you. We also don't want to judge someone. After all, we don't know the reason behind you being given up for adoption. Now, would you like us to tell you the story of a little Turkish boy who captured our heart and came from far away, from another continent, into our family? It all starts in the year of 1993…"

And with these words, Kareem and Amel began to tell him their compelling story and about why and how Şenay had become part of their lives.

Marrakesh, Morocco
May 1993
Amel and Kareem

On a hot May afternoon in the city of Marrakesh, a young woman lay in her bed of the small pink-coloured house. She was covered in sweat. On the tea table next to the bed sat a tray with a hot pot of 'Té de mente' (Moroccan mint tea) that her husband had placed there a couple of minutes ago. On the orange tree that stood in the tiny courtyard outside their bedroom, a bird was twittering happily.

"It happened again, Kareem. I cannot take it anymore. It's obviously not meant to be," Amel said in great distress to her husband Kareem. Her beautiful large, brown eyes looked at him with despair.

"Oh, no, Cherie," Kareem responded with sadness in his voice. He stroked Amel's long, ebony hair, normally shiny and beautiful, but mats at the moment and limp. Her face looked ashen and Kareem was very worried about her.

"I've had three miscarriages now, and in such a short time. Why us, Kareem? Perhaps it's Allah's will that he just doesn't want us to have children?" she murmured.

"Please don't stress yourself, Amel. I'm just as sad as you are. But we are still young and there is always another chance," Kareem tried to calm his wife but not sounding too convincing himself.

"But what if it happens again? What if there isn't another chance? I know I cannot go through this another time. You know I cannot, Kareem. I don't want to die just because I'm trying to have a baby," she said and began to weep.

Amel had married Kareem, her great love, two years earlier after he had asked her father for her hand. She had been 25 and Kareem had been 26 years old. She knew nowadays many people chose to have children when they were a little older, and she wanted to finish her studies before the children arrived anyway, and Kareem had been very understanding. He himself was busy finishing his studies in tourism and catering that year.

"Please try to sleep, ma Cherie, and when you feel better, we will talk about it and try to find a solution, okay?" he soothed his wife, gently stroking her hair.

Amel nodded, turned over and tried to go back to sleep. Kareem stood up and wondered how he could help his wife. He also was keen to have children but he was not the kind of man who would put pressure on her and he genuinely wanted to find a solution to their problem.

He decided he would talk to his brother Tahiri and see if he had an idea about what they could do. Tahiri was two years older than Kareem and he had always been the wiser of the two. Yes, that was it. He would be of help, Kareem was sure.

He left their bedroom and closed the door quietly, then let himself out of his house. He made his way to his older brother's house, who lived with his wife and baby, Tariq, only a few houses down in the same street. Their narrow street was located near the Medina in Marrakesh, the old market. The restaurant where he worked as a Catering Manager since his studies in Tourism and Catering was only a few minutes of walking distance away. It was in the perfect location and it attracted many tourists who came to visit this beautiful city called the 'pink' city due to its pink coloured buildings, constructed of ramparts of beaten clay during the residence of the Almohads in the 12th century.

Kareem knocked on the door of his brother's house and didn't have to wait long until it was answered. They never locked their front door but he considered it polite to knock first and not to just waltz in on his brother's family without announcing his arrival.

"Hello, Kareem! What a surprise to see you this early! Come in, have tea with us," Tahiri's wife Fatima greeted him when she opened the door to their attractive little house.

"Hello Fatima, I'm not disturbing, am I?" he asked.

"No, of course not. Tahiri, Come, Kareem is here!" she called into the house.

Tahiri emerged from the lounge at once and embraced his brother affectionately. The two of them had always been close and now, even as they had both got married, they still had a close friendship with each other's partner. Kareem also loved his one-year-old nephew, Tariq, dearly and spent time with him when he could.

They sat down in the comfortable living room which was carefully decorated with colourful rugs, two armchairs and a very cosy sofa. Three of those typical small Moroccan tea tables sat next to the sofa and the armchairs. The room looked very pleasing in the bright light shining through the window. After a few minutes, Fatima brought in a silver tray with some fresh Moroccan mint tea and two cups and placed it down on one of the small tables next to them.

"There you go. Enjoy the tea. Sorry, I cannot join you today. I'm in the middle of cooking lunch and I'll have to go back to the kitchen. And Tariq needs feeding soon too. Please excuse me, I'll have to go," She smiled.

When they were left alone, Kareem picked up his cup and took a sip of the strongly flavoured tea he loved so much. It took him a few moments to pluck up his courage to ask his brother the delicate question he came to see him for. As it was a very personal matter, it was not normally something he would discuss even with a relative or anybody else for that matter. However, Tahiri and he had always been close since they were children and had no secrets from each other. He looked over to his brother. Tahiri knew Kareem well and he knew that he would say what bothered him in his own time. He waited until Kareem was ready to speak.

"Erm, Tahiri, forgive me but there is something rather delicate that I have come to ask you about. I think I need your help in a certain matter," he began, a little embarrassed.

"Yes, go ahead," his brother encouraged him.

"As you know, Amel and I have been trying for a baby for quite some time. We really want to start a family, we're ready for it. But, erm, you see, Amel has already had three miscarriages so far within a fairly short time, and she is terribly scared it will happen again if she has another pregnancy. She is feeling rather distressed."

"Oh, bro, I'm so very sorry to hear that. I had no idea," Tahiri said, shocked at this revelation his brother had just offered.

Kareem took another sip of his mint tea, and then placed the cup carefully on the tray. "Yes, it has been a rather tough time for both of us, I'm afraid. And I so want to help her. And of course, also myself, as I want a family as much as she does."

"I understand, I really do," Tahiri looked thoughtful. "And how do you think I can help?"

"Well, I thought you might have some ideas about how we can go about it. I mean, having a baby, a pregnancy that will not be terminated in such a way? I know it is nature's way to a certain extent but maybe there is something else we can do? Is there perhaps a special treatment we could try? What do you think?"

Tahiri was thoughtful for a long moment before he spoke again. "Mmh, I believe there is something. They call it IVF treatment. That would be an option, I assume. However, from what I have heard, it might be very expensive. Also, there would be many tests you would have to undergo first before you could go ahead with the treatment. And there is still a chance it might not work. But you could have a try and see how it goes."

"Ah, yes, I think I might have heard of IVF treatments and what it involves. Unfortunately, I don't have a lot of money for this kind of treatment. I really don't want to wait for years until I have a lot of money saved up because by then we might be too old anyway," Kareem said in despair. He ran his hand through his thick hair, a gesture he always did when he was in distress.

"True, yes. Well, it was only an idea. But you know, there is something else I could think of," Tahiri ventured.

"And what's that? Anything that might help us would be good to try," Kareem asked desperately.

Tahiri's heart went out to his brother and he saw how distressed he was. Being a father himself now, he knew how much love and joy a child could give them.

"Have you ever thought about an adoption? You know you could adopt a child and provide him with a good life, a good future. You know, a child that maybe comes from a disadvantaged family, perhaps from India, Asia, or another African country. It might be a child who had lost his parents due to a war or something like that. You would help yourself as well as the child. There are so many poor, unfortunate children in this world, for whatever reason, and they would appreciate being given the chance for a better life and a good education."

Kareem sat quietly and considered the suggestion his brother offered for a while. He stared into space. For some reason, he had not thought of this option before. Yet, he realised, it might be their only chance.

"Actually, no, I've never even thought of it," he admitted to his brother, "but it might be our only chance. You know, the best thing is to talk to Amel and see what she thinks. Perhaps she would consider this and then we could start making some inquiries."

"Yes, do that. After all, she would have to agree, wouldn't she? Amel would have to feel comfortable with it because it would not be your biological child. But that doesn't mean you cannot be his parents and do a good or probably a better job than the biological parents."

"Definitely," Kareem agreed, "however, I would hate it if she didn't feel comfortable with this. I don't want to pressurize her. I'll talk to her in the next couple of days. I just wanted to give her a bit of time because of what has just happened and not stress her out even more."

"Absolutely, you're right," Tahiri said, "anyway, let me know, if and when you have decided you want to go ahead with it because I have a friend in Turkey, Adnan, who knows an adoption agency which is located in Izmir. It's a city on the west coast of the country, by the way. They deal with this subject professionally and they are also good friends of his. Have you met Adnan, by the way?"

Kareem shook his head. "No, I've never met him in person but I remember you mentioned him occasionally. He studied with you, didn't he, and he is often on business trips, also here in Morocco as well, isn't he?"

"Yes, that's the one. We've been friends forever. And don't worry, he is a good person. He would never recommend or do anything illegal, let alone put us in touch with a shady adoption business. That's not his style. It's all very well organised and they have a very good reputation. Think about it, Kareem, and let me know what you two have decided. And if you decide to go ahead, we'll get the ball rolling, okay?"

Kareem stood up. He felt much better after this conversation. He knew his brother would be able to come up with a solution. He was a very wise and worldly man. He embraced Tahiri and made his way through the long corridor to the door. When he passed the kitchen, he waved goodbye to Fatima, who was busy feeding their young son Tariq. With a lighter heart, he set off down the alleyway to his own home.

A few weeks later, on a sunny Sunday afternoon in July, both Kareem and Amel sat again in Tahiri's living room, this time together. After Kareem had announced the idea of adoption to Amel after the conversation he had with his brother, she had, to his surprise, readily agreed to this option.

"I think Tahiri is right. We might be able to give a child a good life, opportunities, and the love he or she needs. We can still be parents, even if we are not the biological ones. I believe there are many babies out in this world who need a loving home, as well as a good education. Yes, why not help one of them," Amel had agreed.

"You know, ma Cherie, I'm so very glad to hear this and that you agree. I was so worried about you. It's just that I didn't want to put any pressure on you. And after all, it's a very important decision for both of us."

They told Tahiri about their final decision to adopt a baby from Turkey and asked him to contact his friend, Adnan, on their behalf. Tahiri got to work and a week later he came back with some good news.

"Great news! Adnan has called me a couple of days ago and he is ready to receive you. He contacted his friends from the agency and was told that there are a couple of newborn babies they received in June, and he is hopeful that one of them will be right for you."

"Fantastic news! We do hope so as well," Kareem said and squeezed his wife's hand.

"What do we have to do now? I assume we need to travel to Izmir soon to meet the babies and then decide on one of them? And what about the adoption papers? How does it work?"

"I would make a flight booking for some time in August and stay over until the adoption papers are ready. They can organise everything for you there and then, no problem at all. And then you can take the baby home with you straight away," Tahiri reassured them.

"Okay, we'll do that. I do hope we'll find a lovely baby who wants to come home with us," Amel said passionately. She was ready to become a mother.

"Also, please let me know your flight details as soon as you've made the booking. I'll send them to Adnan so he can pick you up. Oh, and by the way, I almost forgot to mention it. You're going to stay at my friend's house. He lives in Izmir too. He doesn't want you to stay in a hotel. Please accept his invitation, he insisted on it," Tahiri announced.

"That's awfully kind of him, please thank him in advance. We'll make our flight booking within the next few days, and then we're getting ready to become parents next month! And thank you too, brother, for all your help," Kareem said happily.

"My pleasure, I hope it'll all go well. I can't wait to become an uncle myself!" Tahiri laughed.

Kareem looked fondly at his wife whose beautiful face had more colour in it than it had for a long time. *It would be good for her to finally become a mother and it will make her happy*, he thought.

A couple of days later, they went to their local travel agency in the town centre and booked their flight to Izmir in August. They were ready to embark on their new adventure as parents.

Amel and Kareem
Izmir, August 1993
An Adoption

"You know, Kareem, I'm still a bit nervous about this whole adoption thing. Do you really think it's the right way to go forward?" Amel sounded sceptical and looked at her husband.

"We'll see, but it's maybe the only way for us, love. Please don't worry right now. We'll see when we get there. If it is completely not right for us, then we won't have to go through with it, I'm sure. There is no obligation," he reassured her.

It was an early afternoon one day in late August, when they sat on a plane at Marrakesh airport bound for Izmir in Turkey, where they would be greeted at the airport by Tahiri's friend, Adnan. The couple had not travelled very much before, apart from a few places in their own country, and therefore it was a special adventure to have this journey to another country and in fact, to another continent. After a few hours, flying and circling over the Mediterranean Sea before they were given a slot to land, the plane touched down smoothly at the airport of Izmir. It was dusk already and the lights of the city were beginning to be switched on.

"I hope Adnan is there and will indeed pick us up," Amel said to Kareem when they were in the queue for Immigration.

"Don't worry, Cherie, he will. I trust my brother and I know he would not send us to someone shady and irresponsible who would leave us stranded here. Remember, he had emailed our flight details to Adnan," he reassured his wife.

After a few more minutes, they emerged into the arrival hall and picked up their suitcases. They intended to stay for two weeks but depending on the paperwork involved in the adoption, they might have to extend their stay for a few more days. His supervisor at the restaurant had been very understanding when he told him the reason why they were making this trip to Turkey and had not objected to Kareem's leave of absence.

"Look, there he is," Kareem pointed to a tall, slim Turkish man, dressed in a dark-blue business suit, who was standing in the crowd holding up a sign up with their names and scanning the newly arrivals. Kareem waved to him and pushed their trolley in his direction.

"Merhaba! You must be Kareem and Amel," Adnan greeted them in a pleasant and friendly voice when they approached him.

"Yes, we are, and you must be Adnan, my brother's friend. I'm so pleased to meet you," Kareem shook his hand.

"So am I. Did you have a pleasant trip, I hope?" Adnan inquired and smiled.

"Yes, thank you, it was perfect and the flight was even on time," Kareem said.

"Brilliant, so let's go then. Please let me help you with your luggage. Fortunately, we won't have to drive far. I live only 20 minutes away from the airport."

He grabbed the trolley with the luggage and started making his way through the many people, followed by Kareem and Amel. He led them to the airport parking and steered them in the direction to a large SUV which seemed to be a new model with tinted windows.

"Here we are. It's my company car," he announced and opened the boot to drop their luggage in. Then he held the back seat door open for them to climb in.

When he drove off, Adnan asked, "Have you ever been to Turkey before?"

"No, it's our first time," Kareem replied.

"Ah, so I hope that at the same time you can see a little bit of my city as well, then. It's rather a nice place and by the sea as you know. There is plenty to do here as well. I hope you do like it and perhaps one day you will come back for a holiday."

"Yes, we hope so. It would be nice to see the place where our new baby originates from. It seems very nice from the few glimpses we have seen so far," Amel offered and smiled, looking out of the car window to the busy streets of the city. It had a good feel to it and the place reminded her of other cities in their home country.

Adnan's apartment, he shared with his wife, was located in a middle-class area of the city, in a lovely tree-lined avenue not far from the centre. Kareem and Amel were impressed by the Turkish hospitality and felt very welcome. Over a delicious dinner introducing various Turkish dishes, prepared by Adnan's wife, he informed them about the adoption agency and how they would proceed with finding themselves a baby.

Two days later, Adnan took Amel and Kareem to his friend's adoption agency which was located right in the city centre. However, there was no business name sign on the entrance door to the office which Amel thought was a bit odd but didn't think more about it. They were greeted by a receptionist and asked to remain in the waiting room.

It was a pleasant-looking room that looked more like a family living room than a foreroom of an adoption agency. There were some pictures hanging on the wall that showed pretty Turkish landscapes, including Pamukkale with its famous thermal water terraces, the archaeological site of nearby Ephesus, among several other pictures that showed faces of happy, smiling babies. Amel studied the faces of the children and felt a warm sensation wash over her. Soon, hopefully, she would hold her own baby in her arms that would also smile happily like those children in the photos.

Soon they were called and when they were shown into the office, Adnan introduced them to his friend Khalila, who was also the owner of the agency.

"Khalila, these are my friends, Kareem and Amel, who I was telling you about."

"Yes, hello, I'm very pleased to meet you. I'm Khalila and I hope I can help you find a nice baby who you will take home with you soon," she said and stood up to shake Amel's hand. She was well-dressed in a dark yellow business suit, and the way she spoke, they realised she was also well-educated and spoke excellent English.

"Thank you very much. We hope so too. It took us a while to make this decision to adopt, you see. It's not very common in our country," Kareem explained and Amel nodded.

"I understand. It is rather a difficult decision for many couples, you see. Actually, interestingly most couples who adopt through us are Europeans. It is very common there, you see. I personally believe it is a good way to help a child and if you cannot have your own biological children, you can still be parents and have a family," Khalila agreed.

"That's exactly the reason why we have decided to take this step," Amel offered.

"Congratulations. And you don't have to worry, once you have decided on a baby the adoption papers can be prepared during your stay, and it will not take long. It's all perfectly legal."

"Brilliant, thank you, Khalila," they both said.

"Well, we are lucky at the moment. We have actually received three babies in the past couple of months, two girls and one boy, and hopefully one of them might be suitable for you. First, I will show you some photos of them and then I will take you to the orphanage where they are being looked after in the meantime before being adopted, where you can also meet them and decide. We always make sure that the couples we take there can spend some time with the children because it is important how they feel with them. After all, they will have to be good parents and spend a long time with the child."

Khalila stood up and took out a large folder from the bookcase that stood by the office window and placed the file on the desk in front of Kareem and Amel. She opened it and showed them several photos of the three children she had mentioned earlier. All three of them looked cute and healthy.

"It is quite unusual that we have several babies coming in at almost the same time, normally it is just one or two and then there is a gap again until we receive another one. We do receive older children more often, you see," she explained.

The couple studied the photos carefully. Khalila told them to take their time and get a feel for the children first.

"Forgive me for asking this but what is the issue with those babies? What I mean is that are they orphans, half-orphans or the family cannot look after them? Or maybe the mother was unmarried and could therefore not keep the baby?" Amel wanted to know.

"This is the case with one of the girls, yes. Sadly, the mother was quite young and was unable to keep the baby. She would have been shamed by her family if they had known and she would not be able to get married later on if her future husband found out."

"That's a very sad story," Amel admitted.

"But with the other girl, her parents have died in a car accident only recently. In the case of the boy, we were told that the mother had died in the hospital giving birth but I'm not familiar with the whole circumstances regarding the father but this is what we were told when he was brought to us. We have no other information, unfortunately."

"Okay, thank you for filling us in. How old are they?" Kareem was interested.

"The girl, the one with the single mother, is two months old. The other girl is only one month old, and the boy will be three months old in a few days."

Amel studied the picture of the boy for a very long time, and she felt some kind of strange sensation shooting through her body, a familiarity, a little bit like *Deja vue*. This feeling did not make any sense to her but she knew in an instant that it was the boy who she wanted to adopt. Kareem studied the photos carefully as well and then looked at his wife. Her eyes had a gleam in them that he liked.

"So, what do you think, are you ready to go and see them?" he asked her.

"Yes, I am," Amel said and decided she would tell her husband later what she felt and that she was convinced that the little boy was the right choice for them.

When Khalila and Adnan took them to the orphanage where the babies currently lived, they discussed quietly in the back of the car what they thought about which baby they would likely adopt.

"I love that little boy," whispered Amel to her husband, "I don't know what it is but he had something in his eyes that I feel so drawn to. It's very strange and I have never had that feeling before."

"I do understand, Amel, because the same thing has happened to me," admitted Kareem.

Amel looked at her husband in astonishment. He was not normally so ready to admit to something so easily.

"Are you saying you also think that little boy is the one for us?"

"Yes, I do. Even before we see him, and the girls. They also looked lovely but the connection with the boy is somehow special. However, Khalila seems very kind and for the sake of her, I feel we should see all three children, regardless, what do you think?"

"Oh, definitely, yes, I totally agree. Let's not jump into a decision right away and we can let her know when we are back in her office. I don't want her to think that we are wasting her time," Amel agreed.

"I wonder if they have been given names. That would be good. If not, we'll have to choose a name ourselves." Amel remarked to her husband.

"From what I have heard, I believe you can normally change their name after the adoption, if you like, yes. Maybe the young mother has given her daughter a name but the parents who died, I doubt it somehow that the child's name would be known. Hopefully, the boy already has a name too and that we'll like it."

"Yes, I assume you're right. Let's see what we can find out. Oh, wow, look at that building! That must be it. We've almost arrived! What a lovely place!" Amel exclaimed.

She pointed to a beautiful house that had come into view as they were driven through a garden with exotic flowers; it looked like an old Ottoman palace. Adnan stopped the car in front of the entrance and switched off the engine.

"Here we are, the orphanage. It is a lovely place that is why it was chosen. It's actually an old mansion that they have converted for the purpose and a really nice place with a large garden at the back. Right, let's go and see the children," Adnan announced.

The four of them went in together and waited in a large room that looked like a foyer of a big hotel while Khalila announced their arrival with the manager of the orphanage. As she had called ahead to inform them of their visit and which children they wanted to meet for a possible adoption, they didn't have to wait long until they were picked up.

A middle-aged Turkish lady who was like Khalila, immaculately dressed in a dark-blue silk business suit, who introduced herself as the manager, greeted them kindly and told them to follow her.

They were led up the steps onto the first floor and through a long corridor that led to a large, pleasant-looking room specially designed as a play area for smaller children. There were many toys, cuddly teddy bears in all sizes and several baby books lying around, and two childminders were busy keeping the little ones occupied. Several large and colourful 'kilims' (rugs) with typical Turkish designs decorated the floor and the windows stood open letting the warm air and birdsong into the room.

The scene was very cosy to look at and there was no doubt in Amel and Kareem's mind that the place was run in a professional manner. As soon as they entered, several pairs of eyes were staring at them, curious why all those people were there all of a sudden.

"Come over here, sorry about the mess. The children are having fun. It's their play hour, you see," the manager explained with a smile and guided them to the far end of the room.

"The three babies you would like to see are over here by the window. I understand you are interested in adopting a baby, not an older child? I assume you have already been presented with some photos of them in Khalila's office?" she asked the couple, and they both nodded.

There, in a large baby play nest sat three attractive looking children. There were the two girls that Amel and Kareem had seen the photos of in the file, as well as the little baby boy. When Amel looked at them, her heart began to melt. How sad, she thought that their parents were not able to look after them, for whatever reason. They surely deserved a good home.

She smiled at them and as she did, the little boy looked up and straight at her with an expression of such intensity in his dark-brown eyes that Amel's heart jolted. She knew in an instant, just like she did when she had seen his picture, that this boy was the chosen one. It was almost as if he was the one who had actually chosen them.

Kareem had watched his wife intensely and was aware of her feelings. "He is the one, isn't he? Isn't he gorgeous?" he whispered to his wife looking at the boy.

"Yes, he is, Kareem. I don't know what it is but there is something about him. There is some kind of connection. You could see it too, couldn't you?" she whispered back.

The Manager stopped at the play area. "So, here they are. All three are adorable and no trouble at all. The girls are around two months old and the boy is turning three months next week. Would you like to spend a little time with the children?"

"Yes," the couple agreed, "we would like that very much, thank you. Do we have to come to your office to see you once we have decided?" Kareem wanted to know.

"Yes, of course, and take as long as you like. I'll be downstairs in my office. Once you have decided which child you feel comfortable with, and you are absolutely sure about the adoption, then we can start getting the paperwork organised, even today if you like. I'll leave Adnan and Khalila with you here in case you have any questions," she said and made her way back downstairs.

While Adnan conversed a little with the childminders, Khalila sat down with Kareem and Amel next to the babies and played with them. Both girls were beautiful with large, brown eyes and very fine brown hair. The boy had a wisp of jet-black hair, dark-green eyes, which was very unusual, and was truly attractive. He looked at the couple and Amel offered him her hand. He took one finger into his tiny hand and held it tightly as if he didn't want to let go at all.

"Wow, that's incredible. It looks like he has just chosen you!" Khalila exclaimed.

"Yes, it seems like it. He is so lovely and my wife and I feel a special connection with him. She is already smitten with him. Well, actually, it's a pity we cannot adopt all three of them! They're truly adorable. They all deserve good parents. But since we are only able to adopt one baby, I'm convinced that this boy is the one for us," Kareem confirmed.

Khalila and Adnan, who had rejoined them, nodded and then she said something that baffled them, "You know, he is the only child who was actually given a name."

"Oh, really, was he?" both Kareem and Amel looked at her in astonishment.

"Yes, it is rather unusual here but even more because his mother had died after he was born. I'm not sure about the circumstances but the parents apparently wanted to make sure it was known that his name is Şenay. The name is also mentioned on his birth certificate, together with his birth parents' names. However, of course, if you don't like his name, you are welcome to change it. There is no obligation to keep it."

"Oh, no, not at all, I like his name very much. Don't you, Kareem? It's a beautiful and unusual name, and it really suits him. What's the meaning?"

"It is a lovely name, I agree. It's a typical Turkish name and it means 'Happy Moon'."

"Oh, how beautiful, and knowing the meaning now, we do feel it suits him. His expression is happy and his face lights up the room like the moonlight. We will not change it and we'll bring him up as our son, Şenay," Amel announced and Kareem agreed.

"Fantastic. So, you are happy then and you feel you want to go ahead with the adoption?" Khalila asked again.

"Perfect, yes. I'm also impressed with the orphanage. It looks clean, seems very well run as well and it gives us a good feeling. You understand we wanted to make sure it is not a shady business and it is all legal with the adoption. It was important to come here to see for ourselves and thank you for your help. But since my brother is a good friend of Adnan, I was sure that we can trust him, and you, of course," Kareem said.

"I do understand. One can never be too careful. Unfortunately, there is a lot of human trafficking going on in the world. I would never get involved in anything illegal. After all, you are dealing with human beings and everyone should be respected," Adnan confirmed.

They stood up, waved to the children and said goodbye to the childminders, then made their way back downstairs to the manager's office to start the adoption procedure. There were a few formalities to sort out with the orphanage, as well as the need to make an additional flight booking later on for the little boy to return to Morocco with them and therefore needed the full name of the boy.

The manager was printing out a draft document she had prepared earlier, and then handed it to the couple to check through. "Please verify that it is all in order so that there won't be any mistakes in the original."

There was a knock on the door and an assistant walked into the room with a tray of 'Elma Chai' (apple tea) and placed it on the desk in front of them.

"Thank you so much," Amel said, again touched by the Turkish hospitality she had grown to like very much during her few days in this country.

"Would you like some baklavas to go with the tea?" the Manager asked, "we get them homemade every day from the bakery down the road."

"It's awfully kind of you, thank you, but no. We both have to watch our waistline. The tea is lovely, a real treat," Amel smiled broadly. The assistant left the room and they concentrated again on reading the draft document.

"Once the original document is ready, I will send it to Khalila, as she deals with the adoption side of things. I only deal with the welfare of the children, you see, with their personal documents, and how to release them once they have been chosen," the Manager informed them.

"That's perfect, thank you. When do you think will the papers be ready? It's just so that we can make Şenay's flight booking for him to travel back together with us."

"I would say it will all be ready in approx. four days' time, latest five days to be sure. And by the way, here is his birth certificate, which will be given to you with all the documents, as you've requested," She reached into her file and pulled out another sheet of paper.

"That's brilliant, thank you. And then we come back here to pick him up?" Kareem said.

"Yes, if you come with your signed adoption papers, you can then pick up Şenay right away. We will get him ready and dress him in his best clothes."

Kareem took the birth certificate and showed it to Amel. When they looked at it, they had the confirmation that written next to the birthdate, which was in

June of the same year, was the name Şenay. His birth parents were named as Yasmin Özgűr-Bonerti and the father's name was Metin Özgűr. According to their birthdates, they had been fairly young.

Amel looked at the names for a while. When she read the mother's name, she frowned. It somehow seemed strange to her that the mother's maiden name sounded foreign to her, not Turkish. In fact, it seemed a European name, perhaps even Italian. She was curious to know what fate had befallen Şenay's mother.

"That's interesting," she said slowly, pointing at the woman's name on the document, "do you know, by any chance, where the parents had come from, especially the mother? I don't want to pressurise you, and maybe you're not allowed to say anything. It's just that the mother seemed to have been a foreigner. Well, at least that's what her name suggests."

The Manager took the certificate from her and looked at it. "Actually yes, true, that's what strikes me as a bit odd too, to be honest, and I wish I did know more, Amel. But unfortunately, we were not given any more information regarding the parents apart from the fact that the mother had died. Perhaps, she had moved over here initially to get married but we don't know anything about the father. I'm ever so sorry I cannot give you any more information."

"Okay, well, thank you anyway, I was just curious. There is nothing we can do about it. It's now up to us to make sure that we will give Şenay a good and happy life. We will do our best to give him the education he deserves and that he has a chance in his life and be successful. We promise to do our best. Thank you very much for your kindness."

Kareem and Amel stood up and Amel and the Manager shook hands. Feeling content and tranquil, they were led out of the building. They left in Adnan's car that he had parked in front of the house. The couple felt a rush of happiness when they realised that they had just become a proper family. It was a milestone for them.

"We cannot thank you enough, Adnan. And you, of course, Khalila, for your kind and professional help with this adoption. We are glad that we sought this solution. Şenay is so adorable. He seems a very happy baby," Kareem announced in the car.

"It was a great pleasure to help you. You are very welcome. I'm pleased you have found a baby who will make you happy and that you have become a proper family now. Congratulations!" Adnan's words were genuine and he felt pleased for this nice couple.

It was five days later when Kareem and Amel were driven again up to the orphanage by Adnan. All the paperwork had come through as promised, and they had picked it up early in the morning from Khalila at the adoption agency before they made their way to pick up their new son, Şenay. When he was brought downstairs by one of the childminders they had met during their last visit, the boy looked very handsome in a new, dark blue baby suit and a matching hat that made his dark complexion stand out. His dark-green eyes were shining when he looked at them as if he already knew that today was his special day; the first day of the rest of his life and his first day with his new family. Adnan's wife had kindly presented them with a new buggy seat to put him in so that he was comfortable for the journey and which could also be taken on the plane.

After another week in the country where they enjoyed more of the famous Turkish hospitality, as well as visiting some historic places such as the nearby ancient city of Ephesus and some beaches in the area suggested by Adnan, they purchased some gifts for the family and enjoyed shopping for more baby clothes for Şenay as well as some gifts for Tahiri and Fatima at the local outdoor markets.

It was a hot and humid afternoon in late August when the whole family sat on a plane bound for Marrakesh. Adnan and his wife had dropped them off at the airport, making them promise to consider returning to Turkey in the near future to have a proper holiday and to present them with an older version of their son.

"We came as two people and we leave as three. Oh, I'm so happy Kareem! We are a proper family!" Amel beamed with happiness and looked fondly at her adoptive son, who was sitting comfortably between them in a child's seat, smiling up at her.

He had been very calm and not once did he cry when they had taken him to the busy airport or boarded the plane. It seemed as if he had always been part of this family and that he was a born traveller already.

Marrakesh, Morocco
December 2008
Yasmin

"I can't wait to be on holiday! I truly deserve it!" Yasmin announced to her friend Naila, who was sitting beside her and strapped herself into her seat on the plane that would take them to Marrakesh that afternoon.

She looked out of the tiny window of the plane to the busy London Heathrow airport Terminal and felt a rush of excitement through her body. It was her first holiday in a while. She had been on various business trips throughout the years but there was never enough time to add some additional days as a holiday. Due to her busy schedule at work as a Food and Beverage Manager in London, it had been ages since she had had an opportunity to relax, let alone even think of a proper vacation.

"Neither can I, believe me! I'm so glad we could make it even if we are so busy at work. You have never been to Morocco, have you?" Naila asked and adjusted her seat to the upright position.

"No, it's my first time," Yasmin replied with a smile, "but it is a place I've always wanted to visit. A good friend of mine, who has been travelling around Morocco several times in a rental car actually, told me good things about the country and its inhabitants, and ever since I wanted to check it out myself. It's such a varied country and I'm looking forward to seeing a few places there."

The chill of winter was in the air, and being December, there was a light blanket of snow lying on the ground due to some snowfall they had the night before but it was not enough to be worried about that they would not be able to take off due to a blizzard or ice. The flight left on time and they felt excited that their holiday had finally begun.

Just over three hours later, they stepped out of the plane at Marrakesh airport and a pleasant, warm and sunny afternoon greeted them. Yasmin inhaled the new smells and the warmth eagerly and welcomed it with a grateful heart.

"Great! This is more like it! It's such a difference to the cold and damp winter weather in London, and a nice escape, don't you think?" she said to Naila.

"Oh yes, it is. I like it already. Morocco, here we come!" Naila beamed and followed her friend down the steps from the aeroplane onto the tarmac.

As they were crossing the airport towards the main building, suddenly and quite unexpectedly, Yasmin felt a strange sensation in her heart. It was as if this place had a hold over her as if there was something familiar about it, a special connection. She could not understand why because she had never been to Marrakesh or even in this country before. Maybe because it was somehow similar to Turkey, she mused, because it had a certain familiar feel to it.

Trudging along behind all the other tourists, they made their way to the baggage claim and then looked for the queue for the shuttle bus that would take them to their hotel which was located in town.

A few months previously, Yasmin and Naila had decided to travel around Morocco for a few days to see more of the country and to spend a couple of days on the beach in Agadir, starting and ending their journey in Marrakesh.

"Let's stay in Marrakesh for the New Year's Eve celebration. I've heard it's supposed to be truly special. You know, it's a bit like in *1001 Arabian nights*," Yasmin had suggested to her friend when they were planning their holiday a couple of months ago.

"Sounds perfect to me! And maybe we'll find our Aladdin there as well," she had joked with her friend, her eyes sparkling mischievously.

"Oh well, let's see about that, shall we! But, you know, there are also fantastic and colourful bazaars, so we could go on a shopping spree. It's the perfect place to buy gifts and also leather jackets and handbags which Morocco is so famous for."

Naila had readily agreed to her friend's proposal and felt excited herself to go on this trip. The weather was quite pleasant at this time of year, not too hot, and therefore perfect for travelling around. In the mountainous areas of the Atlas, such as Fez and its surroundings, it was cold and they had snowfalls too throughout the winter months.

On the shuttle bus into town, they took in the different landscape, the olive trees, the colourful exotic flowers, and street sellers offering fruit and vegetables, pushing their carts along the streets. It was a riot of noise and colour. Some sellers had the help of a donkey to pull the cart, and others even offered pretty handicraft items to tourists. The sight of them took Yasmin back to another long-ago moment, and for a while, she felt melancholic, even a little sad.

The moment passed soon, and anyway, she scolded herself, she would not let the past get in her way of this well-earned holiday. After all, it was almost 16 years since her life changed in such a dramatic manner. Having Naila as a close friend since her university days was a blessing, and when they had reconnected in the UK back in 1993, Yasmin had filled her in about the events that had taken place all those years ago in Turkey. Naila had been absolutely fantastic, very understanding and a great help to her. Yasmin considered herself truly lucky to have a friend who proved to be a rock in her life during those very difficult months. She and her attractive Indian friend Naila, with her winning, contagious smile and long, raven black hair, had been inseparable ever since.

She knew that Naila, being of Indian descent, had many contacts and it came naturally to her to help Yasmin find her new job as she worked for the same hotel chain but in a different location. She had put in a good word for her friend and Yasmin was very lucky to land her new position in London in no time. Suddenly, she snapped out of her day-dreaming state when her friend nudged her.

"Oh look, Yasmin, those fruits on that cart! They look so tasty and juicy. I can't wait to try everything here!"

Naila pointed to a fruit trolley standing by the roadside when the shuttle bus stopped at a traffic light. The seller was an elderly man sitting on an old chair beside the cart reading a newspaper. The scene looked very relaxing.

Yasmin laughed, knowing very well her friend's constant eating habits. "Oh, why I am not surprised. If I was eating as much as you do, I'd look like an elephant."

"No, you wouldn't, I'm sure. I just have a different metabolism, that's why I'm so skinny. And you exercise much more than I do."

"Well, maybe fruit might not be so bad for me then, and the hotel gym. I do love fresh fruit juices, and for some reason, exotic fruit always tastes better in the country where they come from, don't you think?"

"Oh definitely, yes. It's just not the same as if you buy them at Tesco. I find it's the same with the olives," Naila mused.

Twenty minutes later, they were driving in the city centre and the shuttle bus was pulling into the drive that took them to their hotel. They had managed to find a great deal with an additional twenty-five per cent reduction due to their jobs at the same hotel chain in London. The bus stopped in front of the entrance and they got off to collect their suitcases.

When they had checked in and found their way to their hotel room, it was as if they had been there for weeks already. Both felt very relaxed and the hotel had a nice, calm feel about it. Yasmin opened the room with the card key and placed her suitcase in front of the bed. It was a little dark inside because the curtains were drawn. She went over to the window trying to find the cord to open them. When she succeeded and opened the curtains, letting the sunlight in, she discovered that there was a balcony hiding behind them. Excitedly, she slid the door open and stepped out on the balcony which she saw contained a small round table with two chairs, inviting them for a drink later. After the coolness of the room from the air conditioning, the warm air of the afternoon welcomed her again.

"Come and look, Naila, it's amazing," she called out to her friend, "guess what, our room is overlooking the swimming pool! I can't wait to have a dip in it!"

"Wow, that's amazing! I've always liked those fancy pools. The imagination of the architects seems endless. This one looks like a huge kidney, doesn't it?" Naila said when she joined her and happily clapped her hands.

Many deckchairs were placed around the swimming pool and on the other side of the pool there was another, small walk-in pool, designed for little children to play in. The whole area was a gigantic, carefully manicured garden with narrow pathways snaking through it. Little pods with tables and chairs were dotted around where an evening drink could be enjoyed, and they were all surrounded by various exotic plants, palm trees and flowers in bright colours. It looked what Yasmin imagined paradise would be. It was truly divine.

When they stepped back into the room, Naila sat down on the bed and tried to pin up her shiny ebony hair into a knot. Yasmin always admired her gorgeous hair that seemed never to be out of shape without her putting any effort into it.

"Right, shall we make a move and try out that divine swimming pool? It's so hot! Such a difference to London, isn't it? I can't wait to cool down in the water. Actually, I might book the Turkish bath for tomorrow morning, too. I've heard it must be such a treat."

"Yes, let's do that, I'm up for it. You'll like the 'Hammam', I assure you. There is one downstairs in the spa area. They give you a massage too, and it's very relaxing, believe me. I've treated myself to it several times when I was living in Turkey. You feel like a new born when you come out. I'll come with you in the morning if you like," Yasmin suggested.

"Ah, yes, I do remember, you told me. I'll definitely treat myself to that. I can't wait. Of course, you must have had some good times there during your time in Turkey."

"Oh, yes, I did indeed, it was divine. And shall we make the reservations for the tours we decided to take at the same time, what do you think? I saw there is a tour desk downstairs, so we can organise it all there. Perhaps, they'll offer us a discount as well because we work for the same hotel chain. We'll try."

"Yeah, let's do that. We don't want to lose any precious time to hit the road in this beautiful country, do we? Where shall we go first? I suggest we travel north first and then make our way to the coast, then south, before coming back to Marrakesh," Naila suggested.

"Sounds perfect to me. Let's go and hit the tour desk now. And don't forget to take your swimsuit and towel for the dip later."

A few days later, on a chilly morning, Yasmin and Naila stood before a gigantic gate in Fez. It was one of the entrances leading into the vast Medina in town. Despite being cold, the sun had made its appearance and it promised to be a nice day.

"Wow! Look at this! I'll have to get my camera out, this is amazing!" Yasmin exclaimed and rummaged in her bag for her camera.

She stared up in awe at the blue mosaic pattern that presented itself on the massive arch in front of her, taking some pictures. "I have a feeling that this is one of those places where you can't control your camera," She laughed.

Just at that time, an attractive young man approached them. He looked in his late twenties and was well dressed in dark blue jeans and an olive-coloured T-shirt. His dark brown hair was neatly combed. He was holding a map in one hand

and the mobile phone case strapped to his belt gave away that his profession was probably a tour guide.

"Good morning ladies, Merhaba," he addressed them in English in a friendly voice.

Yasmin and Naila both turned at once to look at him. "Oh, hello, good morning," they both said at the same time and laughed.

"Please, may I introduce myself, my name is Mohammed, and I work as a tour guide. I specialise in taking tourists into the Medina because it is a very extensive one and therefore it's very easy to get lost in it. It's what you could call a maze. There are more than 8km of city walls encircling this place. Believe me, it is quite a challenge to get around," he explained in immaculate English.

"Oh, that's incredible. We have heard of this Medina before, yes, but we didn't know it was that extensive," Yasmin answered.

"Would you like me to explain a little bit more about it before you decide? Yes? For instance, the ornamented gate here that you have just admired is called the 'Blue Gate' and it is one of the main entrances to the old Medina. This place has an interesting and fascinating past and it's actually the largest Medina in the world."

"Really? Wow! That is pretty impressive!" Naila exclaimed.

"Oh yes, it is. It's also a good place for buying herbs, spices and leather goods. And, talking about leather, there is a tannery here too. If you have not seen this before, it might catch your interest," Mohammed offered.

Yasmin and Naila looked at each other and nodded. "Yes, that would be brilliant and it does sound interesting. We might take up your service," Yasmin smiled.

Mohammed continued to explain more about the old Medina, where 200,000 people lived, and the city of Fez which was founded in the 9th century AD and was also home to the oldest university in the world. Impressed by what they had just learned, Yasmin and Naila decided to take up on his offer to be their tour guide for the day.

"Thank you, ladies, and please do not worry, the Medina is completely car-free. You might come across a donkey or two but that's all. Please follow me now. Step into a fairytale land and let's travel back in time," he announced and led them through the Blue Gate into the ancient walled city.

As it turned out, it was indeed a very extensive tour and they had to admit, without Mohammed's professional guidance, they would never have been able to find their way out. They understood very quickly why it was known as the largest Medina in the world. On their way through the narrow passages, they passed several souk vendors that specialized in spices, herbs, lamps and leather and, of course, silver and gold jewellery. Yasmin bought several spices from one of the friendly sellers, who offered her to try each one. After they had visited the tannery, where Mohammed explained to them the process of leather dying, they decided to go for lunch at one of the many stylish gourmet restaurants with tasty Moroccan tagines and couscous, among other specialities.

The Medina was a labyrinth of alleyways, all so narrow that not even a small car could have possibly driven through. They saw several donkeys carrying goods to the many stalls. Here life was bustling. Souk sellers were sitting in front of their stores, chatting, laughing or drinking mint tea with their neighbours. Some shop owners were calling out to attract people to buy their goods and at the spice stalls, they were introduced to high, colourful mounds of various types of spices. Children were playing in the alleyways, running in between stalls and chasing each other. Women in hijabs and traditional Islamic clothes were shopping for their families and the men working in the souk wore Moroccan kaftans, the traditional garments for men.

It was already 2 pm and their tour was about to finish, so they decided to have lunch in the Medina. When they had chosen a cosy restaurant, recommended by their tour guide, and were guided to a table by a waiter wearing a green Moroccan kaftan, Mohammed handed them each a menu. It was quite extensive and even with Mohammed's explanation, it took them a while to decide on with dishes they fancied, there were so many.

"This is a good restaurant. I come here often. The owner is actually one of my cousins but that's not the only reason. The food here is exquisite, especially their Couscous, Tagines, and homade Baklavas, and the restaurant is always full which is a good sign," Mohammed explained.

"What is a Tagine?" Naila enquired.

"It's one of the main Moroccan's traditional dishes. It's basically like a casserole and it's made with either lamb, chicken or just with vegetables and lots of spices. It's prepared in a clay pot. It's delicious. Try it," Mohammed explained.

"Mmh, that really sounds tasty, I might go for that one actually," Naila said.

"I hope you liked the tour and your feet did not suffer too much. By the way, which hotel do you stay at in Fez? And how long will you be in Morocco?" Mohammed asked.

"Oh, we're actually travelling around the country. We're in Fez for one night and tomorrow we'll be off early to Casablanca by train, then we'll visit some places along the coast, the last stop being Agadir. Then we'll cross the Atlas Mountain into the south to Ouarzazate. Afterwards, we'll return to Marrakesh for another few days," Yasmin explained.

"That's brilliant. It's the best way of seeing a lot of this country," Mohammed agreed.

"Yes, we're looking forward to it. It's been impressive what we've seen so far," Naila agreed, "we've come from Marrakesh, you see, and we'll be celebrating the New Year there, too. Then we'll have to return to the UK, back to work, unfortunately."

"Ah, yes, one cannot enjoy when one doesn't work, I totally agree," Mohammed said and placed the order with the waiter in quick Arabic who had appeared at their table and brought some dates and Moroccan mint tea for them as a starter.

After a short while, their dishes were placed in front of them and they tucked in. "Wow, you were right! This lamb Tagine is truly divine! It's the first time I have eaten it and I can see that this is quickly becoming my favourite!" exclaimed Yasmin.

Mohammed smiled at her. "I'm pleased you like it. It is also my favourite dish and it is their speciality here. You mentioned before that you are going to stay for some more days in Marrakesh, didn't you?" he asked.

When Yasmin nodded, he continued, "You know, I have a friend whose cousin lives in Marrakesh and this cousin owns a restaurant. I have been there myself several times, and believe me, it's a very good address. I'll give you the business card and perhaps you would like to try it out when you are back?"

"Oh, that would be wonderful, thank you, yes," Both Yasmin and Naila nodded eagerly.

"Brilliant. Like here, the restaurant is located in the Medina and you can easily find it. The Medina there is smaller than the one here in Fez. Their speciality is also Tagine among others. It's a very popular place, not just with tourists but also with locals," Mohammed explained and fished out a business card from his shirt pocket.

He passed it on to Yasmin. She took the business card from him and looked at it. "Restaurant Al-Kareem," she read out loud.

"Thank you, Mohammed. Recommendations are always welcome, especially if you are new in the city. We'll definitely check it out, won't we Naila? I assume the owner's name is also Kareem?"

"You guessed correctly, yes, it is Kareem. He has been running his restaurant for quite some time. He went to university with my friend's cousin, you see, that's how they met. They have been friends for a long time," Mohammed confirmed.

Yasmin put the business card into her purse where it would be safe. They finished their lunch, chatting about their jobs in the UK and about their upcoming travels in Morocco.

Mohammed told them about being a tour guide and the daily challenges he came across working with so many people from all over the world. It was clear to them that he loved his job. After a while, they paid and left the restaurant, and Mohammed guided them safely through the maze of narrow alleys back to the entrance at the Blue Gate where they started their tour in the morning.

"Thank you very much, Mohammed, for this amazing tour. You are a true inspiration and very knowledgeable. We hope that you will have plenty of success with your business," the two friends said when they paid him before leaving for their hotel.

"The pleasure was all mine, ladies, it was good to meet you. And when you go for a meal at Al-Kareem, please say hello to my friend Kareem from me," He smiled and raised his hand to wave them goodbye.

"Does this bus have a toilet, do you think? I'm kind of desperate," Yasmin wiggled in her seat, feeling very uncomfortable.

"I'm not sure, I haven't seen one. But there is only one way of finding out. I'm going to ask the driver!" Naila responded and got up from her seat.

It was one week later, when they were on a bus travelling back to Marrakesh from the coastal town of Agadir, a trip that took nearly 6 hours by public transport as it stopped in many small towns along the way, picking up travellers. It was almost 3 hours into the journey when Yasmin started to feel uncomfortable.

When Naila came back she announced, "No toilet on the bus, apparently, but the driver will stop for us shortly. We'll just have to use the natural toilet if you know what I mean."

A few minutes later, the bus stopped and about 10 people ran out. Yasmin realised that it had not only been her who was desperate for the loo. The nearest toilet was, as Naila had said, the natural toilet for the men a little easier to handle than the women who had to find a place further down the embankment and out of sight.

"That feels better," she said, relieved when she returned to the bus, "and this is Morocco for you. I had to go all the way down the embankment and climb back up again. What an experience!" She laughed.

The rest of the journey took them through small, colourful villages and towns, all unique in their own way, with the locals busy going about their daily business. Many street stalls lined the roads where the sellers prepared meals by the roadside, including Tagines, and sold drinks, snacks and fruit to the travellers whenever a bus or a car stopped.

Yasmin was truly taken by this country, and watching the world go by through the bus window she mused, "You know, Naila, I feel so good here, I think I could even live in Morocco permanently. I know it sounds strange but there is something about this place, I don't know what it is but it holds some kind of magic over me. It's a jewel and I'm so glad we came here."

"Wow, that's quite a statement. Perhaps, you lived here in a previous life? It has really captured you, hasn't it?" exclaimed her friend.

"Oh yes, completely," Yasmin replied dreamily.

"Which place is your favourite then? I mean, from those we have seen so far?"

"Hmm, it's actually difficult to say. It's such a varied country and everything is interesting in its own way. But I'd say definitely Marrakesh and Ouarzazate, set in its desert location, stand out, and perhaps also Essaouira, as it located on the coast. Oh, and of course, the Medina in Fez too!"

"So true, I totally agree. I loved Ouarzazate too myself. I was truly amazed to see how the landscape changed completely when we crossed the Atlas Mountain into the desert. I didn't even know before that it was the gateway to the Sahara Desert or that the place featured in several movies."

"That was totally new to me too. I had no idea that Atlas Corporation Studios were located there. And how many times have I watched *The Living Daylights*! Me, as a James Bond fan, should have known!" Yasmin laughed.

Back in Marrakesh, the two friends were getting to know the magical town before they would get ready for the New Year's Eve celebration that would take place at their hotel. During the following two days, they watched the preparations made by the busy hotel staff that included the decoration of the garden and all the on-site restaurants.

It was the day before New Year's Eve, still pleasantly warm and sunny, when they were meandering around the bustling main square, the 'Jemaa-el-Fnaa' which was apparently the busiest square in Africa, according to the travel guide. There you could find anything offered from Henna painting, fruit sellers, tour guides offering their services, snake charmers, orange juice stalls, magicians, as well as many coffee shops that lined the square which was also the entrance to the Medina.

The square was only a short walk from their hotel and when they wandered through it, they noticed several 'caleches', horse-drawn carriages, being lined up alongside the short road leading on the side of the square to the Koutoubia mosque. They decided to venture out on a little tour and give the horse something to do. They chose a 'caleche' with a white horse, haggled for a while about the price with its owner, and when he agreed, climbed up into the carriage.

As they were taken through the narrow streets of the inner city and the Medina, Yasmin suddenly remembered that Mohammed, their tour guide in Fez, had given her a business card of a restaurant in the Medina that he had recommended to them. She quickly looked in her bag, hoping she had not lost the card.

"What are you looking for?" Naila watched her friend rummage around in her shoulder bag.

"Remember, Mohammed, our tour guide in Fez recommended a good restaurant in the Medina? I almost forgot I had the card. I'd love to try out this place before we leave Morocco. I feel like a tasty Tagine again. He said it was one of the best restaurants for Tagine in town. What do you think?"

"Ah, yes, I remember now. It was something like Kareem, wasn't it? I'm definitely up for it!"

"Yes, it's called 'Al-Kareem'. Ah, look, I've found it!" Yasmin held the card under Naila's nose. "Since we're already here, we can try to find it after the tour, shall we?"

When their tour ended, and they arrived back at their starting point, they thanked the guide and paid him, before climbing out of the carriage. Before they set off, they stroked the horse's neck and Yasmin asked the guide for directions to the restaurant.

"Ah, Al-Kareem. Yes, I know it. It is not far from here," he said, pointing in the direction to the far end of the square, giving them directions.

"You go down the narrow street leading down from the square on the right-hand side and keep going until you come to a gold shop on a corner. It's a bit store, you cannot miss it. There you turn left. The restaurant is located a little further down that street, opposite a small hotel. It is well-known, and if you get lost, just ask someone and they will know and help you."

"Thank you, that's perfect. I'm sure we'll find it," Yasmin thanked him and they set off in the direction of the Medina to find the restaurant.

After passing several colourful spice and groceries stalls, jewellery shops, ironmongers and small eating places tucked into the narrow alleyways, Yasmin found herself standing in front of an entrance to a restaurant that looked similar to a gate of an ancient Moorish castle. It was lined on each side of the door with blue tiles from top to bottom.

She stopped and read the sign above the entrance that said 'Welcome to Restaurant Al- Kareem'.

"Oh, look, Naila, here it is. I've found our restaurant," she called to her.

They both wandered through the gate and shortly found themselves standing in a narrow passageway that leads them through to a wide courtyard. In the middle of the courtyard, stood a fountain which was surrounded by various high plants in large terracotta pots. The plants were arranged in groups and the ground where they stood on was lined with tiles similar to those at the first entrance gate but with white and green patterns. Two low-level sofas were placed on two sides of the courtyard, decorated with several red and white cushions. A red and blue Moroccan kilim was lying in front of one. It looked like a cosy living room, inviting them to stay. The sofas were placed underneath some white painted arches that looked like the ones found in an Indian Mogul palace.

They crossed the courtyard and found the entrance to the restaurant at the other end of the patio. They patiently waited until someone would come and take them to a table. After a couple of minutes, a waiter appeared and greeted them in a friendly manner. He was dressed in a white Moroccan kaftan and wore a traditional white hat.

"Good afternoon Mesdames, a table for two for lunch?" he asked.

"Yes, please," Naila replied and he guided them to a small table. As it was still quite early, there were only two other tables occupied at the restaurant. On each table, stood a candle and small pots of tagine for spices, all in different colours, as well as the menu. It was a very pleasant atmosphere.

The waiter pulled out the chairs for them and helped them settle. "Please make yourselves comfortable. The menu is right here on the table. We offer mint tea and dates free of charge for all our guests before the meal. Our tagine speciality today is lamb but we can, of course, prepare you anything else of your choice, chicken or vegetable tagine if you prefer. Please let me know when you are ready to order."

"Thank you, it is very kind. We would love some mint tea," they both said and picked up the menu to study it. The waiter bowed and left for the kitchen.

"I already like this place," Yasmin admitted when she studied the interior of the restaurant, "and did you see that lovely courtyard! It gives a relaxing feeling, don't you think?"

"Yes, it's beautiful, I love it too, and I can see why Mohammed recommended this place. Let's hope that the food is also living up to its expectations," Naila smiled.

All the tables were round, placed at respectable distance from each other, not too close together, and they were arranged in small but open booths to give the guests some privacy. White tablecloths with various Moroccan patterns decorated each table, and each one had a different pattern. On the ceiling, hung several small traditional Moroccan lamps, some in dark blue and others in dark red colours.

When the waiter returned holding a tray with mint tea and dates and placed it in front of them, they were ready to order. A pleasant smell of fresh mint wafted through the air.

Enjoying their tea and dates and chatting about the New Year's Eve party that was planned for the following day at their hotel, they didn't realise how quickly the time passed until suddenly the waiter appeared again at their table.

He was holding a steaming Tagine on a tray and a plate with a huge pile of Moroccan pita bread on it. But he did not serve them alone. He was followed by a very attractive teenager of about 16 or 17 years of age, who held the second pot of tagine in his hands. The boy had mid-length jet black wavy hair, large dark-green eyes and a friendly face. A lock of his dark hair fell over his forehead. Like the waiter, he too was dressed in a traditional white Moroccan kaftan but he did not wear a hat. But what was striking her most was that the boy had deep green eyes, which was unusual for a Moroccan man. They usually had hazel or brown eyes from what she had observed so far. This boy's eyes were the same colour as hers.

When Yasmin looked up to make room for her dish, she almost dropped her cup of tea. She coughed and her hand were shaking violently, spilling some of her tea on the tablecloth when she placed the cup back on the saucer.

"Yasmin, are you all right?" Naila asked, concerned, looking at her astonished.

"Erm, so sorry, yes, yes, I'm fine," she managed to say.

If the waiter was surprised by Yasmin's reaction, he didn't show it. He put the tagine and the pita bread on the table and told the boy to place the other tagine in front of Yasmin.

But she just kept staring at the boy. She couldn't move. This short moment was long enough to take her back to a long-ago time in another country.

"Bon appetite, enjoy the meal," wished the waiter pleasantly and he and the boy retreated. After a moment, the boy quickly turned around and glanced back at Yasmin. When he did, it seemed to her for a fleeting moment that a flicker of recognition crossed his face. But the moment was so brief and passed in an instant that Yasmin was not sure that it had actually happened. Then the boy turned around again and disappeared into the kitchen.

After this incident, Yasmin was unable to speak for a while. She stared at her dish without really seeing it. This could not be true. No, it was completely impossible.

"Yasmin? Yasmin??" Naila's voice seemed very far away. Yasmin slowly snapped back into reality. "I'm sorry…"

"What happened, Yasmin? You look as if you have seen a ghost!" Naila exclaimed.

"Believe me, I might as well have. This boy… this teenager who came with the waiter, he reminded me of someone. But it's impossible," She shook her head.

"Who? Who did you remind you of, Yasmin?"

"Metin! He looked like Metin! You know, my first husband, the Turkish man?"

"Oh my God! Really? Your ex-husband from when you were living in Turkey? I mean, the one you told me was ehm…?" Naila didn't finish the sentence for fear of hurting her.

"Yes, yes, my first husband, Metin. I told you what happened to him in 1993. This boy is the spitting image of him. I cannot believe what I've seen. How is that even possible? This resemblance is so bizarre. I'll have to show you a picture of Metin, so you know what I mean. I would never have thought that I would ever meet someone, who looked so much like him, especially not in another country!"

"Wow, that's quite something," Naila was stunned. "That for sure is strange. And I must say, your Metin was truly a very attractive and good-looking man if he looked like this boy."

"Oh, yes, he was. Very handsome and attractive but he was also kind and gentle and the love of my life," Yasmin said dreamily.

Naila was quiet and waited. She knew her friend would speak in her own time.

"I'm so sorry that I've reacted this way. It just took me so much by surprise. I have not thought about Metin for a while. You know, after that nightmare had happened, and I came back to the UK, I just needed to get on with my life. You cannot live in the past, can you?"

"No, you're right. But I can understand why it has unsettled you," Naila commented.

"Thank you. But Metin's gone, and nothing can bring him back. Now, let's eat, shall we, otherwise our tagines will get cold."

During their meal, which was as delicious as Mohammed had promised them it would be, there was no other sighting of the boy and Yasmin was somehow glad. It had been too much and too emotional for her. She was feeling a little weak, and after they had finished eating, they paid up and headed straight back to the hotel.

For a long while, Yasmin could not forget this strange incident at the restaurant. Back in their hotel room, when Naila was taking a bath, she lay on the bed and closed her eyes. Vivid, flashing images began forming in her mind, making her remember the time when she was living in Turkey all those years ago, and of Metin, her great love.

It was not until later in the evening that she realised something she had completely forgotten, and told Naila when they were at dinner.

"You know, I've just realised that because of this incident today, we totally forgot to ask for Kareem, the owner of the restaurant, and give him Mohammed's greetings! Oh, what a nuisance! We cannot just come back to Marrakesh and let him know another time."

"Oh, yes, true! It completely slipped my mind too. But not to worry, love, we did go there, and the food was as divine as he said it would be. Even if Kareem doesn't know, at least we've checked out the place and Kareem has found some new and very satisfied customers," Naila consoled her.

"You're right; it's too late now, anyway. But I'm so glad we went," Yasmin agreed.

The next day was New Year's Eve and to their satisfaction, it started with a warm breeze and sunshine. The two friends decided to relax in the 'Hammam', go for a swim and take it easy before it was time to get ready for the big party in the evening.

They had made their dinner reservation in one of the traditional restaurants at the hotel where they later took part in the belly dancing performance which was offered as an activity to the hotel guests. Yasmin, who had been taught how to belly dance by her friends in Turkey, drew a lot of attention to herself by the male audience when the professional belly dancer asked her to join. Her skin was glowing and her eyes were shining when she wiggled her belly and for a while, completely forgot where she was, so totally immersed she seemed in the dance.

Even Naila had not known she had this ability. *She dances like a native, so gracefully. How amazing,* she thought, stunned and impressed by her friend's performance, and she realised then how well Yasmin blended into this culture.

Later in the evening, they moved out into the courtyard which had been especially decorated for the event and a large stage had been erected for music and dance groups' performances throughout the night.

They had watched the amazing folkloric 'Tanoura' dance performed by a group of Arabian male dancers, with their incredible ability to turn on the same spot forever, swinging their multicoloured skirts. The music seemed to put them into a trance-like state and they kept whirling for a very long time. Yasmin and Naila were mesmerized by their performance.

And when they welcomed in the New Year 2009 at midnight with the fireworks display, each holding a glass of champagne and hugging each other, they could not have been happier. They made a toast to their lovely holiday that had been blessed with meeting many kind people, travelling through stunning landscapes and cities during their trip through the country, and finishing with an incredible night straight out of a fairy-tale. This was truly a modern *thousand-and-one-night* story.

Morocco, especially Marrakesh, had completely captured their hearts, especially Yasmin's. When she was watching the fireworks display, accompanied with the classical music, that seemed to go on forever, she suddenly became aware that the strange sensation she had felt in her heart when they had entered the country, was more than just a *deja vu*.

There was something much more, something much bigger here in this country, perhaps even in this city, that would keep a hold over her forever, and there was no doubt in her mind that this hold would make her return to Morocco again and again in years to come.

Marrakesh, Morocco
December 2012
Yasmin

"Don't you think one month is too long to be away? I'm so busy at work and I always worry as you know," Yasmin asked Naila over dinner in her apartment one evening.

Autumn in the UK had made its way to winter and the temperatures had dropped considerably overnight. There was the familiar chill of December in the air when Naila had arrived at her small flat in west London. They were sitting in Yasmin's comfortable kitchen over a tasty Indian meal. Naila scooped up some food with her roti and replied.

"No. In my opinion, you need this time. You need to heal. One or two weeks are not enough to get over a breakup! You need to relax girl and get better. You can only do this when you're away from it all. You'll meet other people, see different places, eat yourself silly on Tagine and you already know some of the places anyway from when we were in Morocco before. It'll be good for you, trust me. They'll have to cope without you at work for a while. They're perfectly capable. You haven't had a proper break for ages anyway."

"Yeah, I guess so, you may be right," Yasmin sighed.

"I know I am. And I'm truly sorry it didn't work out between you and your fiancé because you seemed really good together."

"I know but sometimes things are just not meant to be. Well, at least the breakup was amicable. But I should have realised it quite some time ago actually," Yasmin admitted.

"True, unfortunately. But you have made the move now and besides, you'll have a blast celebrating New Year's Eve in Marrakesh again. Remember last time, we had so much fun. And think of the lovely Hammam treatments you are going to enjoy again. You can only win, sweetheart!"

It was only two months ago when she and her partner had broken up after a three-year relationship, and nursing a broken heart, she knew she had to do something for herself that would make her feel better. She had therefore decided to visit Morocco once again, for a whole month this time, and immerse in the culture more that she had found so fascinating when they had been on holiday there together four years before. She had always planned to return to Morocco but due to her relationship and increasingly busy work commitments, her dream had never materialised.

Until now. She was ready. "You're so right! Morocco, here I come again!"

"That's my girl! You'll have to look after yourself!" Naila said, squeezing her friend's hand.

On a cold and frosty Friday afternoon one week later, Naila dropped her friend off at London Heathrow airport to catch her flight to Agadir. She remembered their last holiday together in Morocco with nostalgia. After checking in her bags, the two friends hugged and Naila couldn't help feeling a little sad that she could not join Yasmin.

"Don't forget to call as soon as you've arrived, yes? And have a lamb Tagine on me!" she called after Yasmin before she disappeared through to the departure area.

"Don't worry, I will. See you in a month's time," Yasmin waved to Naila and fished her ticket and passport out of her handbag to enter the departure area.

Yasmin was sitting in a deckchair at the beach that was part of the hotel she had booked herself into in Agadir and was looking out to the Atlantic Ocean. The vastness of the ocean always made her feel insignificant. She watched the 'chameliers', camel owners, who were taking people riding on their camels and there were horses too that could be rented to ride along the beach. It was a peaceful picture. The day before she had taken her chance on a camel and had enjoyed the fun of it. They were such calm creatures.

This time she had deliberately chosen Agadir for the start of her holiday. She needed to relax and nurse her broken heart, and the soothing waves of the ocean were a great help to do exactly that. Besides, she needed a break from her daily busy schedule, never-ending meetings and business travels. One week chilling out by a beach was perfect, before she was going to set off on a roundtrip to see some other places in the country.

When she had stepped off the plane at the airport, the same sense of belonging she had felt in her heart the first time when she had come four years ago, had greeted her. There was a familiarity about this place that she could not quite understand. That was the reason why she had decided on spending time in Morocco again. She had been to many countries and cities on her business travels around the world but no place had captured her heart quite in the same way. She picked up her book again and continued to read.

The train pulled into Marrakesh station at precisely 2 pm and Yasmin grabbed her suitcase from the rack. It was ten days later and she was several experiences richer. It had been a wonderful ride from Casablanca through a landscape of olive groves, desert terrain, viaducts and colourful villages. She exited the station in search of a taxi.

"To the hotel Riad Sol, please," she announced to the taxi driver, who had helped her put her heavy suitcase in the boot and they drove off.

The little hotel she had found on a booking website had immediately caught her attention. The pictures showed a pretty, fairly small hotel with a colourful courtyard with plants and two water fountains and pleasant looking rooms. Each room was painted in a different colour and even the bedspreads were in the Moroccan style. Breakfast was included which suited her fine. The hotel was also located near one of the Botanical gardens, 'Jardin Majorelle' which she liked because she would enjoy spending some time there.

Perfect, she had thought, and had booked it for the rest of her stay in Marrakesh.

The taxi driver stopped the car in front of a typical and quaint Moroccan style hotel that she recognised instantly from the pictures on the website.

"Here we are, the hotel Riad Sol. It's a nice place, you chose well," said the taxi driver and got out of the car to help Yasmin with her luggage.

She thanked him and gave him an additional tip, then made her way to the reception through the lovely courtyard that lived up to her expectations. *If the rest of the hotel is a beautiful as this area, then I'm more than happy to have chosen this place*, she thought.

Behind the reception stood an attractive young man of approx. 20 years of age, with dark hair and a three-day beard. He was just finishing the check-in with an elderly couple, and Yasmin waited patiently behind them for her turn.

"Bonjour madame, good afternoon," said the young man pleasantly in English. He was wearing a black hotel uniform and his name tag told her that his name was Tariq.

"Bonjour," she replied and smiled, "I have a reservation." She fished out her printed reservation page from her shoulder bag and handed it over to him.

"Thank you. Please can I also have your passport? I need to scan it in and photocopy it."

"Of course," Yasmin replied and handed over her passport she had ready in her hand.

"Mrs Özgűr, for two weeks," The young man read on the reservation printout. It seemed to Yasmin that he briefly frowned but the moment passed so quickly that she dismissed it as a trick of the light.

"I hope you like our country. Is it your first time here?" he asked casually as he proceeded with the check-in.

"Yes, I mean, at this hotel. But I have been to Morocco once before, some years ago with a friend. We travelled around for a bit and then celebrated the New Year here in Marrakesh. I love Morocco; lovely people, fantastic food and such great history."

"I'm so pleased you like it, and welcome again," The young man smiled and handed over her passport.

"Mrs Özgűr, all done, you are now checked in. Your room is on the first floor, overlooking the courtyard. It's just up the stairs over there, and then it's the first one on the right-hand side. Do you need any help with the luggage?" he asked and pointed over to the staircase at the other end of the reception to show her where she needed to climb up to the first floor.

"Thank you, it's very kind but no, I'm fine. It's only one floor and my bag isn't that heavy, I'll be all right. By the way, what time is breakfast?"

"Oh, sorry, I almost forgot. It's between 7 am and 10:30 am, and the breakfast room is over there, just behind the reception on the other side, basically," he explained.

Yasmin grabbed her suitcase and made her way upstairs. When she turned the key and opened the door, a pleasant room greeted her with some paintings of Moroccan landscapes, a good-size desk, and a colourful bedspread that looked as if it had come straight out of a Berber village. The window and small balcony were as Tariq had promised, overlooking the courtyard she had walked through earlier.

"Oh, wow, how beautiful!" she announced to herself and placed her suitcase on the floor next to the desk. She decided to rest for a while, and then have a refreshing shower.

Meanwhile, downstairs at the reception, the young man called Tariq felt a little confused. When this attractive, well-spoken lady with the unusual green eyes, Mrs Özgűr, had handed him her reservation sheet, he had a faint feeling of recognition that he had heard this name before somewhere. Mrs Yasmin Özgűr. Her passport indicated she was British, from the UK. She had also said that she had been to Morocco once before.

Now, where had he heard this name before? A guest with a similar name? He could not place it. He knew he had never met her in person. Despite his young age, he remembered faces very well, and he would have recalled meeting a beautiful woman like her. After all, this was a tourist place and many foreigners passed through this hotel. But for some strange reason, this name did ring a bell, if he could only put his finger on it.

"Ah, well, not to worry", he said to himself, "I will ask my father when he comes in later. Maybe he will solve this mystery."

He turned his attention back to his computer to check the reservations from the websites and book them in, the mystery about the attractive lady with the green eyes and the strange name soon forgotten.

"And, how was your trip so far?" Naila wanted to know when they were on their Skype call the next morning. The two friends had been talking online most days.

"It's fantastic! I've seen so many new places, including Chefchaouen, also known as the blue city. You don't know what you are missing! And now, I'm back in my beloved Marrakesh. I have found such a cute, beautiful little hotel," Yasmin updated her friend about the past ten days of her trip.

"Oh, that's lovely! I'm expecting lots of pictures. And I hope you didn't check your work emails all the time. But, tell me, why didn't you choose the same hotel where we stayed last time? You would have had a good discount."

"No, I only checked in with work occasionally, so don't worry, I'm not working. And I chose this little hotel on purpose. I wanted to see Morocco in a different light, you see. All the big hotel chains, as you well know, are kind of the same everywhere in the world. I wanted something different, something more authentic, the real experience. And this place suits me perfectly. It's really cute and comfortable," Yasmin replied.

"Hmm, I can see the point, actually. You're right. You don't want to feel you're back in London when you're on holiday. By the way, have you decided what you're going to do for New Year's Eve yet?"

"No, I'm not sure yet. There will be plenty of events. I might go to see a show that evening, I'll play it by ear," Yasmin said.

After her call with Naila, she showered and got ready to go downstairs for breakfast. It was only 8:30 am, plenty of time. In the dining room, she chose a table by the window and sat down. It was right next to the courtyard, the sun lighting it up like a little paradise. It was a peaceful and gorgeous sight. After she enjoyed a lavish breakfast and a refreshing mint tea, she decided to venture out on a shopping trip to the Medina first to buy a few gifts for her friends and parents. She grabbed her phone and purse and left the table.

As she was going through the door that leads to the reception area, she realised at once that she had left her room key on the table. She abruptly turned around to go back into the dining area to pick it up and just as she did that, immediately collided with somebody.

"Oh, I'm awfully sorry!" she exclaimed, completely embarrassed.

"No, it's me who is sorry, Madame, I wasn't looking," a calm male voice said.

Yasmin looked up at once and straight into the kind eyes of a very handsome Moroccan man, more or less her age group, holding a large folder in his hand. When he studied her, she felt a jolt like a thousand bolts of lightning passing through her.

"I'm… I wasn't paying attention either. I've just realised that I left my room key on the table and was on my way to pick it up," she tried to explain lamely.

They stared at each other for a couple of minutes and she took in his features. She noticed that he was a little taller than her. His dark, almost shoulder length hair was thick and wavy and had some white streaks in it, suggesting he was probably in his late forties. His jaws were chiselled like a sculpture and his lips were full. He was by all accounts a very handsome man. When she didn't move, he looked at her slightly amused and smiled.

"Erm, well, I think I'll have to pick up my key, so sorry again. Have a lovely day," Yasmin stammered, feeling a little unsettled by this man, and returned to the dining room.

"Don't let me stop you, Madame. Please accept my apology again, and I too wish you a wonderful day," he said in perfect English and stepped aside to let her pass.

Back in her room, she first had to sit down to catch her breath. Why did this encounter unsettle her so much? He was just some man, whom she would most probably never see again. However, she wondered, was he a guest too or was he part of the staff?

"Well, never mind. There are many good-looking men in this country. Silly me, I behave like a schoolgirl. He is probably married with children anyway," she scolded herself, then picked up her little backpack and headed out to the Medina for her shopping spree.

Satisfied with all her purchases and having succeeded to finish all her shopping in one day, she decided to pay a visit to the Botanical Garden, the 'Jardin Majorelle' the following day. This exotic, beautiful and tranquil garden being within walking distance from the hotel was a well-known location for locals and tourists alike. It offered exotic plants, palm trees, cacti, little ponds and fountains, and it was like walking in a little paradise of its own that seemed far away from the hustle and bustle of the city. Stunned by the beauty of the place, Yasmin strolled around as if in trance. Mesmerized by this lush, enchanted garden she suddenly found herself standing in front of a blue fountain which was itself set in a small square filled with water. A few meters behind the fountain, there was a two-storey building with pillars on all sides, looking like some sort of a Moorish villa, also painted in a rich, deep blue colour. It looked like a sanctuary.

"It is beautiful, isn't it?" a male voice said behind her. The voice sounded vaguely familiar.

Deep in her thoughts, she hadn't heard anybody approach her. Startled, Yasmin spun around and looked straight into the handsome face of the man from the hotel she had bumped so clumsily into the day before.

"I'm truly sorry, Madame, it was not my intention to startle you. I must apologize again. It seems that every time we meet, I have to apologize," He smiled, revealing a perfectly white set of teeth.

"Oh, hello again, no problem. I just did not expect anybody I know here, that's all," Yasmin said pleasantly when she had composed herself.

"And it is a truly gorgeous place, like a little oasis in the middle of a busy city. I have never seen anything like it. I could just stay here forever," she admitted.

"It is. Did you know that this botanical garden was created over the course of forty years? Have you heard of the fashion designer Yves Saint Laurent? I'm sure you have. It was actually him who bought it in 1980."

"Wow, really? That's so interesting. No, I didn't know that. Thank you. I'm always very interested in history, you see. That's why I come to these places."

"That makes two of us. I come here often, mainly to think but also to relax. This garden has a calming effect on me," the handsome stranger said.

"And by the way, I'm Tahiri Ahmed. I'm very pleased to meet you," he introduced himself.

"Oh, sorry, how rude of me. I should have introduced myself as well. I'm Yasmin. Yasmin Özgűr," Yasmin replied and held out her hand to him, as it was her custom.

This name rang a bell, thought Tahiri. Was it possible that he had heard her name before? He had a very good memory and he never forgot a name or a face. He knew he had not met this woman before but the name sounded somehow familiar.

"Yasmin Özgűr," he repeated, "that's a lovely and unusual name. I'm very pleased to make your acquaintance."

If there had been a flicker of recognition in his face, it disappeared in an instant, and Yasmin was not sure if she had imagined it. Then she recalled the same when she had checked in at the hotel the day she arrived and when the young man at the reception had seen her name on the passport. This seemed strange to her. Why would they know her name? It didn't make sense. Maybe she reminded them of someone? As she had never met either of them, she didn't dwell on it and the impression was soon forgotten.

"Thank you. It's actually a Turkish surname, my married name. From my former husband," she offered, a brief sadness creeping into her beautiful face, "but he died many years ago. Anyway, I'm British, from the UK but with Italian origin through my parents." *Why was she telling him all this?*

"I'm very sorry to hear that your husband died. However, you seem to have a very interesting family history and a very international one too," Tahiri responded. He couldn't help himself but this woman fascinated him. Ever since he had met her the day before, she had captured his thoughts.

"Well, now that we know each other's names, would you mind walking together a little? I could explain more about this place if you like?" Tahiri suggested.

"That would be lovely, thank you. Yes, please," Yasmin agreed, and they set off together.

While Tahiri was filling her in more about the history of the gardens, Yasmin told him about her first time in Morocco four years ago and how much she fell in love with this place and had always wanted to come back.

"Why did you wait four years to return if you liked it so much if you don't mind me asking?" Tahiri was interested to know.

"I…, well, it's just that I was in a relationship for several years and we did other things together and spent our holidays in other countries. Anyway, we have now split up, quite recently in fact. That's the reason why I only came back now and also because I needed some time to myself. You know, the healing, and to decide what I'm going to do about my future," she explained, still not understanding why she was telling her personal and intimate affairs to this stranger she had only just met.

"Bon, I see. I do understand. You see, I, too come here to reflect and to think. My wife, her name was Fatima, died six months ago. She had cancer and that was what killed her. She was only in her mid-forties and such a lively woman," Tahiri explained sadly.

Yasmin stopped and looked at him with compassion. "Oh, that's so sad and I'm very sorry to hear that. It must have been an incredibly difficult time for you."

"Yes, yes, it was. But one must go on. My time to leave this world has not quite come yet. I'm busy at work every day and that always helps."

"That's so true, isn't it? I'm the same, I have a busy job and I throw myself into work. This way I don't always have to think because it would drive me crazy," Yasmin agreed.

"What do you do? You work in the UK, don't you?"

"Yes, I do. I'm a Food and Beverage Manager and I work in London for a big hotel chain. And what about you? What do you do?"

"I'm the owner of the hotel Riad Sol," Tahiri explained humbly.

"Oh, I see," Yasmin managed, feeling embarrassed that she had never thought of this possibility. She had assumed that he was perhaps the chef or another member of staff or even a guest when she had met him the day before.

"Don't worry, Yasmin, if you have not guessed right away. I don't wear a name tag that says Hotel Owner. I like to keep it low key," Tahiri laughed, amused by her obvious embarrassment.

"No, I mean, I do understand. It's just that yesterday…," she began.

"I know but I didn't want you to worry that you had just collided with the owner of the hotel. I felt embarrassed myself. I don't usually chase after women and bump into them with my financial papers. I was going out to meet with my son to discuss some finances with him.

You must have met him? He sometimes does the reception cover."

"Your son? Ah, yes, I see. He is the handsome young man who checked me in, I believe?" Yasmin smiled, her eyes twinkling.

"Yes, that's Tariq. He studied in the hotel business and I employed him as my Assistant Manager. One day, well, I hope so anyway, he'll be taking over my business."

"That would be fantastic, Inshallah, as I believe you say. Your hotel is such a lovely and peaceful place."

"Thank you for the compliment. It took me a while to refurbish it and bring it up to the standard as it is now when I bought it. But I wanted to make sure that my guests feel well-catered for and that they have a pleasant stay in a typical Moroccan surrounding. After all, we are well known for our Moroccan hospitality."

"You have done a brilliant job as far as I can see. I already feel calm and well-catered for. Believe me, I know what I'm talking about as I'm also in the catering and hospitality business and I have seen many different establishments. It is a lovely place. In fact, this is why I've chosen it. Because it's authentic and has a true Moroccan feel to it."

Yasmin and Tahiri carried on walking and spent the rest of the afternoon together. When they arrived back at the hotel, he stopped before the entrance and looked at her in a more serious manner.

"Yasmin, I have spent a lovely afternoon. I would like to thank you very much for spending time with me. It has been quite a while since I have had a good conversation with a woman. Would you like to meet me for a meal sometime and we could continue our conversation?" His kind eyes looked at her expectantly.

Yasmin was surprised and she agreed at once. She liked this man and like him, it had been a while since she had a proper, interesting conversation. And now, he was asking her out on a date! This was more than she had bargained for.

"Fantastic, I'm honoured. So, shall we say, tomorrow evening at 8 pm? I will meet you outside the hotel, it's better. I can take a night off, don't worry, it's no problem."

"Thank you, Tahiri, I'll be ready by 8 pm," Yasmin smiled and her heart jumped a beat.

She could not believe it. Her heart sang and she felt alive. She was going on a date with this handsome, interesting man! She felt like the luckiest woman in the world.

Back in her room, she lay dreamily on her bed for a while and in her thoughts went over the events of the afternoon again. This was the owner of the hotel. She was wondering, was there some serious intention on his part, perhaps for a relationship? Would it turn into something serious? Well, time would tell. For some reason, he didn't strike her like a player or a womaniser but a genuine, caring man. After all, he had been married and he obviously had children, too. Well, at least one she had learnt, his son Tariq.

On their first dinner date together the following day, Tahiri proved himself like the perfect gentleman and Yasmin felt like an Arabian queen. She enjoyed the attention he was giving her. She could not help it but this man completely fascinated her. Good conversation, mutual understanding, and they came from the same line of work as well, so they could share some funny stories. During the following three days, they spent more time together and soon they both realised that they had very much in common.

When New Year's Eve approached and she only had a few days left in Morocco, she told him that she would have to fly back to the UK as her long vacation was nearly over. They were sitting in a nearby café and had a tray of Moroccan mint tea in front of them.

"Why don't we celebrate New Year's Eve together?" he suggested, taking a sip of his tea.

"Yes, I would like that very much, Tahiri," Yasmin replied, overjoyed. She didn't have to think twice.

"Lovely. That's settled then. I have a little party planned at my hotel where all the guests are invited for a first cocktail drink and snacks. I hope we can have dinner together and I will introduce you to my son. Of course, only if you don't mind," he announced.

"Thank you, Tahiri, I would like that very much. I hope he will like me," she replied.

"Oh, I'm absolutely sure he will. I haven't told you this yet but I also have a daughter. Her name is Ayesha and she is three years younger than Tariq. She is 17 years old and a lovely girl," Tariq offered.

"A daughter, Ayesha. What a beautiful name. Is she also working with you?" Yasmin asked, not recalling having seen any women working at the hotel yet.

"She is lovely, yes. And no, she doesn't work with me. In fact, she is still studying, also in the catering business. During the semester holidays, she works with my younger brother who owns a restaurant in the Medina, to get some work experience."

"I very much look forward to meeting her too. She sounds very nice."

"I would have introduced her to you too but she is busy at the moment due to some staff shortage at the restaurant, and she also has to work on New Year's Eve. They have a lot of bookings for the night," Tahiri explained.

"That's understandable. They'll be rushed off their feet," Yasmin laughed, glad that she was on holiday herself and could escape the New Year's Eve rush this year.

Tahiri was studying her, without her realising it. So far, she had not mentioned anything about her having children. He knew she was 42 years old and therefore, it would seem likely that she would be a parent. But then, she said that her husband died several years ago. He decided to ask the delicate question.

"And what about you, Yasmin? Do you have any children? Forgive me for asking, and if it makes you feel uncomfortable, you don't have to answer," Tahiri probed.

"Don't worry, it's okay. I… well, no, I don't have any children, no," Yasmin answered. Her secret was deeply buried in her heart and it stayed there. She stared into her tea cup, trying not to get too emotional.

"That's sad. I understand. Again, forgive me for asking, please. I didn't mean to intrude."

"You have a right to ask. Sometimes, it is just not possible to have children or something happens beyond your control," she explained, having a far-away look on her face.

Tahiri nodded. He understood very well. Completely unaware to Yasmin, he had suddenly realised where he had heard her name before. He knew that he never forgot a name and certainly not when it was in connection with something so important. When he had returned to the hotel that day after the Jardin Majorelle, he had checked her reservation and found out her age as well as her full name. It was Yasmin Özgür-Bonerti.

And so he had known at once. That was it! He recalled that it was the name mentioned on the birth certificate of the biological mother of his nephew, Şenay. His birth date matched and also Yasmin's birth date. Although, he had only seen the adoption documents a couple of times when his brother had brought the adopted baby back full of pride and showed him the evidence papers, and later when Kareem had asked him to store all the documents at his house during the refurbishment of his house, this name stayed in his head. He could hardly believe this strange coincidence.

So, what had happened? This was a complete mystery. Yasmin said she didn't have any children, yet it was evident that she had given birth to a baby boy in Turkey in June 1993. She also mentioned her husband, who obviously must have been this Metin Özgür, had died many years ago. This puzzled him. What was the connection? How did he die? What did he die of? And when exactly?

He could not shake off his feeling that something terrible must have happened all those years ago. Something that made Yasmin give up her son for adoption. Or was it possible that she didn't even know her son had been adopted? Perhaps, he had been taken away from her? But how? He concluded that she must have lived in Turkey for quite some time, certainly in 1993 in order to give birth to a child there. She must have left the country soon after Şenay was born and returned to the UK afterwards if she was working in London as she said she did.

He knew then that he would leave no stone unturned and would find out what happened to this lovely woman all those years ago. He would solve this mystery. He would have to go about it very carefully because the last thing he wanted was to stir up some old history that quite obviously had hurt her in some way or upset his brother and his sister-in-law who had done such a good job of raising their adoptive son and loved him dearly as if he was their own flesh and blood. Şenay and Tariq were very close and always had been, from a very early age. It would also come as a shock to them.

When Tahiri and Yasmin welcomed in the year 2013 with the fireworks, he knew for certain that he had fallen in love with her. Looking at her fine features and deep green eyes, she had completely captured his heart. Yasmin, who was standing next to him in the hotel courtyard watching the fireworks go off all over the city, counting down to the New Year with all the guests, felt very much the same. So much had happened to her in such a short time. She could hardly believe it. Trying to forget about an old love, she had found a new one. Her whole life had changed in just one month.

"Happy New Year 2013, mon amour!" he whispered and kissed her on the cheeks.

"Happy New Year to you too!" she said and her eyes shone when she looked at him. She still could not believe that his passionate, handsome man had become her partner.

Tahiri had introduced her to Tariq that very evening and he was genuinely happy for them. His father had suffered for a long time because of the loss of his mother and he deserved all the happiness he could get.

Yasmin had learnt that Tariq was 20 years old and that he had spent part of his studies in London before coming back to Morocco to work with his father. That explained why his English was so immaculate. She was curious to meet Tariq's sister Ayesha, hoping she was as nice as her brother.

On the day before her departure to London, Tahiri had taken Yasmin out to a very special place on a final date. It seemed an expensive restaurant and Yasmin was not used to this treatment. But Tahiri had something extraordinary planned. When they had finished their meal and waited for the dessert as if by magic, he produced a small box and placed it in front of her. He looked at her with great fondness, his kind eyes shining.

"Yasmin, mon amour. I know we have only known each other for a short time but I feel you are my woman. We have so much in common and I love you. We are not so young anymore and I don't want to waste any more time being on my own. Would you do me the honour of becoming my wife?"

This was like a bombshell and totally unexpected to her. Yasmin was stunned and she had tears in her eyes. She just got engaged!

"Oh my God, Tahiri! This is more than I could have imagined! Yes, yes, I would like to marry you! And I love you too!" she almost shouted and opened the box which revealed a lovely engagement ring with a small diamond that glittered in the lamplight.

"Merci, Yasmin, you are making me a very happy man. You don't have to rush into anything. Go back to London for now and perhaps come to Marrakesh, if you can, in a couple of months' time. We can then spend more time together and start planning for our wedding and our future properly. Please don't make any hasty decisions for now. I know you cannot just drop everything and leave your job and your life in England."

"I will, Tahiri. This is all a bit overwhelming now. But I will come back here, maybe around April time for two weeks, if that suits you? I also suggest that you come to the UK afterwards. Perhaps you can travel back with me and spend a few weeks with me in London? I would like to introduce you to my parents and my friends," Yasmin suggested.

"Of course, I was going to suggest the same thing, actually. It is important that I also know your country, your surroundings and, of course, your friends and family. I will leave Tariq in charge of the hotel for that time," he agreed.

"Thank you so much, Tahiri. When I move here, do you think it will be easy to find a job here in my line of work? I would like to work, you see, I'm used to it," she asked.

"Oh, do not worry about this, my dear. There will be a lot of opportunities for you here, especially in Marrakesh. After all, our country thrives on tourism and there are many big hotel chains here too, as well as smaller places, depending on what you choose. I have a lot of contacts, you see, and so does my brother, and there won't be a shortage of job offers for you, I can assure you," Tahiri said confidently.

Yasmin agreed. She would not worry about this yet anyway. It was in the future and still several months away. There was a lot to sort out beforehand. Her mind wandered back to the first time when she entered Morocco, as well as the second time, having this overwhelming sensation of familiarity and belonging. This magical country was going to be her new home. It was a new beginning and an exciting future for both of them.

A couple of days later, it was time for Yasmin to return to the UK. In the morning, Tahiri had taken her to the airport and they were waiting at the check-in to drop her suitcase off. When the boarding of the flight to London was announced, Tahiri held her tightly in his arms. They stood behind a pillar, away from the eyes of other travellers to have some privacy.

"Bye mon amour, my fiancée. I will see you in April. And let me know about your flight details as soon as you make them so that I can come and pick you up. Please say hello to your friends for me. I will meet them soon, Inshallah. I love you."

"Goodbye Tahiri, I will, yes. And I'm looking forward to our new adventure and to planning our wedding together. See you soon. I love you, je t'aime," She hugged him tightly before she made her way to the departure gate.

As she strapped herself into the seat on the aeroplane, she was thinking of Naila, and how to break the good news to her. She would not believe this fairy-tale like a story straight out of *One-thousand-and-one-nights*. She had found her Aladdin like Naila had predicted a long time ago. Smiling, she opened her novel and settled into the story as the plane took off into the Moroccan sky.

Marrakesh, Morocco
April 2013

It was a bright, fresh morning in London and the cherry trees that lined her road where she lived were in full glorious bloom. How quickly the last months had passed. Yasmin was standing in her small flat, staring at the clothes in her wardrobe, trying to figure out what she needed to take on her next trip to Marrakesh. After her holiday in December, she and her fiancé Tahiri had agreed that before she would move to Marrakesh later in the year, she would return to Marrakesh again for a holiday in order to spend time together so that they could get to know each other better before taking the big step.

Never in her life could Yasmin have imagined that she would fall in love again. She had never even expected to even see Tahiri again after her vacation last year. Yet, there she was. When Tahiri had proposed to her so unexpectedly in January and produced that lovely ring, all she had managed to say was a "Yes! I would like to marry you!"

Now, Tahiri and she were in contact several times each week via Skype, making plans for their future together and he had arranged to return to London with her after her holiday in order to meet her family and friends before their wedding.

Satisfied that she had packed everything, she closed her suitcase and called a taxi to take her to Heathrow airport, as Naila was on a business trip and unavailable to take her this time. When Tahiri had insisted to pick her up at the airport, she readily agreed, a big change from trying to find her own way to places and hotels in a foreign land. Soon she sat on a plane again, ready to begin another milestone in their relationship.

Meanwhile, at Marrakesh airport, Tahiri checked the arrivals board and learnt that Yasmin's flight was on time and he didn't have to wait for long to hold her in his arms. He found a chair nearby and sat down. As he was waiting, he started to reflect on the past couple of months, and he knew that there was something very important he had to do. He had to tell her the truth, the truth about his nephew, Şenay.

It had first been his son Tariq, the Assistant Manager at the hotel 'Riad Sol' he owned, who had mentioned the name Yasmin Özgűr to him and thought that it sounded somehow familiar, without him knowing that Yasmin and his father had already become well acquainted. When Tahiri had finally broken the news to a stunned Tariq about starting a relationship with Yasmin, he confirmed that he was right assuming that he had heard her name before and that Yasmin was indeed the birth mother of his nephew.

Tariq remembered that afternoon, years ago, very well when he and his cousin quite unexpectedly came across Şenay's adoption documents and how they learnt about the names and details of his birth parents. As unbelievable as that was, this seemed more than a coincidence.

When Tahiri was certain about who Yasmin really was, however, at the same time being convinced she was unaware of her son living in Marrakesh, he still wanted to make sure he had all the facts correct before he was going to tell her what he knew.

"That's what it was! I do remember now. But I'm sure, Abee that this lady has not come to find her son here if he is actually her son. She told me she had only been to Morocco once before several years ago with a friend," Tariq had said.

"I believe you are right, son. She told me the same," agreed his father.

"And besides, she would have started looking for her child years ago, don't you think? After all, Momo, I mean Şenay, is nearly 20 years old."

"That's true, yes, I totally agree. She surely wouldn't have waited for decades to do it," Tahiri nodded.

"What do you suggest we do, dad? After all, she is going to be your wife and she deserves to know the truth. She is a very nice and genuine lady."

"I totally agree. When I decided to take my chance with Yasmin and asked her to marry me, I knew that eventually, I will have to tell her the truth. I don't want to start a marriage on lies or dishonesty. So, first I think I should tell my brother and Amel about what I know. And then we'll have to find a solution of how to break the facts to Yasmin. I don't want to shock Şenay either, you know. He had a terrible shock when he first found out."

"You're right. In any case, she would eventually find out the truth anyway, one way or another. So, I would say it's better if she learns it from you, rather than from anyone else. That would be more of a shock," Tariq added.

"The other thing is, although we nicknamed him 'Momo', Ayesha has always called him by his real name because she liked it. And Mrs Özgűr, Yasmin, would find out through her. You don't want that to happen. And also, we don't know the circumstances why she had given her son up for adoption in the first place. Maybe she could not have him because she was too young, unmarried or whatever the reason was. It could be anything. She might be very happy to learn that he lives here. Perhaps, you should also find out what happened from her side? She might have a story to tell herself."

Astonished, Tahiri looked at his son. Sometimes young people can be much more realistic than the older generation, Tahiri had to admit to himself, astounded by the logic in his son's words.

"I know you are right, Tariq. We don't know anything about her circumstances and what made her do it. Thank you for your honesty. I will discuss it with Yasmin as soon as she is back. I know I'll have to break the news very carefully," Tahiri replied.

"Yes, father, that's a good plan. And you will also have to break that fact to Şenay. He has a right to know too, as soon as possible. It's his real mother and when he finally meets her, it won't come as such a shock to him," Tariq pointed out.

"A very good point, yes. I'll do that, of course. But first I'll have to discuss with Kareem and Amel and we can perhaps all be involved in this. They have been his parents and I'll follow their guidance. We're all a family and we should stand together in this. I'm sure Şenay will understand. He already knows he has been adopted, so only the fact that his birth mother has turned up through a twist of fate, is new to him," Tahiri commented.

After a while of contemplation, he had figured out what he would do. First, he would take Yasmin to his brother's restaurant 'Al-Kareem' for dinner and introduce her to Kareem there, before he would invite her to his brother's house. Yes, that was the best solution. As Şenay was also working there as the Assistant Head Chef, she might even meet him briefly at the restaurant.

And he would have to play it by ear. If Şenay was too busy at work and unavailable, well then, it would have to be at his brother's house. After all, they had a wedding to plan together and it was best to do this within the family as also

Ayesha was going to be quite involved in the process as one of Yasmin's bridesmaids. He would just have to make sure Şenay was informed about the facts before he met Yasmin.

A sense of joy washed over him and he was grateful to have found such an amazing new partner after his wife Fatima's death almost a year earlier when the cancer she had battled with for nearly three years had won. After his wife's death, night had fallen on his world and he had buried himself in work to ease the suffering and pain in his heart. His children Tariq and Ayesha had always encouraged him to try and find a new wife and were happy for their father when he told them he had met someone and it was serious.

"Please forgive me, my dear Fatima, and understand that I have found a new wife. She is a good person. Please give me your permission to move on. I will never forget you and have always loved you. I hope you are happy in paradise. Please, I am asking you to give me your blessing for a new marriage," he said a silent prayer to his wife in heaven and feeling a sense of peace in his heart, he knew she had heard him and approved.

A couple of weeks after his conversation with his son, the day had come when Tahiri had agreed to meet with Kareem and Amel in their home. Şenay had been asked to join them. They had all gathered in their living room over a cup of tea. Şenay was looking at his parents expectantly, not understanding why he also had been summoned to this family meeting.

"So, tell me, what is the big secrecy then, you want me to know? Mum, Dad, Uncle Tahiri?" he asked curiously.

The two brothers and Amel looked at each other briefly and Kareem nodded to Tahiri to speak first.

Tahiri cleared his throat and began, "As you know, Şenay, I have been grieving for Fatima for a long time. She was an amazing woman and a good mother to my two children. But she is gone and nothing will bring her back and at some point, I have to move on. So, in December last year, I met a woman. She was on a holiday and happened to stay at my hotel for a couple of weeks. She is a little younger than me and very nice, a very genuine lady. We are getting to know each other and we seem to have a lot in common, not only our profession. She is also in Tourism, by the way. Well, what I want to say is, in fact, I have already asked her to marry me and she has agreed."

"Wow, uncle, that's fantastic! I'm so happy for you!" Şenay exclaimed at once and stood up to embrace his uncle, genuinely pleased for him.

"So, tell me more. Who is she? What's her name? Where is she from? And when is she coming back to Marrakesh?"

"Oh, easy, so many questions at once!" Tahiri laughed. "Well, Yasmin is from England but with an Italian background. In fact, she works in London. She is in her early forties, well-travelled, and speaks several languages. She is coming to Marrakesh again in April for two weeks and during that time, I want to take her to some more places. You know, to introduce her properly to our culture. After all, this country is going to be her new home.

We are planning to get married later this year and she will be relocating to Morocco by then too."

Şenay knew his uncle well and sensed that there was more to his story otherwise they would not have asked him to join in this conversation. The way he looked at his uncle, Tahiri knew the time had come to tell him the truth.

"There is, well, a bit more to this story," he continued, looking straight at his nephew, "as you have known for quite some time, Şenay, you were adopted as a baby and you know also that you were born in Turkey, in Izmir to be precise, as it is noted on your birth papers."

Şenay nodded slowly, not quite understanding what that had to do with his uncle's new wife-to-be. She was from England, as he had just learnt, not from Turkey. How could there be a connection?

"It is probably a bit hard to understand, and an incredible twist of fate, what I'm going to tell you now as you will see shortly. Well, what I'm trying to say is that my fiancée's full name is Yasmin Özgűr-Bonerti. Does that name ring a bell perhaps?"

"Not really, no, it doesn't," Şenay replied, still not comprehending.

"Try to think again, very carefully. Have you not heard this name somewhere before? Or maybe you have seen it written down somewhere?" Tahiri tried to help his nephew along the way.

Şenay stared at him and after a few minutes, it suddenly began to dawn on him. This could not possibly be?

"Yasmin Özgűr-Bonerti?" he repeated slowly, and as a faint recognition crossed his face, he realised that name did indeed ring a bell. He recalled an incident many years ago in his cousin's house. But this was too much of a coincidence, surely?

"I think I'm beginning to understand what you are saying, uncle. When I think about it, I believe I might have heard this name before. Is it by any chance the name of my real mother that's mentioned on my birth papers?" he asked slowly.

"Yes, it is Şenay. Yasmin is your birth mother," Tahiri confirmed.

Şenay's face showed at once the shock he was in, and he could barely speak. *Not again,* he thought. *Has this tale come to haunt him? Was this never going to end?*

"But, but… how is this even possible? How did she come here to Morocco? After all these years? Did she come to find me here? After all, she didn't want her baby! But you said she is English, so what is the connection to Turkey then? I don't understand."

He buried his face into his hands. This was too much. This woman, Yasmin, Tahiri's new wife, was the mother who gave him away as a baby. She was the mother who rejected him. He felt betrayed all over again, also by Tahiri. How could he do this to him? His father realised the torment that was going through his son's mind and tried to soothe him.

"Şenay, please look at me and listen to me. Şenay?" his father spoke gently.

Şenay straightened up. He didn't want to upset his father and his mother and he greatly respected them. The least he could do was listen to what they had to say.

"As you probably recall, we discussed this subject many years ago already. The truth is that we don't know what happened. There are no certain facts we are aware of, other than that you were given up for adoption. We don't know either why she had given birth to you in Turkey. Perhaps, she was working there at the time or visiting or got married there.

Maybe there was even foul play involved. She might not have rejected you at all. Yasmin might not have wanted to give you up for adoption. You see, when we adopted you, we were told at the orphanage in Izmir where we picked you up that your mother had died after giving birth."

"What? You were told my mum was dead? Why?" Şenay looked at his father in disbelief. Nothing made sense to him anymore. This whole story involving his birth and adoption began to look somehow sinister. A nagging feeling formed in his stomach that his father might be right, that indeed foul play had played a part.

"Yes, that's true, I swear. And not until we know the whole truth, meaning from Yasmin herself, we cannot blame her for anything. She might be a victim in this case just as you are. Perhaps, she was told that you had died. Or perhaps it was a case of mistaken identity. These things happen. We simply don't know. And even if this had been a misunderstanding, if she had indeed given you up for adoption, she might have wanted to find you soon after and to get in touch with you somehow. I'm quite convinced that she would not have waited 20 years to do so, let alone to travel to another country to find you. She would have needed to know also in which country she would need to look for you. In fact, I'm sure that Yasmin is quite unaware of the fact that you are her son."

"I see," Şenay replied slowly, "it somehow makes sense what you are saying."

"Yes, it does. So please can you go gentle on her when you meet her? Have an open mind? Please can you do this for us? Give her a chance. She needs all our support as she doesn't know yet either who you are. Tahiri will have to tell her soon."

Şenay looked at his father's gentle face, then across to his mother. There was an element of truth in it, he had to admit, what they were telling him, and he couldn't help being curious who this mysterious Yasmin was; his biological mother and the story behind his birth in another country which was combined with his adoption. He agreed, seeing that his parents were right.

"Yes, mum, dad, I will do that. I see that you might be right. I will talk to her. Maybe she has something to tell me too," he agreed.

"I'm sure she does. She must be a lovely person, otherwise, I'm quite sure that your uncle would not have taken up with her or asked her to be his wife. Just ask her questions and see what facts you learn from her, okay?" his father reasoned.

Şenay nodded and with this conversation, they agreed that first Tahiri would inform Yasmin of what he knew before Şenay would be introduced to her. The two of them would need to spend some time together to get to know one another and to catch up on two decades as well as finding out what mystery it was that surrounded Şenay's birth and adoption in the first place.

When Yasmin emerged from the arrival area and was approaching him, it brought Tahiri back to the present. They embraced happily and he guided her through the busy airport to the car park where he had parked and they drove to the hotel. They had agreed that she would stay at his hotel for the first two days and they would then decide if she wanted to relocate to his house for the rest of her stay.

When Yasmin had settled in and at her agreement later moved to her fiancé's house, Tahiri took her to several sites within Marrakesh during the course of the first week of her holiday. He planned to show her more of the new home country she was soon going to move to and to help her familiarise herself with the city better. He also suggested Arabic classes with a private teacher, a close friend of his, who would help her with the language once she had settled in. As she already spoke fluent French, the second language spoken in the country, it was easy for her to communicate with those people who didn't speak English or to haggle with the sellers in the Medina shops.

One day, Tahiri announced he wanted to take her to the Koutoubia mosque which was located just off the famous Jemaa El-Fna square, in the Medina quarter, and on the other side of the street where the horse-drawn carriages were waiting for their tourists.

"You will see, it is a wonderful place and very historic. The mosque is the largest in the city and actually dates back to the mid-12th century."

Standing together in front of the ancient building, Yasmin stared in awe at the impressive minaret that stood 77 metres high into the sky and was an important landmark of Marrakesh. It was decorated with arch motifs and was topped by a spire and metal orbs. It was a gorgeous sight.

"It's beautiful, can we go in? I've brought a headscarf with me," she whispered to Tahiri.

"Of course, come, the entrance is just here," he said and guided her to the main entrance of the mosque.

Inside, they found themselves between a group of tourists who also admired the place. Red carpets decorated the floor of the hall and large chandeliers were hanging from the ceilings. Yasmin watched some people come out of the big hall, who appeared to have completed their prayer. A sense of peace washed over her. She knew something had just happened to her inside this mosque that seemed almost like a palace and a little paradise on its own.

"Tahiri," she began, "I have a very important request. I have, actually quite some time ago, decided to become Muslim. I think it even happened the first time when I came to Morocco. I would like to learn more about the religion. And I would therefore like to take my 'Shahada', the declaration of faith, to make it official. It would also help our marriage, don't you think?"

"Mashallah, that's wonderful, Yasmin! This is an amazing and very important step. What made you decide?" asked Tahiri.

He was quite stunned by her sudden revelation. He had not expected it and would never have pressurised her with such an important decision. He strongly believed that it was people's own will to choose the religion they felt comfortable with.

"Well, it's quite simple. I feel I have been guided here, to this country I mean, by an invisible force. It was like a pull, you can say. A pull towards... I don't really know but it has been there right from the first time I came to Morocco in 2008. It's a sense of belonging that I could never quite explain. It never happened to me before. It seems to me that I was guided here to find the truth. I don't know, does that make sense?" Yasmin tried to explain.

"Oh, yes, it does. Believe me, Mon amour, I do understand," Tahiri agreed, feeling a chill down his spine that made him realise that very soon it would make even more sense to her because of the most important revelation he had yet in store for her.

"Thank you, my love. So, will you help me with this, please? I would really like to take my Shahada before I go back to the UK."

"Bon, of course, I will help you. Welcome to the faith, Yasmin. You will not regret it, I promise you. As it happens, I also know the Imam of this mosque well, and we can do this any time you like. I will check with him when he is free," he confirmed.

As they stepped back out into the bright sunshine and the busy street, Tahiri knew this was the time for his next big move. He would take her for lunch at his brother's restaurant. He looked at his watch and it told him it was nearly 1 pm.

"Well, now, Yasmin, would you like to go for lunch? It would be good to have a bite, I feel quite hungry. I don't know if I have told you but my brother Kareem owns a restaurant in the Medina. As it happens, my nephew also works there, and so does my daughter Ayesha in her semester holidays. It's not far, only a few minutes walk from here. We could go there if you don't mind and I'll introduce you to him? What do you say?"

Something stirred in Yasmin's memory. Did Tahiri say his brother's name was Kareem? Where did she hear that name before? Well, she would soon find out.

"Yes, actually, I feel quite hungry too. Let's go to your brother's place, then," she agreed.

Five minutes later, they walked through the courtyard to the entrance of the restaurant called 'Al-Kareem' in the Medina. When they were approaching, Yasmin realised at once that this was the same restaurant she and Naila had lunch at, more than four years earlier. She also recalled a strange encounter with a teenager here that had unsettled her for a while. So, Kareem was in fact Tahiri's brother! What a strange coincidence!

"Al-Kareem is your brother's restaurant?"

"Yes, Kareem is the owner. He bought the restaurant many years ago. It's a family business, as two of my cousins also work here, in addition to Ayesha and my nephew. Why do you ask?"

"It's... well, actually, it's a very strange coincidence. You see, I have been here before. It was during my first visit in Morocco, in December 2008, when I was on holiday with my friend Naila. This restaurant was recommended to us, believe it or not, by our tour guide in Fez and we came here for lunch once. The food was delicious," she explained.

If Tahiri was surprised by her statement, he didn't show it. This was indeed a strange twist of fate. Could it be? Could it possibly be that she had also met Şenay here? She must have done, he concluded, as he had already helped out at his father's restaurant at the time. But if she had, she would have certainly mentioned him, he was sure, even if she hadn't known who he was. He was now even more convinced that Yasmin has no idea that her son was living in this city, perhaps not even that he was in this country.

"By the way, do you know what Kareem means? You see, the name of the restaurant was chosen for two reasons."

"No, I don't know. I thought it was a name?"

"Yes, it is a name but it's also the Arabic word for 'generous'. You will find this name mentioned in our religion a lot. So, that's why my brother chose it for his restaurant as well as of course, it's his own name. He thought it fitted well."

"Oh, how lovely. That's a great idea, especially because it's also his name," Yasmin agreed.

The same friendly waiter from years before, probably Tahiri's cousin Yasmin assumed, greeted them at the entrance and embraced Tahiri.

"Merhaba, Tahiri, good to see you. Please come over to this table here. I'll let Kareem know right away so that you can introduce your fiancée. I'll tell him he personally should serve you today. Of course, Tahiri you don't have to pay, it's on the house."

A few minutes later, a slightly younger version of Tahiri but equally good-looking and slim built, came out of the kitchen and a wide smile lit up his face when he saw them. It was obvious that the two men were brothers. They had the same nose, the same smile, and the same colour hair. The only difference was that Kareem was slightly taller than Tahiri and his eyes had a lighter colour. Yasmin had been told by Tahiri that Kareem was two years younger than him.

"Tahiri! My brother! It's so good to see you! It's been a while," he exclaimed and the two brothers hugged each other tightly.

Before Tahiri could say anything, he turned to Yasmin. "And this is the beautiful lady in question. You must be dear Yasmin. My name is Kareem. I'm the younger brother. I'm very pleased to finally make your acquaintance. Tahiri has told me a lot about you."

Yasmin smiled at this very warm welcome. She immediately liked this man, so like her fiancé, who was going to be her brother-in-law and greeted him with equal warmth. He had a pleasant demeanour about him.

"I hope it was only good things Tahiri has told you about me. I'm very pleased to meet you, too Kareem," she said pleasantly in French and held out her hand to him.

"Come, come, please sit down, and if you let me know what you would like, I will bring it personally. You're my special guests today. It's been a rather quiet day so far but this might change, you never know. For now, please enjoy the mint tea I have just freshly prepared a minute ago and some dates and oranges. I'll bring it over in a minute," he informed them when Yasmin and Tahiri sat down. It was the same table that she and Naila had occupied the last time.

"Thank you, Kareem. Is my nephew here too?" he asked, trying to sound as casual as he possibly could.

"He is, actually, yes, I'll ask him to come and greet you in a minute. But he has a delivery to take away, I'm afraid, so he cannot stay long," Kareem responded.

"That's okay, no problem. I was just wondering as I wanted to introduce him to Yasmin too. But we will have more time when we come to your house the day after tomorrow anyway. Is that still on?"

"Oh yes, of course, it is. It's our rest day at the restaurant and the only time really when we are free at the moment to enjoy some time together. Well, I'll now fetch the tea and some oranges for you. I'll be back in a minute," Kareem said.

"Merci, it's very kind. I'm looking forward to the tea and the oranges," Yasmin said and placed her handbag underneath the table. Kareem disappeared back into the kitchen.

"Your brother seems very nice. It's so obvious that you're related," Yasmin commented.

"Yes, everybody says that. We've always been close and we are lucky to have such a good relationship and a close family. Not everybody has that privilege," Tahiri confirmed.

"You're so right, love. Sorry, I would like to go to the bathroom to freshen up and wash my hands before lunch, if you don't mind? I feel a bit hot and sticky actually."

"Of course, mon amour. It's just over there, see, where the white screen is? The door is behind it." Tahiri pointed to the other end of the restaurant to a screen that separated the dining area from the doors behind. Yasmin stood up, grabbed her handbag and made her way to freshen up.

Unknown to Yasmin, a young man came out of the kitchen just a few seconds after she had disappeared into the toilet and quickly walked over to the table where Tahiri was sitting. Şenay greeted his uncle in Arabic and embraced him.

"It's so good to see you, uncle. Is Yasmin here?" he then asked, looking around and sounding a little nervous.

"Yes, she is but she literally just went to freshen up. I really wanted to introduce her to you. But not to worry, we can do this when we come to your place," Tahiri responded.

"Oh, that's a pity. I do feel a little nervous about the whole thing, actually. Does she know who I am? Have you told her yet?" Şenay asked, glancing in direction of the toilets, hoping to meet his birth mother shortly.

"No, not yet. I'm planning to do this later today. That's why I wanted her to meet you first. Did you know that she has been to this restaurant before? It must have been just over four years ago. She came with a friend."

"Oh really? Wow, that's such an incredible coincidence! You know, when I think about it, I might have done, actually. I do recall something, quite vaguely. I once served a lady many years ago, who seemed a little unsettled when she saw me. I remember it because she had spilt her tea. And there was something else. Her friend called her Yasmin. So, that must have been her then! Oh my God! I did feel a connection somehow when I looked at her but of course, I would never have thought there could be a reason."

"That is truly an amazing coincidence, yes. Well, I'm now quite convinced that she had no idea who you were either or that you even lived here in Morocco. We still don't know any of the circumstances of your adoption. But I will find out. I have to tread very carefully though because obviously, I don't want to shock or hurt her. And hopefully, she can then help fill in the gaps for you," Tahiri suggested.

"That would be very helpful, yes. I don't know anything about my heritage and where I come from. But now, I'm so sorry, I must dash. I have a delivery to take out and I can't wait any longer. Bye, uncle Tahiri, and see you the day after tomorrow," He hugged his uncle again and swiftly returned to the kitchen to pick up the delivery order.

Right at this moment, Yasmin reappeared from behind the screen and caught a glimpse of a slim young man with black hair and a hint of a moustache, who was just disappearing into the kitchen. She was wondering who he was. Maybe this was Tahiri's nephew he mentioned? She returned to their table and sat down. A couple of minutes later, the same man came out of the kitchen carrying a large bag of food parcels.

"Momo!" a voice called out from the kitchen and the man turned around. While doing so, he was revealing his face and his features. The voice from the kitchen called something else to him but it was in Arabic and since Yasmin didn't speak the language, she didn't understand what was being said. The other man came out, holding a leather bag in his hand that he handed over to the man he called Momo.

Yasmin stared at him, unable to speak. This was the slightly older version of the same young man, she was sure now, who she had met more than four years earlier in this restaurant. This was Tahiri's nephew? But the resemblance to Metin was even clearer now. She didn't understand. How could this possibly be?

Tahiri was watching her from the side and saw something like recognition dawn on her face. He was convinced then that she must have met him before, that time with her friend all those years ago in this very restaurant. However, she must be totally unaware of who he really was. He was also quite sure that Şenay must have felt the same kind of recognition even if he had not made the connection. How could he anyway? He had no idea who his birth mother was or where she came from, apart from having seen her name mentioned on his birth certificate.

"What is it? Are you okay, Yasmin?" he asked her gently, squeezing her hand underneath the table.

"Yes, yes, I'm fine. It's just… I don't know what to call it really. Is this young man, this Momo, I have just seen leaving the restaurant, indeed your nephew?"

"Yes, he is. A bright young fellow. He actually came over to the table to say hello when you were freshening up but he couldn't stay long because he had this delivery order to take out."

"Oh, I'm sorry. I left at the wrong time, didn't I? I had no idea."

"Don't worry about it. When we meet at my brother's house the day after tomorrow, I will introduce you properly, when we have more time, and you can have a good chat then. It's always a bit rushed at the restaurant but I thought, I'll try and see if he is available. You do look a bit as if you have seen a ghost though. Are you sure you're all right?" Tahiri asked, fully aware of what was going on.

"Don't worry, I'm okay. He just reminds me of someone, you know. Someone I knew a long time ago. It is very strange though, because it happened in another country, far away from here. That's why it has unsettled me a bit. Please don't worry, everything is fine," she assured him.

Tahiri nodded. He decided that he would tell her who Şenay was this very evening. He could not wait any longer. He would have to prepare her for meeting his nephew properly. It was of great importance that Yasmin knew the whole truth but hoping it would not come as too much of a shock to her. Perhaps once she was aware of this fact, she would also unravel the missing details around the mystery of his adoption and her time in Turkey. She had never spoken about it so far. The more he thought about it, the more this story intrigued him.

About twenty minutes later, Kareem reappeared from the kitchen and brought over their steaming chicken tagines. He wished them 'Bon appetite' and they tucked into the delicious food that Yasmin remembered so well from last time.

When they left the restaurant two hours later, Tahiri suggested that they went back to his house straight away as he had something important to talk to her about. Intrigued what this could possibly be, Yasmin agreed eagerly because she had something of similar importance to tell him too.

She had also decided on her part, back at the restaurant, to finally break her silence and to tell Tahiri her whole story about her time in Turkey, her first husband Metin and her baby, both of whom she had lost so many years ago through such tragic circumstances. She knew by now that Tahiri was a kind and understanding man and deserved to learn the truth about this important part of her past before they tied the knot.

Unravelling the Truth

Later in the afternoon that same day, Tahiri and Yasmin were sitting on the veranda of his house with another tray of steaming fresh mint tea sitting on the tea table in front of them. It was a pleasant and still hot early evening, the sun just beginning to set behind the horizon. Yasmin had settled into a comfortable chair with soft cushions. This was the house she was going to move to in a few months' time and she already felt very much at home. She picked up her cup and took a sip of the mint tea.

"Yasmin, there is something very important that I must tell you," Tahiri began, breaking their comfortable silence.

"There is no easy way to say this but it must be done," He sighed, trying to find the right words. He composed himself and reached over to take her hand into his.

Yasmin's heart began to beat fast. What was it that he had to tell her? Had he ever committed a crime? Been in prison? Or did it have something to do with their engagement? She looked at Tahiri with a terrified expression on her face.

"Oh, no, no, Mon amour," Tahiri soothed her, guessing what her facial expression was implying. "This is not about us. Well, not really in that sense anyway. But it is something very important. It's actually about you. And it's about my nephew too."

"About me?? And your nephew?? Momo? The one I have seen at the restaurant today?"

"Yes, it is. You will understand when I'm telling you. Please just listen to me what I have to say and you will see why it is important that you know this. Trust me, Yasmin."

"You're scaring me now, Tahiri."

"It's not as bad as it seems. It is about Şenay, Yasmin. My nephew."

"Şenay?" Yasmin repeated slowly, not understanding.

"Yes, Şenay, my nephew, Kareem's son."

"Your nephew, Şenay?" Yasmin felt stupid repeating his words like a parrot. "But…but I thought your nephew's name is Momo? That's what they called him at the restaurant."

"No, Momo is just his nickname. It has been ever since he was a child and somehow it stuck. His real, I mean, birth name is Şenay. And there is something else. He is, well, not Kareem and Amel's biological son. They adopted him as a baby."

"I don't understand," Yasmin said again, her face was ashen.

This could not be true. Even as Tahiri's words sank in, she could still not quite make the connection, despite deep down in her heart she felt something stir.

"Yes, Şenay was adopted as a baby. You see, Kareem and Amel could not have children, so they asked me if I could help them somehow if I had any ideas. I put them in contact with one of my close friends, a university friend in fact, who lives in Turkey and had connections to an adoption agency there. Şenay was only three months old when my brother and Amel went to Izmir to adopt him. His official first name on the birth certificate was listed as Şenay, and since they liked the name, they decided not to change it."

"Turkey?? He was adopted from Turkey?" Yasmin whispered as she slowly began to realise the truth and the enormity of what she was told.

"When was that, I mean which year?" she asked, afraid of learning the answer.

"The adoption was perfectly legal, and it was completed in August 1993. And there is something more to it, as you might guess now. The names of the birthparents mentioned on his birth certificate were a Mrs Yasmin Özgűr-Boncrti and a Mr Metin Özgűr. The birth date of the mother matches your birth date, Yasmin."

Yasmin was beginning to feel sick. This was a nightmare but at the same time, a true miracle. Her son was alive! She had been right! All these years, she had been right.

"Do you see what I'm trying to tell you, Yasmin? You are Şenay's birth mother!"

It was a long time until Yasmin spoke again. This was a shock and the last thing she would have expected. Tahiri didn't push her. He knew she would speak in her own time.

"My God, that's almost too much to take in, I can hardly believe it," she was feeling very emotional and slowly beginning to recover from the shock.

"So, this must be the reason why I have always felt there was a connection to me in this country. It was like I was guided here by some invisible force like I tried to explain to you before. Oh my God! That's a miracle, Tahiri! And because his colleague called him Momo, I didn't make the connection when I saw him at your brother's restaurant today."

"Yes, that's why. Well, you couldn't have known. I was also very careful not to call him by his real name. I always referred to him as 'my nephew'. And you would not have expected it anyway, that's another reason," Tahiri added.

"Not at all but also because he is quite tall and therefore appears older than his age. You know, when I went to your brother's restaurant in 2008 with my friend Naila, as I mentioned, I did actually meet him. He served us with another waiter, I assume your cousin? He was only 15 years old then but looked older. I just thought at that time, that the resemblance to my former husband Metin was so uncanny. But nobody called him by his name, so I wouldn't have known anyway. But tell me, how did you find out all this?"

Yasmin was going over the events of her last holiday and then that very afternoon when the truth was finally being unravelled. Then something else occurred to her.

"Does Şenay know about me? Is he aware of who I am?" she whispered.

"Yes, he does. I have told him, together with my brother and my sister-in-law. As soon as we knew who you were, we decided to break the news to him too. After all, you are going to by my wife, and I wanted you to be aware of all these facts. But also, it was important for him obviously, to learn about his heritage and what his country of origin was. This is so important for a person."

"And how did he react? It must have been such a shock for him too, no? And how did Kareem and Amel react when you revealed my true identity?"

"Oh, they understood very well. After all, neither of us expected this and nobody, including you, was aware of the incredible trail of events. And so, we made the decision together to tell you. After all, Şenay is a grown man now, not a baby, and they knew you would not stir up anything. Also, I was quite sure by your reactions that you had no idea that your son was living in Morocco. You would have mentioned such a significant detail and not have kept it from me."

"Yes, of course, I would have. Thank you for telling me, so that I'm not thrown into the deep end, especially when I meet him at your brother's house. I also want to thank Kareem and Amel for raising my child in such a good way. I cannot be more thankful to them," Yasmin said, still finding it hard to believe what she had just learnt.

"I'm sure they will be happy to hear that. And that's precisely why I decided to inform you about it now. But let me tell you how I found out about all this in the first place. It's quite a story, believe me," he continued and started to recount her, the events of this discovery.

"When you checked into my hotel last December, Tariq, my son, who you know, worked at the reception at the time, told me that he recognised your name from somewhere but he could not remember where from. So, I verified your name from your passport copy we obviously keep on file when you check-in, and I finally realised that it must have been from Şenay's birth certificate which I confirmed as well later on at my brother's house."

"You saw his birth certificate? Why was it in your house and not in his parent's house?"

"Well, you see, there is another twist to it. It's kind of a funny tale somehow. It was some years ago when Tariq and Şenay were snooping around in my home office. It was just before Tariq's birthday and he wanted to find out if I had bought him some birthday presents! He knew that I normally keep them in my office," Tahiri smiled at the memory.

"Oh, I see, that's boys for you. So, they were mischievous." Yasmin couldn't help but laugh herself.

"Yes, but he didn't find any presents because I hadn't bought him anything yet. But by chance, they found Şenay's original birth certificate and adoption papers there as they were wedged in a drawer in that wardrobe. My brother had given me all his documents to store when he was refurbishing his house but he had forgotten to take this particular envelope back home. This way Şenay found out that he had been adopted as of course, he had no idea up to then. His parents explained to him why they adopted him and he understood. But then, when I realised who you were, I asked Kareem and my sister-in-law if they gave me the permission to tell you the truth. After all, Şenay is a young man now, and even if you came here in search of him, I was sure you wouldn't try to claim him back. Also, I didn't want to have any secrets from you. You're going to be my wife."

"Oh my God, Tahiri, that's almost unbelievable. It's more than I could have ever imagined. Thank you so much for telling me the whole truth. You know, I'm truly blessed that I have found my son. My lovely boy, my Şenay, who I thought died long ago," Yasmin exclaimed, having listened to Tahiri's narrative almost breathlessly.

She spoke with such compassion, Tahiri was completely stunned. He could not believe what he was hearing.

"What?? Died?? You thought that Şenay had died? How, when?" it was now Tahiri's turn to look aghast. This statement was a lot more than he had expected to hear. He looked at Yasmin expectantly for a revelation.

"Oh, so many questions, love. Believe me, I'm so overwhelmed by this whole story, this secret, that I find it myself almost unbelievable."

"Take your time, Yasmin, there is no rush," he said, not wanting to pressurize her.

"Yes, well, you see, Tahiri, there is something also from my side that I need to tell you now. It's of equal importance that you know this," Yasmin exclaimed and took a deep breath to compose herself.

What she was about to tell Tahiri was her story, a part of her life that she had not spoken about for almost two decades. The only person, apart from her parents, who knew her full story, was Naila. It took her a lot of strength to mentally go back to that time and to reveal those tragic events in 1993 that had completely changed her life.

"You see, the reason why I thought Şenay was dead is because I was told at the hospital, the night he was born, that it had been a stillbirth. They told me that my baby had died, that he had never taken a breath, Tahiri."

Shaking violently, tears streaming down her face, she vividly remembered those short moments that night in the hospital corridor when she came across that nurse. Tahiri, truly worried, put his arms around her, comforting and soothing her.

"Oh, Allah, what happened? How absolutely terrible! How could they do this to you? Why did they tell you this? Obviously, your baby was not stillborn! No wonder you were so shocked when you saw Şenay for the first time in 2008 and you realised the resemblance to your husband. It must have been like a ghost haunting you."

"Yes, believe me, it was but because I didn't know he was alive, I only thought that the resemblance was so surreal. And now you have told me the whole story about his adoption. I thought I was going mad," Yasmin responded, gulping for air.

"I can well and truly understand. So, what happened to him then, at the hospital? He must have been abducted? But by whom? I cannot think of anything else." Tahiri shook his head, not comprehending that someone could do this to a mother. How cruel this was. His heart went out to his love.

"I don't know exactly what happened, Tahiri, I truly don't. But I can imagine somehow, knowing what I know now, what might have happened that night and the reason why he was taken from me. You see, there is something else I need to tell you. Something so horrible that took me a long time to process because it completely broke my heart. That's why I couldn't speak about it for such a long time."

"What happened, my God, Yasmin?" whispered Tahiri and grabbed hold of her hand, finding it hard to believe there was even more tragedy involved in her strange story.

Yasmin slowly opened up, and with tears in her eyes, she started to recount those fateful series of events that unfolded in Turkey in the year 1993 which changed her life forever.

"Well, my tale, full of deceit and loss but also of great love, begins as far back as August 1991, when after university I started working on a cruise ship. It was followed by my employment in a hotel on the west coast of Turkey, in 1992, and my marriage to Metin, my first husband, in 1993…"

Metin's Fate
Manisa, Turkey, June 1993

Totally unaware of the fate that had befallen Yasmin, Metin was fighting his own battle several miles away from Izmir. Having been lured to Manisa by his parents under false pretences the month before, he had not realised what his parents had done until it was far too late. When they had arrived home at his parents' house, a massive row had erupted between them and then his parents had locked him up in his room. Metin had protested heavily and had never in his life been so angry. He was a grown man.

"What do you think you are doing? Mother, you are not even ill! Why did you bring me back here? You have been lying to me! Why?? I have a job and a family. I need to get back to work, to Kusadasi. Not only will Yasmin miss me, wondering what has happened to me and be worried sick but I have a busy job and cannot stay away. My boss will be manic!"

His father had screamed at him, "You do not talk to your parents in such a tone! And I am telling you, you will not go back there. I forbid it. You will not go back to this woman. As we have told you before, a so-called modern woman is not right for you. You will marry the woman we have chosen for you. She is a good, respectable and educated Muslim girl and comes from a good family."

"No! I will not! I don't care who I am talking to. I have already told you that I am a grown man with my own life! In case it has escaped you, I AM already married and I have a family!" Metin shouted.

"What did you say?" roared his father.

"Yasmin and I got married in April in a legal ceremony. She is my wife. We are legally married, and therefore, I cannot marry someone else. Also, Yasmin is pregnant and our baby will be born in June," he said triumphantly.

Selda, Metin's mother, went pale. "What? Have you gone completely mad? Not only have you gone against our wishes and culture but you have impregnated this woman?"

"In case it has escaped you what I have said. She is my wife, mother, whether you like it or not! She is my family and she is a respectable and educated woman too."

His mother and father looked at each other. His mother's lips were tightly pressed together, a sign of her being very angry. When Metin's father started to speak again, it was full of venom.

"In this case, we will make sure this child will be adopted somewhere else. We will not have it that you will be back with this person, whether there is a child or not. We will take care of it. There is no more to be said."

And that had been the end of it. Metin could only stare at his father. He found it hard to believe what he had just been told. There was no more communication about this subject. His parents had stormed out of the room and Metin had been locked in ever since with no way of getting out or attempting to make a phone call, let alone trying to escape.

He was shaking so badly, he had to sit down on his bed. *Why are my parents doing this to me?*, he asked himself. He was terrified of what would happen to Yasmin once she had given birth to their son. What would happen to their child? What did his father mean when he said that he was going to sort it out and to give his son away for adoption? How? He didn't know when Yasmin's due date was or which hospital she was going to give birth at.

His heart was aching beyond imagination. There must be a way of getting back to Kusadasi and to Yasmin. He had to warn her, to protect her, and his child. She must be worried sick from not knowing what had happened to him. He knew the baby was due any time now. He thought back to their last afternoon in her office at the hotel. He had told her not to worry, and that everything would be all right. How wrong had he been! And how right she had been when she expressed her concerns to him, he realised sadly.

"I should have listened to Yasmin," he announced to his bed, "she knew instinctively that my parents were up to no good. I really believed they had accepted my choice by now."

It was at that moment when Metin decided that he needed a plan. Yes, that was it. And he would put it into action as soon as possible, perhaps even as soon as tomorrow. This decision gave him some energy. He knew it was his last chance. What he needed to do is to somehow make a rope and then he would jump over the balcony and escape this way. His plan obviously needed to be carried out during the night. He stood up and crossed the room over to the balcony door and tried the door handle. It was not locked. He sighed in relief. That was some good news at least. His parents had forgotten to lock the balcony door and this would now become his escape route. They could not keep him here and under lockdown as a prisoner in their home. He would fight it, whatever the cost, even if it was going against his own parents. His love for Yasmin was much stronger.

He stood by the window for a long time, trying to figure out how he would put his plan into action in the best way and return to Kusadasi without being seen once he got out of the house. If he ever got out of here, that was. As he was staring across the car park and the entrance gate to his parent's property, he suddenly became aware of a movement between the trees that lay beyond the parking area of the house and near the entrance gate.

What was that? No, this could not be, he thought. *I must be mistaken. My mind is playing tricks. I'm losing my marbles.*

He looked again in the same direction. Then he saw the movement again. It was very slow and not clear but it was obvious that there was somebody out there. No, he was not mistaken. His heart sank into despair and a horrible feeling crept into his heart when he realised who this person was.

Uncle Bekim, he thought, horrified.

Metin had only seen his uncle Bekim a few times since his university days, and when he lived abroad during his work on the cruise ship, he had not been in touch and therefore had not seen him for several years. Uncle Bekim was a policeman in town and had been for many years. He was also well-known for being corrupt. Metin had always disliked him, even as a child. There was something dark and evil about his character and therefore, he had always kept away from him as much as he could and when he was working abroad, he forgot that he even existed.

Now there, between the tallest trees behind the gate to the house, there stood uncle Bekim. He was almost hidden in between the trees but Metin knew in an instant it was him, even though he had put on several kilos since he had last seen him. It was also clear that his uncle has a rifle with him, which was slung over his shoulder. This was indeed very bad news. From his uncle's position, Metin's room with the balcony was in good view and he could be easily seen and watched if he was getting close to the window or get on the balcony. That meant, if he tried to escape, he would immediately be spotted.

Metin started to feel sick and a horrifying thought crossed his mind. If he tried to escape, there was no doubt in his mind that his uncle would see what he was doing and undoubtedly attack him and shoot him. Bekim would not hesitate, he was sure of it.

Uncle Bekim was his father's brother and taller as well as bulkier than him. His father must have installed him there to keep watch and to make sure Metin would not be able to escape. He was also convinced that he had paid him a large sum for his so-called 'service'.

All life went out of Metin's body. He felt weak. What a terrible nightmare this was. He closed the window and went back to his bed to lie down. Overcome by grief, he buried his head in his hands and wept. Why were his parents so hostile? The cruelty of what they had said to him about his wife and child hurt him more than anything.

He would never have thought that he would have to fight this kind of battle for his love when he proposed to Yasmin on their last night on the cruise ship. She was the love of his life and he would never give her up, no matter what. But now, he realised in despair, he would have to find another way, a different plan, that would make an escape possible.

"I'll have to deal with this tomorrow," he said to himself, "there is nothing I can do now but tomorrow I will make a decision. Oh, I so wish I could get in touch with Yasmin somehow. I must warn her."

He was determined to find a new way of escaping. He was desperate. Then he remembered the note he gave Yasmin before he left Kusadasi, with his aunt Esma's contact details on it. She would have realised by now that something had gone horribly wrong at his end and would take action. He was convinced that his wife would get in touch with his auntie and they would somehow find a solution, a way to contact him and try to rescue him. Maybe that was it. He would have to just wait. He also realised that, if Yasmin was about to give birth soon, if she had not done so already, she would not be able to act straight away.

He settled into his bed and prayed that he would be rescued soon or be given some guidance from Allah about making his escape. Finally, he fell into a deep but troubled sleep full of nightmares.

Yasmin's Fate
Izmir, June, 1993

It was in the evening of the second day after she had given birth, when Yasmin was discharged from the hospital. Apparently, they needed the bed and as she was not ill, she had to leave, they had told her. Yasmin had woken up after a disturbed sleep on and off for almost two days and full of nightmares where she kept hearing her baby cry. She had not eaten anything in the past two days. After she had packed her few belongings into the holdall bag, she was ushered out of her room with no communication from the nurses and no explanation regarding the birth. Nothing was said about her baby and the nurse working that day was a different one than the one who she had met in the corridor the day before. She could feel in her bones that her baby was alive but where had he been taken? How could she ever find out the truth?

When she exited the hospital, her legs felt very weak and her stomach and scar still hurt as well from the caesarean operation. The fact that she had not eaten for a long time didn't help her condition either. She had no idea how to get to Kusadasi and she was too weak to even contact her friend Hűlya. Besides, what would she tell her?

There is no baby, they said. He died after I gave birth. But I heard him cry. I know he is alive and somewhere.

Her friend would probably also think that she had lost her marbles. No, she would have to find another solution. Then it came to her. She knew what to do. She looked in her purse for the little note with Esma's phone number on it. She carefully took it out. Esma had told her to contact her once she had given birth and that they would try to find Metin together and bring him back to her. She had to call Esma and tell her what happened.

However, first of all, she had to find a public phone somewhere. Perhaps, she could stay at Esma's house for a few days until she recovered. She looked around but there were no public phones in the vicinity. She would have to find a shop as they normally had payphones, where she could make a call. Gathering her bag, she started limping along the rather dusty road until she found a small convenience store a little further down from the hospital where she asked if she could use their phone. The shopkeeper took her to a small room behind the counter and pointed to the phone.

"Thank you, it won't take long," she said and started dialling Esma's number.
"Esma, it's Yasmin," she said weakly when it was picked up.

"My girl, you sound dreadful! What happened? Where are you? Is the baby okay?" Esma asked full of concern when she heard Yasmin's weak voice.

"There is no baby," said Yasmin in a small voice and began to sob.

"What??"

"There is no baby. They told me that my son has died after I gave birth."

"And you believe them? Do you have any evidence of this? They would have to give you a birth certificate in any case and the proof that he has died and why, Yasmin."

"No, none at all and there is no document. I haven't been given anything. But I don't have any evidence that he is still alive either. I heard a baby cry, Esma! It was my baby! I know, I just know that my baby is alive!" Yasmin said hysterically.

"I can't believe that this is happening, love, I'm so very sorry to hear that. Are you sure he is alive? You didn't see him actually after the birth, did you?" Esma inquired.

"No but a mother knows! I did hear him cry and I just know."

"But where did they take him? And who has taken him? Did you ask the midwife or a nurse in the ward if they have seen anything?"

"Yes, I did but you see, they had moved me to another room after I gave birth and there was no other woman there. I was alone. It wasn't in the maternity ward anymore. I was taken to a different room in a different area of the hospital."

Esma had a horrible feeling in her stomach. If it was true what Yasmin was telling her, that she had heard her baby cry and she was convinced that her son was not dead, she had a fair idea what might have happened. She just did not know how to break it to her. She knew she had to be very gentle with this poor woman.

"Listen, Yasmin, I'll pick you up. Where are you? Please stay where you are and I'll be there as soon as I can. Don't move from there. Then we will decide what we are going to do next, okay?" she said gently.

"I will, thank you, Esma," Yasmin replied and gave her the location of the little convenience store where she would be waiting to be picked up.

She went to pay the shopkeeper who gave her a curious stare. She ignored it. She was not in the mood or had the energy to go into any explanation. She exited the shop and made her way to the dusty roadside outside the store in wait for Esma to pick her up.

It was one week later after this fateful event and Yasmin was still staying with Esma and her husband. She had been very ill and exhausted from her nightmare and Esma had simply insisted that Yasmin remained with them in Izmir and not to go back to Kusadasi. She wanted to nurse her back to health first. She had even called the hotel herself and told Yasmin's boss that she would not be back at work for a while. Fűgen had been appalled when she heard the sad news but had been very understanding. After all, her friend would have been on maternity leave anyway and therefore it made no difference that she did not return to her job for a few months.

When Esma was confident that Yasmin had become a little stronger, she consulted her about the plan she hatched of how to find Metin and bring him back. It was a pleasant, balmy evening and they were all sitting on the large terrace of their Izmir flat which was overlooking the sea, having dinner. Yasmin had grown to like this place and it soothed her. She slowly recovered her health and had begun to eat again, even if it was only small portions.

"This is what I thought we should do," Esma announced, "because I don't think we have many options. On top of this, we cannot leave it too late either, otherwise, he might not even be there anymore."

"Yes, I totally agree. What do you have in mind? I just hope that Metin is still alive," Yasmin sighed with a heavy heart.

"You know, I strongly feel that he is, although, we don't know really what happened to him," Esma reassured her and Yasmin believed what she said.

She took Yasmin's hand and placed it gently into hers. "Despite everything, I don't think his parents would have done any harm to him. Not at this stage anyway."

"Why do you say that? Because I'm not so sure about it."

"Well, first of all, they want him to marry this other woman, right? That rich Muslim girl, according to what you have told me. If he was dead that would not be possible, would it? And secondly, his father wants him to take over the restaurant at some point as well. And that would not be possible for the same reason either."

"Yes, that makes sense," Yasmin admitted slowly.

"So, in this case, I assume he must still be there. I mean in Manisa and in his parent's house. Or maybe somewhere else…" Esma let it linger.

"…but that would not make sense at the moment. Well, not unless they had forced him to marry this other woman already," Yasmin finished for her.

"Exactly! So, what do we do?"

"We'll go to his parent's house to find out somehow if he is still there. Then we'll find a way to kidnap him."

"Yes, we do. I think it is also easier if I approach the property myself because it would not be good for you if they spotted you in the area. You'll stay away from the proximity and wait until I give you a signal. I'll see what I can find out. We will need quite some time and it's also better obviously to approach the house when it's dark. As soon as we have assessed the situation properly, we will put the second part of the plan into action."

"I agree, yes. Let's do it soon," Yasmin sighed.

They had plotted the final details over the following few days until they both were comfortable that their plan could be put into action. Yasmin started to feel stronger as the days passed, and although the loss of her baby was always at the back of her mind and completely devastated her, she tried to accept her fate and prayed that he had found a nice place in heaven if he had indeed died.

"You know what completely devastates me," she said one day to Esma, "because I will never read him a bedtime story, and bathe him and sing him lullabies. I will never see him play with other kids in the playground. Metin will never play football with him and we will never see him grow into a young man or attend his wedding."

"I know, Yasmin, and I'm so sorry," Esma said, feeling Yasmin's pain through her words.

"I don't know how to even break the news to Metin if I ever find him again. The loss of a child is the worst thing that could possibly happen to a parent. I would never have thought that this would happen to me, to us. He will be as devastated as I am."

They had been looking forward to having a family and to moving to Europe together. Now their child had been torn from them and their future was uncertain again. She was beginning to get a nagging feeling in her stomach that their idea to rescue Metin would not go as smoothly as they were hoping. She tried to push those thoughts away but she was not successful. Anyway, she knew she had to at least try.

The Last Battle

About a week later, Esma and Yasmin decided it was time to carry out their plan. It was early evening when they set off on their journey to Manisa in Esma's car. It was just beginning to get dark and when they arrived, Esma decided to park the car in a hidden spot at the nearby large country park, however, not too far from Metin's parent's house so that they could make a quick getaway if needed.

"It is safer here, Yasmin. You are not likely to be spotted if you decide to get out of the car. But please be careful. You don't want to create any danger for yourself," she said.

"Don't worry, it'll be better if I stay here, I do understand. Do you know where to go? Have you ever been to their house?"

"Yes, I have, years ago and only once but I know the area quite well and I know how to find it. It's not far from here and I know a shortcut. Don't you worry love, let me deal with this. It's dark now and I'll be protected by the trees as well," Esma assured her when she got out of the car.

She grabbed her flashlight out of the boot and a black jacket with a hood she had taken with her to be on the safe side so she could not be recognised. She zipped it up, put the hood over her head and switched on the flashlight. She looked around to decide which direction it was best to go and where she would most likely not be seen.

"Okay, wish me luck," she whispered to Yasmin and kissed her on the cheek.

"And if anything happens, I'll flash the light three times as a code so that you know I might need help. But only in that case, you will leave this area, okay? Listen, girl, don't put yourself in any danger."

Yasmin nodded. "Okay, don't worry. Good luck. Please be careful as well."

She watched Esma slowly disappear through the trees. Sitting completely in the darkness, she wondered if Metin indeed was still at his parent's house. She missed her husband so much. Their times together had been magical and so full of love.

"I love you, Metin, please be strong," she whispered into the dark.

Before she had met Metin, she had not known true love. She only had one relationship and it had not been serious, more like a friendship, during her years at university. They both had other plans to pursue after uni and at the time it never occurred to her to have a family yet or even to get married. She felt she was far too young. So, they had said goodbye to each other but parted in friendship. When she had met Metin, although she was still young, she had known in an instant that he was the one and it was obvious that he felt the same about her.

A faint light from the moon was shining through the trees. Being this far out of town, there were no streetlights and not many houses stood in the area either that would offer any light. How long would she have to wait? Should she get out of the car and try to approach the house as well, despite Esma's warning?

What if anything happened to Metin's aunt? She would never forgive herself. After a few minutes, she made her decision. She would have to help her and at least not be far away so that she could assist her in case she needed help and also Metin if she was able to get him away.

If she got out of the car and followed her, she decided it would be better if she had also a flashlight. She opened the glove compartment and searched around. Knowing Esma, she always had two items of a kind. Maybe she'd get lucky. And she was. There was a small, camping flashlight in the compartment. It was one of those used for hiking, the kind you stuck on your forehead and was adjustable with a strap, a headlight. She took it out and inspected it. It seemed fine. She tried to switch it on and it worked.

"Perfect, this will do," she announced to herself. She put the lamp on her forehead and adjusted it to make sure the strap was not too loose, and then switched it on. She released her seatbelt and got out of the car. The night was eerily quiet but very warm. Now, in which direction Esma went, she wondered.

When her eyes had adjusted to the darkness, she could just about make out a pathway on the right-hand side of the car that wound itself into the woods. *Probably a hiker's track*, she thought. After all, this area was well-known to people who wanted to get out of the city for a walk and breathe in some fresh air. It was clear to her that this must have been the path that Esma took as she knew the area well. Yasmin decided to slowly make her way along this pathway and at the same time remain at a safe distance of Metin's parent's property.

Since Esma had taken the car key with her, she would have to leave it unlocked and hoped that nobody would be in the area who would think of stealing it. Well, she shrugged, there is nothing she could do and hoped that Esma would forgive her. She would have to take potluck. Her flashlight only had a low beam and slowly and carefully, she set off along the path she had spotted.

Suddenly, she heard a noise. It was more of a rustling sound. She stopped in her tracks and listened. She was afraid to breathe. Was there someone? What if someone had seen her and followed her? There, she heard the noise again. She stood completely still and tried to listen. But then the night was quiet again and she assumed it might have been a fox or a bird making its way to the bushes.

She carried on. The trees were very tall in this part of the park and she could not see further than just a few feet due to the faint beam of her flashlight. Occasionally, a branch brushed her forehead and she hoped she would not have many scratches.

A few minutes later, she came to a crossroads and she could make out a second path that went off to her left-hand side as well as another one to her right-hand side. She paused.

Think now, which path is the one leading to the house? she asked herself. The one she had been on was slightly wider, so she assumed that must be the one people most likely took when someone was hiking in this area.

In any case, the last thing she wanted was to get lost in these woods and not finding her way back to the car. She was not familiar with this forest and she would definitely be in severe danger if she lost her way. She knew she would have to keep her wits about her and try to find some little landmarks to get her bearings, even if it was dark.

But just before she could decide which path to take, she suddenly heard a loud noise. It seemed quite near. Shocked and terrified, she stopped dead in her tracks and looked around her. She could not make out anything further ahead as it was all in the darkness.

She had no idea where the noise had come from. Again, she heard a rustle in the bushes. Now she was truly petrified. Was somebody there? Would someone harm her? A terrifying thought crossed her mind. It suddenly seemed not such a good idea to have come out after all. She sent a silent prayer to heaven for protection.

Quickly, she switched off her flashlight and stood still. Could she hide somewhere? She looked around but could not make out anything in the faint moonlight. She was scared to death. There was nowhere she could go or hide. If there was someone in the bushes nearby, they would bump into her and she would have jeopardised the whole operation due to her stupidity.

Then all of a sudden, she heard several people shouting something in Turkish. No matter how hard she tried to listen, she could not make out how many voices there were. She also realised that without knowing, she must have been a lot closer to the house than she had imagined.

Then Yasmin froze. There was one voice she recognised in an instant. It was unmistakeably Metin's. So, that was the proof that Metin was still here! Had Esma found him already and made it possible to get him out of the house? She felt a glimmer of hope spark in her heart. Yet, she did not know what to do. If she carried on walking, she would put herself in a very awkward position, and certainly also Metin and Esma. She decided to stay where she was. Then she heard another round of shouting.

"Metin, quick, run, run! I'm over here!" she heard Esma yell in Turkish. Her voice carried a horrible urgency.

"I'm okay, coming, coming," she heard Metin shout through the trees.

Then one gunshot blasted through the night, and another. An eerie silence followed. Yasmin was shaking. The whole world seemed to stop in an instant.

"Nooooo! Noooo! You son of a bitch!" she heard Esma screaming. She had never heard her so angry.

Oh my God, what had happened? Yasmin was truly terrified now and convinced that she and also Esma were in severe danger. *Was it Metin who had been shot? But who was it who shot him?*

Then another angry voice suddenly cut through the darkness. It was full of venom and it gave Yasmin a shiver down her spine.

"Get lost, Esma. You don't belong here. This is none of your business!"

Whose voice was this? It was unfamiliar to Yasmin. After a couple of minutes, she heard Esma shout again in a very angry voice.

"You killed him, Bekim! You killed your own nephew! How could you? You nasty piece of work! You killed Metin! Go to hell!"

Bekim?? Metin's uncle, the policeman? What was he doing here? A horrifying thought crossed her mind. She remembered Metin telling her that he was a corrupt policeman and that he had never liked him. Was it possible that he was involved in the kidnapping of this nephew, together with his brother, Metin's father and his mother? The other voice must have been the one of Metin's father.

And his uncle had now shot Metin and very possibly killed him. Yasmin felt as if her heart had just been ripped out of her body.

"Metin, my Metin, noooo! What am I going to do without you?" she wailed to herself.

There was more shouting coming from the direction of the house, and at once, the porch lights came on and shone through the trees. Yasmin realised how close to the house she was. There were more voices coming from the house and Yasmin knew that it was Metin's mother who had come out. Unfortunately, she could not understand what she or his father was saying as it was very rapid and with her limited knowledge of the Turkish language, she could not make out the complete meaning of the words. However, she could imagine what they were saying and she became aware at once that their plot of rescuing Metin had gone horribly wrong.

Despite everything, she was convinced that Metin's parents had not wanted their son dead, only to teach him a lesson. It was too late for this now. Due to their evil nature, they had now not only lost their only son but also their heir to their business. They were also murderers.

Without wasting any more time, she turned around and started to run back along the path where she had come from. She fumbled with her headlight and finally was able to pull it off her head. She knew she could not be seen here. She stumbled along the path and suddenly fell to the ground over a fallen branch. Ouch, that hurt, she almost screamed.

She bit her lip and felt it bleeding, and when she got up, her ankle hurt very badly. It might have been sprained. She limped further along the path as fast as she could.

What if Bekim found her here and shot her too? He would know at once what they had been up to. Without switching on her flashlight and just using the light of the moon, she tried to find her way back to where the car was parked. She reached the car a few minutes later, panting and trying to catch her breath. With trembling hands, she opened the car door, threw herself onto the passenger seat and buried her face in her hands. She felt sick.

"Metin, Metin," she screamed inside the car, "why did you have to die? Why? My only love, why did you die? What did he do to you?"

Only a few minutes later, the driver's door was ripped open and Esma dropped into the driver's seat, fumbling with the car keys. Her hands were trembling badly. Out of breath, she threw her flashlight onto the backseat.

"Yasmin, we must leave at once. Something very terrible has happened. We're in grave danger."

Yasmin was unable to speak. Every bone in her body felt numb. This is what death must feel like, she thought. I might as well die too.

Esma started the engine with trembling hands and shot off into the darkness with screeching tyres. For several miles, they drove in total silence. Yasmin could not think. She stared ahead but not seeing anything. She did not feel anything anymore. Silent tears streamed from her face and her body was shaking. When Esma glanced over to her, she realised instantly that Yasmin knew what had happened. When they were close to approaching Izmir, it was the first time that Esma spoke again.

"You have been there, haven't you? Although I told you to stay back in the car, you still got out. Do you realise the danger you were in and that you could have been shot too?"

Yasmin only nodded. She tried to ask a question but words failed her. She looked over at Esma and noticed that she had dirt on the front of her jacket and there were also some large, dark wet spots that looked like fresh blood.

Esma drove into the parking garage of her house and switched off the engine. They sat in the car in silence. Neither of them spoke for a while.

"Metin is dead, isn't he?" Yasmin asked in a very faint voice.

"I'm so very sorry. There is nothing I could do. He died in my arms," Esma said sadly and took Yasmin's hand.

"Please tell me exactly what happened," Yasmin whispered and looked at Metin's aunt.

She was devastated about her loss, not only her baby but now also her husband. Her family did not exist anymore. She didn't even want to begin to imagine what experience it must have been for Esma who had seen her nephew shot in front of her eyes and holding his dead body in her arms.

"Okay, since you know part of it anyway," she said and slowly started to recount the events of those two hours in the woods.

"I went along that path, the one you also came on obviously and decided to first approach the house from the back and to assess the situation and also to find out where Metin was. If he was still in the house. I know the area like the back of my hand, you see, because I spent a lot of time in those woods as a child. I knew which room Metin would most likely to be in if he was still at the house, and I saw a faint light coming from it. I took a potluck and threw some small stones at the window."

"Was it the room with the balcony?"

"Yes, yes, it was that one. Then, after a couple of minutes, I saw Metin appear in the window. He must have heard the noise from the stones. He could not make out at first who I was but then he recognised me. He seemed very surprised. I assume that he realised I had come with you because he had given you my phone number to get in touch with me if anything happened to him, right?"

Again, Yasmin nodded. She knew Metin well and he must have known that they had come together to his rescue. It must have given him hope.

"So, I made some gestures for him to get out via the balcony. I saw him nod but also he was trying to tell me something. But I didn't understand what it was. Now, of course, I do," she said sadly.

"It was him telling you that his uncle Bekim was lying in wait with a gun and would shoot anybody and him, if he was trying to escape," Yasmin said.

"Yes, that was it. But how could I know this? Then I moved back into the trees again behind the house to hide and waited for him to come out."

"And somehow he did manage to come out?"

"Oh yes, he tried. I suppose he thought he had nothing to lose. I saw that he had put two bedsheets together and tied them to the balcony railing. Then he climbed down. So far so good. Bekim must have been somewhere else for a while or not looking at the house at that time or whatever, and so Metin made it safely down from the balcony and started running in my direction. And that's when it happened."

"I heard the gunshots and some people screaming. I must have been closer to their place than I thought," Yasmin confirmed.

"Only then I did realise that Bekim had been on the watch, and must have been for a long time and that he would shoot if he saw Metin escape. I'm sure he was in with the conspiracy with Metin's parents and being corrupt as he is, he must have been paid well by his brother to take such an action and shoot his own nephew."

"But did he kill Metin? Why?"

"When I saw that Bekim had shot Metin, I ran to him and tried to rescue him, to take him further into the woods. But when I tried to grab him, I realised at once that he was already dead. Bekim had fired two shots and one of them into his heart. I'm not sure if that was intentional or if he was just meant to hurt him.

In any case, he is a very nasty and evil person. How could you kill a family member? How could you conspire to such a thing?"

Esma shook her head. She was still in shock herself, having witnessed this incident which would certainly stay with her for the rest of her life. Her heart went out to Yasmin. She was such a lovely person and now she had not only lost her child but her husband too.

"I'm so very sorry, Yasmin. I was trying to help and I was convinced that we would rescue him and get him back safely. I did it for you. Metin was a very kind man with a good heart, and I have always liked him. He was sincere, responsible and just a lovely person."

"Esma, it is not your fault. You did everything you could and for this, I'm very grateful. I will always remember my loving husband, the love of my life. I could not even tell him that I had given birth to a son or what happened to me at the hospital. Maybe it's better this way. He didn't even know I was there too, and ready to take him into my arms again."

"I know, my love, I know," Esma said with great compassion.

"What makes me so very sad is that we had planned to start a new life in Europe once the baby was born, to be safe and have a family, maybe another baby in the future. I feel my life is over before it has really begun. It's the expectation we had of a great future, and the hope, which is now truly shattered."

"It is absolutely terrible that this has happened. And one thing is for sure, I will never be in contact with anyone from that family ever again. They are such evil people. I hope that one day there will be justice and that they will go to prison for what they did," Esma said with a passion that surprised Yasmin.

Yasmin's heart was aching and for a long time, the pain was unbearable. She wept the whole night and could not find any consolation in sleeping. Her head was spinning when she collapsed onto her bed. She started to feel sick and leaned to one side and vomited on the floor. *Sorry, Esma*, she thought. *I'll clean up tomorrow.*

Because now, she didn't care, nothing mattered anymore. The golden future with the man she loved and their baby would never happen. And nothing would matter ever again.

For a long time afterwards in her nightmares, she was tormented and relived the events. She kept hearing those gunshot sounds over and over, then the eerie silence that followed Metin's last words, and the shouting of the people involved during that fateful night. When she eventually woke after her restless sleep, she was drenched in sweat, many times accompanied by a migraine, often not realising where she was until she was fully awake.

In the days and weeks after the incident, she often sat on the balcony of Esma's apartment, staring out onto the calm Mediterranean Sea. It reminded her of happy times, of love, of hope and promise, and of the short life they had shared together. When she listened to the gentle waves of the sea, it soothed her troubled mind.

Not long ago, they felt they were invincible together. They had exciting plans for their future in Europe and their family. Now, with her husband's death, night had fallen on her world. Her heart felt tormented and great sadness washed over her again, giving her the feeling that she was drowning in a deep sea of emotions. She was sure that she would never find a love like Metin ever again. It had been so unique, so gentle and special, full of life and hope. He was only 27 years old when he died. What a waste of a beautiful, prosperous young life.

Nearly two months had passed after that fateful night when Metin was killed. One evening, Yasmin, Esma and her husband were sitting on the terrace enjoying their dinner when she announced her final decision.

"I meant to tell you for a while," she began, "I have made the decision to leave Turkey for good. After all that has passed in the recent months, there is nothing here for me anymore. I have to move on."

Esma looked up from her dinner plate and nodded, not at all surprised about Yasmin's announcement. "I do understand, and I have expected something like this. So, what are you planning to do?"

"I'm going to return to the UK where I will stay with my parents for a while before looking for a new position in another hotel chain where I can pursue my career. After a long time of considering my options, I know that I have no choice but to leave this country in order to move on with my life. You know, I cannot bear to be reminded all the time of the heartbreak I have been put through in the recent months. I really only have one choice."

Having lost a lot of weight, she looked like a shadow of her former self. Her eyes were sunken and lost their sparkle. Esma was terribly worried about her and tried to convince her to eat more and to find her strength again.

"You are right to move on, Yasmin," Esma agreed, "you need to gain strength and work will help you, and also to see your parents because they will give you support as well."

"Yes, that's another reason why I have decided to return to England. I'm also going to have counselling to help me with my nightmares and migraines. I have to hand in my notice at the hotel too as my boss doesn't know yet. She will probably be disappointed but I hope she'll understand why I have made this choice," Yasmin explained.

Fügen had indeed been very understanding when Yasmin had handed in her resignation at the Grand Ephesus hotel. Her boss had been, just like everyone else, completely shocked by the incident and the terrible fate that had befallen her dear friend. She gave Yasmin a fantastic reference that would help her find a new position in Europe, and told her to keep in touch and that she would always have a job at this hotel should she ever return to Turkey. Yasmin knew that this would never happen but she thanked her kindly for the offer.

On a hot day in mid-August, at the height of the Turkish summer, Yasmin sat on the plane at Izmir airport bound for London. Esma and her husband had insisted on taking her to the airport to see her off.

"Are you sure you're all right, Yasmin? Is it not too early to travel just yet? You still seem quite weak," Esma's voice had been full of concern.

"Yes, thank you, please don't worry, I'll be fine," Yasmin said when they had been standing in the queue at the check-in desk.

All her belongings were packed in her two suitcases. They were the same two suitcases she had arrived in this country with Metin what now seemed a lifetime ago.

"Please Yasmin, look after yourself, and keep in touch," Esma said, hugging her.

"I will, I promise. And thank you so very much for all your support and help. You have been so good to me. I honestly don't know what I would have done without you. I will never forget your kindness," she said with tears in her eyes.

"Let us know about your new job and new adventures. And of course, your new address wherever you will move to, okay?"

"Don't worry, I will, as soon as I have sorted myself out. I might go abroad again to work but that depends on my opportunities. I haven't decided yet. For now, I'll stay in the UK to make a fresh start. My work will keep my mind off the grief. Time will heal, I hope." She hugged her two friends tightly and then disappeared through the departure gate.

Yasmin looked out of the window as the plane took off from Izmir airport towards the Mediterranean Sea in the direction of her home country, and despite everything, she felt a great sadness coupled with a sense of relief about leaving Turkey. She had loved Metin's homeland, just as she had loved him, as well as the tasty food and the beauty of the place. It was an interesting, varied country with many amazing sights and a great, ancient history.

Many people she had met here, including Esma and her husband, Hűlya and Fűgen, as well as her work colleagues at the hotel, had been very kind to her and she knew she would miss them dearly. And for the last time, she said goodbye to Metin, her loving husband and the life they had together, cut short by such a terrible series of events. She said a silent prayer to their little baby, Şenay, who also was torn from them far too early and wished him well wherever he was in heaven.

Marrakesh, April 2013

"And that was it. I have never been to Turkey since," Yasmin ended her tale.

Tahiri had sat very still, totally stunned by Yasmin's narrative. His mint tea had gone cold, totally forgotten on the tray, so immersed had he been in her story.

"Oh Allah, I'm so very sorry to hear about this tragedy, mon amour," he said with great compassion. His eyes had started to water, hardly believing what he had just learnt.

"It must have been absolute hell for you," he added, shaking his head.

"Believe me, it was. I had nightmares about that night for years, not to mention the night I gave birth. I needed some counselling for quite some time to get over it, actually. It was hard work to get on with my life and to find some kind of normality again. But eventually, I got better and I could put it behind me," Yasmin admitted.

"Yes, no wonder, I can well imagine. Poor you, having to go through something like this. And so, in August 1993 you left your husband's country behind and moved back to the UK. Have you ever heard again from anyone from his family? And what about Esma? She seemed to be such a caring and special person. It must have been such a terrible shock for her too, having Metin die right there in her arms. I cannot even begin to imagine what it must have been like."

"She is a lovely person, and it was terrible for her too. Well, we have been keeping in touch all these years, as best as we could with our busy schedules. But even she didn't have any more information regarding the murder of my husband, no."

"I understand," Tahiri said.

"She completely distanced herself from that family, you see. Mind you, even before that happened, she didn't have much contact with them," Yasmin explained.

"Yes, no wonder, given the circumstances. I would have done the same! But has nobody ever found out who it was that kidnapped Şenay right after he was born?" Tahiri was wondering.

"No, I have no idea at all what happened or who could have possibly arranged it."

"The way I think about it, there must have been someone working at the hospital who got involved, and perhaps was even bribed into that kind of operation. In fact, I'm sure of it, one of Metin's relatives, perhaps? Şenay couldn't end up at that orphanage all by himself. Someone must have contacted that adoption agency way before he was born," Tahiri was thinking out loud.

Yasmin stared into space. Trying hard, she forced herself to recall the events of the night at the hospital when she gave birth. Then suddenly she remembered something that she thought was odd at the time but had forgotten all about it.

"I think you may be right, Tahiri. Now that you mention it, there was something. When I got to the maternity ward, you know my friend took me in a taxi, there was a midwife there expecting me straight away. I think her name was Zeynep, something like that. That's what her nametag said anyway. She addressed me by my name even before I even had the chance to check-in. How did she know my name if she had never met me before?"

"I agree, that is kind of odd," Tahiri nodded. "Is there something else you remember? Think carefully. Anything?"

"Actually, there is, yes. I was forced into having a caesarean operation. They gave a strange reason for it; I don't really remember what it was. I basically didn't have a choice, even though I wanted to have a natural birth. They just wouldn't listen to me."

"And I assume the reason for this was because you would not immediately be awake at or after giving birth or remember much because of the anaesthetic," Tahiri explained.

"That must be it! Yes! Now it all makes sense! And when I finally woke up, I found myself in a different room in another ward! It wasn't in the maternity ward anymore. I had been moved. But my stomach hurt from the stitches, you know, from the caesarean operation. I could barely move. They must have hurried. I remember I was worried that they hadn't done a good job and I would somehow get an infection if it didn't heal properly. And, actually, yes, there was something else," Yasmin remembered.

"What was it? Try to go back to that night," Tahiri encouraged her, really wanting to find out what seemed like a crime that had been committed.

"There was this nurse. She said her name was Gül. I met her in the corridor when I had managed to get up and was trying to find my baby. She was kind, actually."

"Was there something strange about her?"

"No, no, it wasn't her. But, well, she told me when I asked her where my son was, who I had just given birth to, she said that he had died, that he'd been stillborn. This statement seemed kind of strange to me… it was almost as if she knew more than she was letting on, just bizarre. How could she have even known that I had a stillbirth? The nurses don't normally attend the births of the children in the maternity ward, do they? It's the midwives, isn't it?"

"That's a very good point, Yasmin. Well done. Now that you remembered some important facts and you have told me the whole story, I get a much better picture of what could have been like a conspiracy. It certainly was a crime that has been committed, whichever way you look at it, Yasmin."

"A conspiracy? Do you think so?"

"Yes, I do. Think further back, the experiences you had long before you even got pregnant. Also, given the fact that Metin's parents quite obviously didn't want you to be his wife or have his baby. They tried to put all obstacles in your way of being together. They must have had something to do with it. In fact, I'm convinced of it."

"Do you really think so?"

"Oh yes, absolutely. There cannot be any other explanation, Yasmin."

"Maybe you're right…," she admitted slowly, recalling that one time she accompanied Metin to meet his parents in Manisa and how hostile they behaved towards her.

"I'm quite sure I am. Even if it seems far-fetched somehow but I think I have an idea of what might have happened that night, and how Şenay ended up being given up for adoption in the first place. Listen, this is what I assume must have happened…"

When Tahiri had her complete attention, he laid out to her his view of events that might have unfolded, and probably started as far back as when she married Metin, that were leading up to the crime on that fateful night of Şenay's birth.

A Clandestine Operation
Izmir, Turkey, July 1993

The night when Yasmin had given birth and subsequently was convinced that she had heard her baby cry, a clandestine and illegal activity took place at the hospital, completely without Yasmin's awareness. It was this event that would devastate the young mother beyond imagination and change her life forever.

A few months into Yasmin's pregnancy, she and Metin had decided that the baby's name would be Şenay. It was a pretty name they both liked and the beauty of it was that it could be a girl's as well as a boy's name. The meaning of the name was 'Happy Moon' in Turkish. Before she had been given the anaesthetic for the caesarean operation, she had told the midwife that they had already chosen a name for the baby and it would be Şenay. She wanted to have this name mentioned on the birth certificate as well as both parent's names. Despite not knowing yet what fate had befallen Metin, she wanted to make sure that Şenay knew who his parents were.

What neither Yasmin nor Metin could have known was that the midwife, who had delivered her baby, was a relative of Metin's father. She was, in fact, his cousin and he had worked out a plot with her. After the incident at Metin's home, and knowing that Yasmin was about to give birth, his father had taken action regarding his so-called taking care of the baby.

The midwife, a woman in her late thirties called Zeynep, had been bribed by Metin's father into taking Yasmin's baby away straight after birth. The instructions were that she had to take the baby to a car that waited in the rear area of the hospital which was not accessible for patients, only for the ambulances, so she would not be seen by anyone.

A friend of his would wait for her there in a car and she would hand over the baby to him. His friend would then take him to an orphanage in town that he knew of. Once the baby was there, he would then call the adoption agency and give the green light for the child being given up for adoption. He would also take care of the papers that would state that consent had been given for the baby to be given up for adoption by forging the signatures of the parents.

However, first Yasmin had to be enticed into having a caesarean operation because that way she would not see her baby or hear him cry when he was delivered. Yasmin was then to be told that her son had died at birth. He was stillborn, if anyone, including Yasmin asked. Because Yasmin would still be weak from the anaesthetic, and basically be unconscious, she would not notice when she was removed from the maternity ward straight after she had been given birth, to another wing of the hospital. Then she would have to be again sedated for a while longer so that she would not remember anything.

"You have to make sure that you have no one watching you, therefore you must work at night," Mr Özgűr had told Zeynep.

"But what if the baby is born during the day? I would have to wait for much longer. And what if I'm not on shift that day?"

"If the baby is born in the day, you'll just sedate the woman again and leave the baby in the baby room. And you change your schedule so that you're on shift that day. Cheating should not be difficult for you. I know you've done it before and you can come up with something," Mr Özgűr had insisted.

Zeynep knew he was right and she had no choice. She had twice before fiddled with the schedule when she needed to get away and no one had noticed.

"I will pay you handsomely, so you will do this job, no questions asked, understand? Then, when you have the baby, the birth certificate and all the papers, you will take him to my friend's car which will be waiting for you outside the hospital as I have explained earlier. I will give you the car model and registration number shortly, so you will recognise it. After this, your job is done. My friend will take the baby to the orphanage. He knows where it is located. And not a word to anyone, ever, do you understand?"

Zeynep nodded and agreed to this deal because in her job as a midwife she earned very little money and although she worked long hours, and sometimes even overtime, she was never able to make ends meet. This so-called 'deal' came in very handy for her, especially as she had two teenagers herself who she wanted to put through university. She would not have them lead a miserable life as she had.

The adoption agency that worked with the orphanage, dealt mainly with couples from other countries who were unable to have children and would seek help from agencies that were not so expensive. The charges for adoptions in

European countries, as well as being a long process, would be much higher, and for many young parents, such an amount would be impossible to pay. It would also mean that the adoption procedure would be much quicker. A further advantage would be that an adoption to another country from Turkey would mean that the baby's origin could not be traced so easily.

It was shortly after 2 am, the same night, one of the night nurses, a young woman called Gül, came into the maternity ward to check up on the young mothers to see if everything was all right or if they needed help with anything. After a quick check, she was convinced that nobody was in need of anything, so she left the ward and made her way back to the babies' room to check on the little ones. The babies' dormitory was situated on the same floor, at the far end of the wing. When she entered, the room was very quiet and all babies were asleep. When she looked at the tiny creatures her heart melted. They looked so cute, so innocent, and she was looking forward to having her own child one day.

"Bless you, my babies," she whispered to them, "sleep well. Now, I'm going to have my well-earned coffee."

Just as she turned to leave the room, she hesitated. Also, there was a movement she became aware of in the corner of her eye but she dismissed it for the light in the room playing tricks on her. Still, something wasn't right here. First, she couldn't decide what it was, and then the realisation hit her. One of the little beds was empty. She had missed it at first because that cot was the last one of the fourth row of beds and therefore the furthest away. That's why she had not seen it right away. She rushed over to the cot and read the name label that was attached to the headend. It said 'Şenay Özgür' and the birth date was the very same day. This baby had just been born! *How bizarre,* Gül said quietly to herself, *why is his cot empty? Where was the little boy? Had he already been given to his mother? In the middle of the night?*

She looked around the room and noticed that at the far end of the room, where the sink and also two chairs stood, the curtain was drawn. Now, that was strange. Normally this curtain was left open. Why was it drawn now? It was night-time and normally nobody would need the area for cleaning at this time. There again, the movement. The curtain was twitching. There was no doubt in her mind now. It was only a slight movement and it could be from a draft if the window was open.

She looked properly and it happened again. No, it wasn't from a draft because the window was closed. She was now sure there was a person hiding behind the curtain and something rather sinister was going on. She knew that apart from her, there should not normally be anybody in this room at this hour. So, who was there?

Tiptoeing and holding her breath, she slowly approached the curtain. She jerked it open. There, behind the curtain she discovered her colleague Zeynep, the midwife on shift tonight, holding a bundle in her arms wrapped in a light blue blanket. A large bag was hanging over her left shoulder. She looked as if she was going somewhere. The look on her face told Gül that she was quite obviously very annoyed about having been caught out.

"What are you doing here, Zeynep? You're not supposed to be in here," asked Gül and was shocked when she looked closer at the bundle in Zeynep's arms.

"Isn't this Mrs Özgűr's son? Why are you holding her son? I saw that his cot is empty," Not understanding why her colleague was hiding behind a curtain, holding someone's baby.

"None of your business, go away," came the short, unfriendly reply.

"What do you mean none of my business? Where are you taking Mrs Özgűr's son? Put him back in his cot! He was only born tonight and he needs to sleep. He will be taken to his mother in the morning."

"No, he won't. He is coming with me. I have special orders. I'm paid for this and this baby will be given up for adoption. He will not go back to his mother. Now go," Zeynep hissed.

"What do you mean he is not being taken back to his mother? He is a new born and needs his mother! He needs to be nursed! And what do you mean by an adoption? Did Mrs Özgűr agree to have her son adopted??" she asked in disbelief.

"Yes, the parents don't want him. I was also told to put Mrs Özgűr in another ward tonight as soon as the baby is gone. She will not stay in the maternity ward."

"What?? I don't believe you!" Gül was mortified to hear her colleague's statement.

When Zeynep didn't reply and given her hostility towards her, she knew at once that this was a very bad sign. It was an illegal operation and must be stopped somehow. Her mind was racing. She must do something, anything to stop Zeynep from taking this baby.

"Are you crazy, Zeynep? You cannot steal someone else's baby! And it is my business too. I also happen to work here, in case it has escaped you!" she almost shouted.

"If you don't keep quiet about this, I will report you for misconduct and I will have you dismissed," Zeynep hissed at her colleague, as rude as she had always been.

Gül opened her mouth to say something but no words came out, she was too shocked. She also knew she could not lose her job. It was her first one since university and she depended on her work.

"Now, let me through. And if anyone, you hear me, anyone asks you what happened to this baby, you will tell them that he has died. He was stillborn. The same applies for his mother if she happens to ask. And you don't breathe a word to anyone about what you have seen. Do you understand?"

With this threat, Zeynep pushed Gül rudely aside, ran towards the door and disappeared into the hallway and out of sight. Gül stumbled and almost fell over one of the chairs. Holding it for support, she gathered herself and stared after her colleague, stunned, not believing what she had just witnessed. A baby started to cry, obviously woken and disturbed by the sudden noise.

Gül had been placed in the same maternity ward where Zeynep was working as a midwife, only six months previously. The two women had disliked each other from the start. Gül was a good worker and strongly believed in justice and integrity. She also loved her job, was ambitious and dedicated to her work. She knew there was no way she could let this go. After a couple of minutes, she composed herself and ran after her colleague. The baby was still crying but she had no time to soothe him.

"Oh blast, the coffee has to wait for a while and sorry babies, I have to sort something out," she announced to the small creatures and rushed through the door that led into the corridor and peeked out. She had to make sure nobody saw her and would question what she was doing. The corridor lay in semi-darkness, the light only coming from the night lamps mounted on the ceiling. It was eerily quiet and nobody was in sight. Then she heard footsteps far away but paid no attention. It was probably another nurse doing her round.

Gül knew she had to try to get this baby back somehow. She did not believe a word Zeynep had told her and was convinced that the baby had been kidnapped. If the parents had indeed agreed to have their son adopted, for sure it would not be during a clandestine operation, in the middle of the night, without the mother giving at least a signed document to prove it and to be handed over with her baby.

She felt horrible for the young mother, who would for sure not know that her baby had been stolen from her. She would be completely devastated when she woke up in the morning and her baby was not given to her to be nursed. Gül looked down the corridor left and right. Where did they go? She quickly calculated. She assumed that Zeynep was probably trying to leave the hospital through one of the back entrances to give the baby to someone who was waiting out there and obviously didn't want to be seen. If she was quick, perhaps she could stop them from this disaster happening.

And then what? What would she say to them? Suddenly, she realised that her rescue plan might not be so straight forward as she had thought, and she might put herself in a dangerous situation if she was trying to stop them.

Well, she thought, *at least I would have tried. It's worth the risk, especially for the mother. I'm sure they won't kill me because of it.*

She turned right and ran along the corridor. She didn't bother using the lift and took the staircase, taking two steps at the time. Once she tripped and nearly fell down the last flight of stairs, had she not grabbed the handrail in the last second. Her ankle began to hurt but she hardly took any notice. Out of breath, she reached the basement and ran towards the back entrance, near the A&E section of the hospital, which was used by the ambulances.

She jerked the door open and found herself standing among two ambulance vans parked in front of the entrance. They were locked up. She looked around but didn't see anybody. She didn't hear a sound. It was eerily still. Where did Zeynep go? Slowly and quietly, she slid between the vans and crept a few steps further to see if she could see something that would give her an indication of where Zeynep had disappeared to.

Suddenly, she heard an engine rev up, then tyres screeching at the far end of the ambulance car park. A car speeding away quickly, she realised. She now ran the last metres between the vans in direction of the noise but still didn't see anything. The car must have been parked further down behind the other vans, hidden from sight, lying in wait for Zeynep to bring the baby. It was the right position for a quick getaway.

And now it was gone, with the baby in it, of course. It was too late to save him.

Gül stood still for a moment. There was nothing she could do now to save Mrs Özgűr's son. The little boy had been taken away and she had no idea where.

"The poor mother," she whispered to herself, a feeling of helplessness wash over her.

Slowly, she turned around and made her way back into the hospital. *Would it be possible to report this kidnapping incident to her boss? Would anybody even believe her? Probably not. Her boss might even have taken part in it!* She had heard of such incidents before and knew that once this had occurred, all traces would be erased and honest people, who would have tried to help, would be dismissed as liars or worse even be killed. *This is corruption,* she thought sadly and shook her head, then turned around and went back through the same entrance and up the stairs. She had no choice but to return to her ward to complete her rounds for the night.

A few hours later, just before Gül was finishing her shift, she was walking along the corridor of another ward, when suddenly a door burst open and a young woman came stumbling out, almost bumping into her. She seemed in great distress and it was obvious she was very weak. She could barely stand up and held on to the wall for support. When she noticed Gül, she began to speak almost hysterically.

"Nurse, please, do you speak English? I gave birth a few hours ago but my baby is not there. Please can you take me to my baby? I know I had a son. Where is he? My name is Mrs Yasmin Özgűr-Bonerti."

"I do speak English. Mrs Özgűr, please calm down and listen to me. My name is Gül. I'm the night nurse on shift tonight. Please, you must go back to bed now. You are too weak to wander around the hospital and besides, it's the middle of the night. You need to rest. Come, I'll take you back to your room."

She gently took the woman's arm and guided her back into the room, then helped her get into the bed. Suddenly, the woman grabbed her hand.

"Please tell me, Gül, where is my baby? I know I've given birth to a son, and my husband and I agreed a long time ago to name him Şenay. Where is my son, please?"

"Mrs Özgűr, there is no easy way to say this," Gül began to explain as it dawned on her who this woman was. She knew she had no choice but to tell her. She looked at her with compassion, very concerned about the young mother.

"What? What happened to my baby? Tell me!" her face was ashen.

"Your son has died, Mrs Özgűr. He was stillborn. There is nothing we could have done to save him. He didn't breathe. I'm ever so sorry to give you this bad news."

"Nooo! I know my baby is alive! I heard him cry! I heard him! I didn't imagine it. He is somewhere! You are lying to me! I don't believe you!" the woman was screaming now.

"I'm so very sorry but your son died. I truly wish I could give you better news. Please go to sleep now, Mrs Özgűr. I'll give you a sedative so you can sleep better," Gül said, trying to calm the distressed mother.

"I don't want to sleep! I want my baby! Tell me where my baby is!"

"Please madam, please calm down. Trust me, you will soon feel better. You need to rest now and soon you can go back home," Gül tried again to calm her.

She helped the woman, who was obviously in pain from the birth, lie down. Then Gül quickly took a vial from the trolley that was standing next to the bed and pushed a needle into the young mother's arm to give her the sedative. She gently covered her with the duvet to make her comfortable and left the room. Outside in the corridor, she paused for a while, feeling very sorry for this young, distressed mother. It broke her heart. She wondered where her husband was. Why did her husband not come to visit her?

When she made her way back along the corridor to complete her round, she suddenly remembered something. When she had caught Zeynep with the baby in her arms, she had noticed that she had had a bag slung over her shoulder. Only it didn't register at the time. What had been in that bag? Was it more than just a spare blanket and a baby bottle? She wanted to be sure about what she suspected.

She turned and ran back to the babies' ward and straight to the cabinet where she knew all the documents of the newly registered births were kept. If she could find those birth documents, she would have proof that the baby was alive. This way, she would be able to tell Mrs Özgűr that her son has not been stillborn. She jerked each drawer open where the papers were kept in alphabetical order, and rummaged around. For sure, something must have been kept there. Occasionally, she looked up just to make sure nobody would come into the ward and see her and question what she was doing.

But there was nothing. No documents for Mrs Özgűr, no documents for her son. There was no proof at all that she had ever given birth to a son.

"Oh no, no, no. So that was what Zeynep had in the bag. She did a thorough job and also stole all the documents that proved the baby existed," Gül exclaimed to herself, collapsing onto the nearest chair.

She stared at the filing cabinet as if it could give her some answers. What a nightmare. She would not be able to prove to the young mother that her child was alive. In fact, she could not even prove that there had ever been a baby at all. Tears filled her eyes.

A strong dislike turning into hatred for her colleague Zeynep crept into Gül's heart. She was the true culprit in this whole incident together with whoever it was that helped her steal this baby. How desperate she must be. And all this for how much money, she wondered. This was sick. She stood up, closed the filing cabinet so that no one would find out she had been nosing around and left the dormitory. She looked at her watch and saw that her shift was over, and then she went to the locker to change into her civilian clothes before going home.

When she put on her shoes, she swore she would find a solution, anything to help the young mother. Perhaps, she could find out more regarding this incident through another source and give Mrs Özgür some information before she left the hospital.

Maybe another mother from the same maternity ward where Mrs Özgür was first stationed, had seen her giving birth? There must have been several other women in the ward at the same time. All she needed was one witness. That would be enough. The very least she could do was tell her that her son was still alive and what really happened that night, even if Zeynep threatened her with dismissal. Yes, she would do that. It was what her conscience told her. It would calm the young mother somehow, even if she didn't see her baby anymore. At least, she would know that her son had not been stillborn and that she had not been hallucinating when she had heard her baby cry.

But when Gül returned to the ward for her night shift a couple of days later after her day off, she was told that Mrs Özgür had been discharged from the hospital and with her, the whole mystery involving her son's birth and disappearance had left with her.

Tahiri and Yasmin
Marrakesh, September 2013
A New Future

Yasmin could barely contain her excitement. She felt like a 16-year-old girl all over again, with butterflies in her stomach and counting the days until she was reunited with Tahiri.

She could hardly believe how much her life had changed in the past twenty years.

"I have come a long way, that's for sure," she announced to herself when she sorted out her last bits and pieces in her small London flat that she was going to take to her new future in Morocco. Her flight to Marrakesh would leave in three days and her life would change in a way she would never have imagined. Her last pieces of furniture were sold and today, her last day in her flat, her bed was going to be picked up by her friend Albert, who had just moved to a new home. Later on, she had arranged to drop the keys with the estate agent and would then spend the remaining two days at Naila's place.

"Oh Tahiri," she told him when they skyped two days before, "you can't imagine. The past few weeks have been manic! I've now handed in my notice at the hotel and had to train my replacement. My voice is hoarse now. And now I'm so overwhelmed with the wedding preparations. It doesn't seem to end!"

Tahiri had laughed. "Wait until you arrive here, the pre-wedding parties and everything leading up to the wedding takes up to seven days."

"Oh, my goodness, really? That's like the Indian weddings, isn't it? I've been to so many of those, with Naila you know, and I loved them. They're fantastic."

"Yes, it's pretty much like it, and I'm sure you will enjoy it," he had confirmed.

Their big event would take place at the end of September at the Hotel Riad Sol, just a week after her arrival. Tahiri had already made the arrangement with the Imam at the mosque to sign the wedding contract the day before, which was the shorter part of the wedding.

When Tahiri had come to visit her in the UK in July for one month, she had proudly introduced her fiancé to her friends and her parents, who were very pleased to see their daughter finally happy again and with a new prosperous future, as well as a new job to go to. Due to an unexpected vacancy at a big hotel in Marrakesh, the same hotel chain she worked for in London, her supervisor had agreed to a transfer straight away, and she could work there in her usual line of business. She was due to start one month after her wedding, which gave her enough time to settle in and to enjoy the honeymoon with her husband.

Yasmin had another surprise for her parents. When she had filled them in with the news of her son, Şenay, whom she had found again in such an unexpected and incredible twist of circumstances, they had not believed her first. But when Yasmin had produced a copy of his birth certificate as well as a photo of him and showed it to them, they both cried, overjoyed that her daughter had not lost her child. Now they were looking forward to meeting their only grandchild, even if he was already a young man. And Yasmin, who had found two more children with Tahiri, finally had a proper family.

Her parents fell in love with Tahiri, the kind stranger who had swept their daughter off her feet. They were going to travel to Morocco, their first time in that amazing country, they heard so much about through Yasmin, a few days after her so that they could get to know their grandson, Şenay.

Yasmin's colleagues at the hotel had given her an amazing and quite unexpected leaving party, and with just her friends in London, she enjoyed a pre-wedding party because not all of them were able to travel to Morocco. She was given a very good send-off which had touched her heart deeply.

Both her friends Naila and Carol, who had kept in touch after their time on the cruise ship and was working also in the UK, were going to travel to Marrakesh to be her bridesmaids. They had all been working with her on the busy task of the wedding invitations. Albert, her old friend and flatmate from her university days, happened to be an amateur photographer, and he had agreed to be their official wedding photographer and helper at her wedding in Marrakesh. There was one more bridesmaid to join them. It was Ayesha, Tahiri's daughter, who would assist her with choosing her wedding dress, act as her hairdresser and apply the henna to her hands and feet before the big day, as was customary in their country.

Yasmin was so immersed in sorting out her suitcases and deep in thoughts that she jumped when she heard her mobile phone ring in the depth of her handbag.

"Hey, how is the beautiful bride, what are you up to? Finished packing?" She heard Naila's familiar voice when she answered.

"Oh, nearly, yes. I'm just about to decide if I have more clothes to get rid of. My suitcase is already bulging," She laughed.

"Don't worry, just tell Tahiri to build an extension to his house, and then you'll be fine!"

"He might have to just do that," Yasmin smiled. Naila was always thinking of practicalities.

"Listen, why I'm calling. I just wanted to ask you what time I shall pick you up tonight. What time did you arrange with the estate agent to drop off your keys?" Naila asked.

"He is coming at 6 pm, so any time after that will be fine. Don't rush back from work, Naila, I can wait," Yasmin said.

"No worries, 6 pm is fine with me, I'll see you then. Sorry, got to rush. I have a meeting to attend," she said and rang off.

Three days later, Yasmin was sitting again on a plane at London Heathrow airport bound for Marrakesh. This time it was her last. It was early afternoon but the sky was grey. Rain was beating against the little window and she was looking forward to stepping into the sun on her arrival in Morocco. Despite the rainy weather, she felt tearful when she watched the rolling hills of England slowly disappear underneath when the plane took off, and when she saw the river Thames for the last time.

Naila had dropped her off at the airport and she missed her already. *Well, I'm going to have a new exciting life on another continent again*, Yasmin thought, *but I will for sure miss my friends sorely*. Soon after she fell asleep, exhausted from her last stressful days in London, and only woke up when the flight attendants were bringing the lunch and drinks.

Meanwhile, Tahiri was impatiently standing at the airport in Marrakesh looking at the arrival board. It told him that Yasmin's plane arriving from London was on time. His heart felt at peace because he knew that this time his fiancée would stay for good and they had a life and future together. He sat down on a nearby chair and his thoughts travelled back to a few months ago when he met her and decided to take his chance with her. He knew he had made the right decision.

An announcement over the loudspeaker brought Tahiri back to the present. He checked the arrival board again and it told him that Yasmin's flight had just landed. He also had another surprise in store for Yasmin that she didn't expect. He was not waiting alone. Next to him sat his nephew Şenay, busy with checking and answering his work emails on his iPhone. When the announcement came, he also looked up, nodded to his uncle and together they made their way to the arrival gate to greet his mother.

When Yasmin stepped out into the arrival hall, pushing her heavy trolley with two huge suitcases on it in front of her, she broke into a wide, surprised smile when she saw Şenay standing next to her fiancé.

"Wow, what an extraordinary reception!" she exclaimed and stopped the trolley.

Smiling, Şenay stepped forward and embraced her first. "Merhaba, Yasmin, I mean mum, welcome back! I hope you had a good flight?"

"Yes, it was perfect and no turbulence. It's so good to see you both," she said emotionally and hugged her son tightly, then Tahiri. She felt so safe in his arms and in an instant, her old life and sufferings from the past left her like a snake shedding off her old skin, transforming her into a newborn person.

When they were travelling to her new home in Tahiri's car, weaving through the busy afternoon traffic of the city, she looked over at Şenay and her heart melted with love. He had indeed turned into a beautiful and handsome young man. When she saw Amel and Kareem next, she would especially thank them for their kindness and for raising him for her. They had done a very good job. She was happy and thankful that she had found him, her only child, the boy who she had thought was lost so many years ago.

She was also aware now that she had been guided to Morocco by some special force, and why she had experienced this sense of familiarity and belonging of this place every time she entered this country. It was her destiny. She had been guided by God, through some incredible coincidences, so that she could be reunited with her son. He was the spitting image of his father, apart from his eyes which were as deep green as hers, giving away their Italian heritage. He was also a little taller.

I'll have to tell him more about Metin, his father, she thought. *He has a right to know who he was and that he was a good, caring man, who had truly loved me, and I know he would have loved Şenay dearly, too.*

During her last visit in April, when she had learnt the truth about her son and his adoption, and Tahiri had learnt her own story about Metin and the events in Turkey at that time, they had made arrangements for her to meet Şenay at his parent's house over a family dinner. It was the first time that Yasmin would also be introduced to Amel and gets to know Kareem properly as she had only briefly met him at his restaurant.

When she had entered their pleasant house, also painted in the same reddish colour as the rest of the buildings in the city, and only a short distance away from her fiancé's place, she was astonished how similar it looked to Tahiri's house. It was a beautiful building with a large front terrace where she noticed many plants in terracotta pots placed along the walls and a table with several chairs stood in the middle of it. The veranda was lit with a warm amber glow from several Moroccan lanterns hanging on the beams. Soft Moroccan music played from the speakers next to the entrance door. Yasmin recognised the singer. There was also a settee, decorated with the familiar dark-coloured cushions, standing against one wall underneath a canopy. The entrance door to Kareem's house was located next to the canopy.

The table was decorated with traditional Moroccan plates and bowls which were generously filled with oranges and dates. A colourful tablecloth lay on the table. A vase was placed in the middle of the table, as well as a large jug of water with ice and two jugs with orange juice. It looked very inviting.

She felt immediately at home with her in-laws-to-be and their lovely house. So, this was where her son had grown up and had lived for the past 20 years. It was a place full of love, tranquil and beautiful.

She was still standing next to the entrance, taking in the beautiful sight when a young man stepped out, who she instantly recognised from two days before at the restaurant. She knew now that this handsome young person was her baby, her son Şenay. Her heart instantly filled with unconditional love for him. A shy smile appeared on her face and her eyes lit up.

Şenay – A Reunion April 2013

When Şenay came out of the house and stepped onto the terrace, he found himself looking straight at Yasmin. She noticed that he was only slightly taller than her. Their eyes met and recognition passed between them in an instant.

"Merhaba, erm, Yasmin, I'm Şenay. I'm very pleased to meet you," Şenay said kindly, looking for the first time properly at this woman, who was apparently his birth mother and at once was completely mesmerized by her. He had not expected this. It was quite emotional for him. There was no way you could not like Yasmin, he knew that now. What a beautiful woman she was. He noticed that her eye colour was the same as his.

"Merhaba, Şenay, I'm very pleased to make your acquaintance too," Yasmin responded kindly, not quite knowing how to react. Should she embrace him? Kiss him on his cheek? Was that acceptable here? He was a grown man and she didn't want to embarrass him. She looked at him and smiled. She need not have worried. He came over to her and embraced her tightly.

"You are my birth mother," he said emotionally, his eyes wet, he couldn't help it.

"Yes, I am. And I'm so very blessed to have this great opportunity to finally meet you," Yasmin said, also having tears in her eyes.

Tahiri, Amel and Kareem had come out as well and joined them. They all looked at each other, smiled and nodded. The meeting had gone well so far. It was Tahiri who spoke.

"Şenay, we would like to give you a bit of time with Yasmin to get to know her, if you don't mind. I'm sure you will have plenty of things to talk about and learn about each other. Please sit down and we'll bring out some tea and dates for you. Don't worry about the time, okay. We will have our meal afterwards."

"Thank you, mon amour," Yasmin said, looking at Tahiri with shining eyes, "yes, Şenay and I have a lot to talk about and I'm sure he has many questions for me too."

As Tahiri, Amel and Kareem quietly went back into the house, Yasmin and Şenay went over to the settee and sat down next to each other. Yasmin placed her hands into her lap and studied her son, for a moment, unable to speak because her emotions were in turmoil. She let the moment linger and finally picked up her courage. Şenay studied the expression on her face and felt nothing but deep love for her.

"There is so much I want to tell you, Şenay. I don't even know where to start!" She laughed, still feeling a little clumsy.

"And I'm sure you must have thousands of questions too. The whole thing must have come as much as a shock to you as to me," she added.

Şenay, feeling a little awkward himself, now that he had finally met his mother, composed himself and tried to help Yasmin.

"Yes, you could say that. Well, actually, I do have loads of questions myself, yes. First of all, if I may ask, there is one thing I was wondering about. I know now obviously that you are my mother but please tell me, who was my father?"

"Oh, my goodness, that's a very appropriate question. I can't believe that I've almost forgotten about the most important fact. I've just been so overwhelmed about the recent events, you know," Yasmin replied.

They both laughed heartily and the ice had broken. As they sat comfortably next to each other, Yasmin asked Şenay if he wanted her to continue speaking in English or if he preferred French.

"English is fine if you don't mind because it gives me more practice," he replied.

"Lovely, English it is then. Your English is brilliant, by the way. I'm very impressed actually. Right, okay. First, let me begin with a tale of a great love. It all starts with a love called Metin, a kind young Turkish man of 26 years of age, and a young woman, just out of university. They meet on a cruise ship leaving Southampton in the UK for their work in the summer of 1991…"

Şenay's eyes opened wide when his mother revealed the story to him right from the start when she and Metin had met, followed by her life in Turkey through to the tragic death of his father, the nightmare around Şenay's birth and how she was told her baby had died.

"And that's why I eventually left the country and returned to the UK. There was no point in staying in Turkey and being reminded of all the horrible events there. I just had to get on with my life and besides, it was work that kept me sane," she ended.

Şenay had sat very still, stunned and totally immersed in this almost unbelievable story that his mother recounted to him.

"Oh, by Allah, Yasmin, I mean mum, how absolutely horrible! What happened there was a crime. I was kidnapped. I had no idea, well, how could I anyway. I'm so sorry I could have ever doubted that you loved me or be angry because I thought that you had rejected me."

"You could not have known, Şenay, it's impossible. They told me that my baby had died. Imagine! That night, when you were born, they took you away from me right away, I mean straight after I had given birth, then moved me to another ward so that I would not recall I had given birth in the first place. But I knew! Because I subconsciously heard my baby cry, I was so sure, also, of course, because of the stitches from the caesarean. You know, the worst thing that a mother could be told is that her baby had been stillborn."

Şenay saw the sadness in her eyes and on an impulse hugged her tightly. He felt such compassion for his birth mother. He could not even imagine what she must have gone through. It had been true, he realised now, when his father Kareem had reasoned with him that they didn't know what happened, why he was given up for adoption and he even provided the suggestion that her child might have been taken away unwillingly. And now he learnt that his mother indeed didn't even know! He told her what his parents had discussed with him.

Şenay shook his head and looked at his mother. "You know, this was such a mystery to me. My parents were told at the adoption agency that you had died, that they had no information on record at all about my father and you were told that it was me who had died! Unbelievable! This is worse than any soap opera!"

"Yes, it is. And so, I missed out on holding my baby in my arms, bringing him up, watching him take his first steps, saying his first words, meeting his friends. But you see, deep in my heart, I have always known that you had not died. That it was all a lie. Because I had heard you cry that night. But of course, nobody believed me and they thought I had gone mad. And there was no way I could have found you or could have found out what happened to you."

"I believe you. You know, it's weird but somehow, I have also felt deep in my heart, even if I didn't admit it, that you were somewhere out there. Have you got any idea who might have been behind this?" Şenay asked, feeling very emotional.

"Well, when I think about it, I might have a theory, yes. You know Metin, your father who was killed, his parents didn't like me. In fact, they were absolutely horrible to me, even hostile. I only met them once. They wanted him to marry someone else. One of those arranged marriage things, you know. And I strongly believe that it was his father, who was behind the abduction. Perhaps even with his uncle, this policeman Bekim, I don't know. There is no other explanation. It is even the theory Tahiri came up with when I told him. What I don't know is that how they arranged it. That's still a mystery, unfortunately."

Şenay nodded, understanding now as all the events unfolded. "From what you have told me, it seems like it. But mother, the main thing is that we have found each other and now we can have a life together. I think it's such an amazing quirk of fate what has brought you here to Morocco and that you have found Tahiri too."

"Oh yes, it is. And through him, I've found my life, my son, a new future, and I finally got justice. And for Metin too. And most importantly, I know I'm not mad." She laughed.

"No, you're certainly not mad. You are so beautiful too. And it seems my father was a nice man. It's so sad I could never meet him," Şenay contemplated.

"If it helps, I know he would have loved you. He was so excited about having a child. You are the spitting image of him. He was only a few years older than you are now when we met. You know, he was only a year younger than Tahiri and a year older than Kareem."

Şenay nodded. "I believe he would have loved me, yes. Perhaps you can show me some photos sometime, if you have any. Thank you so much for telling me all this. The mystery is finally solved and all the pieces of the puzzle have come together. It's always difficult when you don't know the whole story. You make all sorts of assumptions."

"I understand. It's only natural. And thank you also for listening to me, Şenay and for accepting me. I could not be more proud of you. You are beautiful, intelligent, and you will be successful, I have no doubt about it. I cannot thank Kareem and Amel enough for bringing up my son with so much love and giving you such a promising future."

"I love you, mum. My parents, I mean, Kareem and Amel..." Şenay began. "It's okay, love, they are your parents. The only thing that's changed is that you now have two mothers. And three sets of grandparents too," Yasmin laughed.

"Thank you. Well, my parents could not have any children and that's why they looked at an adoption. But sometimes, and I have never told anyone this, not even my parents, I used to have nightmares. It was mainly when I was younger. I dreamt I was abducted and screamed but couldn't do anything about it. That's so strange, isn't it?" he revealed.

"My goodness, yes," Yasmin said, shocked by what he had just told her, "you know, it's psychological, meaning that many things that happened to us in early childhood that we have no control over but it's being revealed in dreams. Do you still have those nightmares?"

"Not anymore, no. And that's the most bizarre thing. The dreams stopped when I was about 16-years-old. You see, I vaguely recall an encounter many years ago," he paused and looked at his mother.

Yasmin's heart nearly stopped and she paled. In an instant, she knew what he was about to tell her. "And what was this encounter?" she whispered.

"It was actually at my father's restaurant. I think I must have been 15 years old then and I was already helping him out during my school holidays, so it must have been perhaps December. There was this beautiful lady, who had come into the restaurant and she was with a friend, an Indian lady. I served her together with my father's cousin, and when she looked at me, well, stared at me, she almost dropped her tea cup and spilt some of her tea. It was as if she had seen a ghost. I thought it was rather strange at the time but then her friend called her Yasmin…" Şenay finished.

Yasmin finished the sentence for him, "And the name sounded somehow familiar to you? But why?"

Şenay nodded. "First it was that the woman seemed somehow familiar to me, although I had never met her. But later, I recalled my birth certificate and that my mother's name listed on it was Yasmin. And then, there were her eyes. She had the same intense dark green eyes as I have. But I couldn't understand what happened because I have never come across anything like this. But soon I forgot about it until you turned up again."

"I know. And it was indeed me. That's so extraordinary. You see, I had the same feeling at the time. You were right. I was in December 2008, and the lady I came on holiday with is my friend Naila, who you will meet at the wedding. She knows my whole story and all about you too. You were the spitting image of my Metin. Actually, you still are. That's why I could not believe what I saw. I couldn't make the connection; it just wasn't possible, for obvious reasons. This is Morocco, not Turkey, so what would my son do in this country? This is beside the fact that he was supposed to have died. Also, you were quite tall for your age and I assumed you were at least 16, perhaps 17-years-old. My son would have been 15 in that year. I just thought at the time it was a strange coincidence," Yasmin explained.

Şenay and Yasmin were still in deep conversation and looked up in surprise when suddenly they found Tahiri standing in front of them. Yasmin's face was lit up and her skin was glowing. He had never seen her more beautiful and, in an instant, he knew that their meeting had been successful. He smiled at the pair.

"Hello, you two. I see you have done some bonding and I'm so very happy for you. Are you ready for dinner now? It's all prepared," Tahiri asked.

It was beginning to get dark and they hadn't even noticed. A bright silver moon began to rise in the darkening Moroccan sky and cast its light over the city. It was almost like a sign from heaven, just like that night many years ago when Şenay was born. She felt calm in her heart and knew she had finally come home.

"Come Şenay, my son. Look at the moon. How bright and happy it looks, illuminating the sky, like your name suggests, 'Happy Moon'. Isn't it nice?"

With these words, Yasmin took her son's hand into hers and stretched out the other hand to her fiancé. They both stood up and smiled at each other, mother and son, so alike and reunited at last. Kareem and Amel came out onto the terrace now as well, each carrying a couple of steaming dishes smelling incredibly inviting.

"Yes, we are ready for dinner now. We do have something to celebrate, don't we, Şenay? There are no more secrets in our lives and the shadows of the past have gone. Everything is all right now. What a lovely family we are! We can only be thankful for this beautiful blessing."

As Yasmin and Tahiri's wedding ceremony was going to take place in just a few days, everything seemed so manic with many last minute tasks to complete.

"First, we are going to have the 'Hammam' day," Ayesha explained to Yasmin, taking her through the itinerary of the following days.

The two women were sitting in Yasmin's bedroom in Tahiri's house, going over all the wedding preparations that had to be organised during the coming days. Yasmin's parents and friends would arrive in three days' time, and they had to be on top of things by then.

"The 'Hammam' day?" Yasmin wondered, looking at Ayesha for an explanation.

"Yes, that's one of the best parts of the wedding preparations, believe me! It's only for the girls and it always takes place on the first day of the celebration. We celebrate for about seven days, you know. We are going to enjoy the whole day in a Hammam and get ourselves pampered. It's divine! It's then followed by other pre-wedding parties, as well as of course, the henna painting," Ayesha filled her in.

"Oh, wonderful, that's amazing. I love the Hammam. I've been many times, you know, here as well as in Turkey. And in Indian weddings, the henna painting is a tradition too. It's such a wonderful idea and I'm so looking forward to it."

"It is, and you know the henna painting of your hands and feet is supposed to bring you luck in the marriage," Ayesha explained further.

Tahiri's daughter Ayesha, being in charge of the preparations of the bride's side of the wedding, was in her element. She was a bright and beautiful young lady now, quite ambitious, and still in her studies in Catering and Tourism. She was working part-time in her uncle Kareem's restaurant in her semester holidays in order to get her work experience. Her aspiration was to open her own restaurant sometime in the future. Yasmin was impressed. It seemed like an incredible touch of fate that they were all in the same line of business.

A week later, the big event finally arrived. The day could not have been more beautiful. Sweltering hot for her friends and parents, who came from colder climates, being nearly 30 degrees C by the early afternoon, the weather was perfect for Yasmin. By the time Yasmin and Tahiri had come back from the mosque where they had gone to sign their wedding contract with Kareem and Amel as their witnesses, their friends and other family members had completed decorating the hotel and the courtyard for the special event. It looked magical, ready to receive the couple later.

Yasmin and Tahiri were back in their house by lunchtime in order to get dressed and ready to make their appearance at the party. In the living room, Tahiri and Kareem went over the final preparations for the catering of the traditional food that was going to be served, while Yasmin was trying to get dressed in her wedding gown.

Her heavy, turquoise and gold coloured wedding gown with glittering beads all over, that she had purchased with Ayesha's advice a week before was an operation of its own to put on, such was the size of it. Ayesha laughed when she saw how much Yasmin struggled to wriggle into it and was trying to guide her on how to step into it properly. Once she had succeeded, her movements were restricted and it was difficult to move around.

"Well, these gowns are not made for you to go on a hike, Yasmin," Ayesha laughed. "You don't have to do much, just sit there and enjoy."

"I agree but I still have to be able to dance somehow in this thing."

"Don't worry, you'll be fine, you won't have to jump up and down. Just take it easy."

Yasmin knew Ayesha was right, and when she looked at herself in the long mirror, she admitted that she looked rather smashing. She saw how much the turquoise of the dress was enhancing the colour of her green eyes and her black hair. *I could almost pass as an Arabian queen*, she thought to herself when she turned around a few times to check if it all sat properly on her body. She then sat down at the small dressing table and applied her lipstick and checked her make-up while Ayesha busied herself with pinning up her long dark hair in the traditional fashion so that she could finish her hairstyle for the train to be attached to the hairpiece.

Meanwhile, their bedroom was beginning to look like a beehive with her friends and her other bridesmaids, Naila and Carol, zooming in and out of it, bumping into each other, laughing and excited about all the buzz of the event. The house seemed like Clapham Junction. Just as Yasmin and Ayesha had finished applying their make-up, and were ready to leave the room, the door burst open and Şenay stepped in. Seeing his mother standing in the room already in her full attire, he looked stunned.

"Wow, mum! You look absolutely amazing! The true Moroccan queen! Your wedding gown looks perfect on you," he exclaimed, mesmerized by the sight of his beautiful mother.

"Thank you, my love, for the compliment. I do feel happy and rather special," She smiled.

"And you deserve it!"

"She actually looks much more like our cousin rather than your mother, doesn't she?" Ayesha observed.

"Oh, thank you so much but I'm a little too old to be your cousin," Yasmin laughed.

"Well, Yasmin, you certainly don't look old enough to have a 20-year-old son. You're a true inspiration to all of us!" Ayesha exclaimed and kissed her fondly on the cheek.

"I feel so very blessed that you came into our life," she added, "you will make dad very happy and you're good for him. He suffered a lot, you know after our mother died, and also before when she became ill. She couldn't do much anymore because of the cancer."

"It's so sad, love, I know, and hopefully she has found a nice place in Jannah, in paradise, where she is happy and where she can watch over you and see how well you have turned out. She wants you to be successful and from what I can see so far, she has done a pretty amazing job with both you and Tariq," Yasmin commented emotionally.

"Thank you, Yasmin, you're such a good soul," Ayesha whispered, fighting back her tears.

"Okay, mum, let's go, everything is ready now. We don't want to be late," announced Şenay and took his mother by his arm, leading her out of the house into the car that was waiting outside to take them to the hotel for the party.

He was proud to have been asked to give his mother away to his uncle and his grandfather and his parents had agreed to it, and in fact, encouraged him, he realised that he was in the lucky position to have not only one mother but two, as well as three sets of grandparents. When his mother had introduced his Italian grandparents to him after their arrival, he had felt as if he had known them all his life and he knew the feeling was mutual.

Later in the afternoon, Şenay carefully and full of pride, led his mother through the archway into the courtyard of his uncle's hotel, underneath the colourful garlands of flowers and decorations through to the dining hall and towards her husband Tahiri, who was waiting for her. Smiling and proud of his gorgeous mother, Şenay passed her over to him.

When Yasmin had stepped into the hall and saw how many guests were waiting, she was almost reduced to tears. Never would she have expected such a reception. She slowly took her husband's arm and walked over to their seats with him, her skin glowing, eyes bright and shining and full of love, and her three bridesmaids following behind her. She noticed Albert, who was busy capturing every movement they made with his camera, and they both nodded and smiled.

She looked up into Tahiri's kind face. This lovely, passionate man, who had captured her heart and always touched her so gently, whispering many loving words into her ear during their love-making, was now her husband.

"Hello, mon amour, my gorgeous bride," he said, his voice full of love.

This was truly the most beautiful day in her life and the beginning of a new chapter for them. A new life, that included her long-lost son Şenay as well as her parents, who had agreed to live in Morocco for two months every year to spend time with their grandson and their newly found Moroccan family. Yasmin had been truly blessed and she felt she had already entered paradise. Her parents, standing next to Tahiri, blended into this culture very well. They could not be happier to see their daughter finally happy and glowing again like the woman she had been long ago. "Good luck," they whispered to her.

Everybody started clapping for them, the food was brought out, and the music began to play. The wedding party began and was soon in full swing and with it, a new and bright future.

Epilogue
Marrakesh, 6 Months Later

Yasmin was standing in the kitchen preparing her breakfast before going to work. Her husband Tahiri had already gone out and she still had another hour and a half to spare until she was due at her work. She was in the process of making her coffee when she heard footsteps coming up the small path to the entrance door. Then the doorbell rang.

"Who might that be? A visitor perhaps, this early?" she wondered, wiped her hands on the tea towel and went to the door to answer it.

It was not a visitor but the postman who she found standing at the entrance and with a friendly greeting, "Bonjour Madame", he placed a letter into her hand, then left with a smile and said, "Have a lovely day, Madame."

She returned the greeting and closed the door behind him. *Not many people write letters these days*, she thought, *why didn't they just send me an email?* She was even more curious now, looked at the envelope to find out a clue where the letter came from and took it back into the kitchen.

The postmark told her that it came from Izmir, Turkey. Instantly, a smile crossed her face and at once she knew who the sender was.

Through all those years since she left Turkey, Yasmin had always kept in touch with Esma, Metin's kind aunt, who had helped her during her darkest, most difficult time in her life back in 1993, when she tried so hard to help her to find Metin and reunite them. Although, there were large gaps when they had not been communicating due to their busy schedules and it was also the reason why they had never thought of asking each other for their email address. She made a mental note to include her email address in her next letter to Esma. But every so often they wrote to each other by mail and shared their stories and events happening in their lives.

That was the reason why Esma knew that Yasmin now lived in Morocco, had found a new husband and was married again and was also aware of the good news about finding her son, Şenay, so unexpectedly. Even to this day, when Yasmin remembered that fateful night in Manisa all those years ago so very vividly, she shivered just thinking about it.

She grabbed her freshly made coffee, put some sugar in it and sat down at her kitchen table, then tore the letter open. A sheet of paper fell out, a photograph of a young man she did not recognise, and some newspaper cuttings of a Turkish newspaper.

She put them all aside on a pile on the kitchen table and slowly, she started to read, curious what news Esma had to tell her this time.

My very dear Yasmin,

I hope you are doing very well with your new exciting life and your new job in Marrakesh. It's brilliant that you could get a transfer so easily and it saved you from a long period of job hunting. The hotel sounds very fancy. And you have already been promoted to team leader of your team! Well done! I'm so very proud of you. I have always known that you would be successful in your career. You have always been very committed to your work. And so much has happened to you in the past few years. I hope you will be able to start your own business together, your B&B hotel you have mentioned, in the future too. By the way, how is the Arabic language course going?

It sounds that your husband Tahiri is a very kind man from what you have told me and he is looking after you. It's so important that you have someone who truly understands you. I am overjoyed learning about your good relationship with your son Şenay. It's so exciting. He must be so happy to have two mothers in his life!"

Yasmin felt a warm sensation developing in her heart. She had written to Esma shortly before her wedding and had told her about her new life she was going to start with Tahiri and her move to Marrakesh, how happy she was to have found her son and that he had grown into a nice young man, and how lucky he had been to have found such good and kind adoptive parents. She continued to read.

"All is well here in Izmir and pretty much as you remember it. The city is as busy as ever and has grown considerably since you have left, with many new *edifices and shopping centres being built. You'd love it! The place also attracts many tourists which is obviously good for the economy.*

My husband is fine also and is sending his love too. Imagine, he has now published his first book! Yes, dear, it has finally happened! I'm so very proud of him. He has been working hard to achieve this and deserves the success.

But now, I won't keep you in suspense any longer, here comes the bombshell. You will never guess...! Well, I'm not beating about the bush...

What I want to tell you is that Metin's uncle Bekim has been accused and convicted of murdering Metin in 1993! And that's not all! His father, Hassan, has also been convicted of second-degree murder and conspiring with Bekim to shoot his son if he tried to escape that night! They are now both in prison for life. His mother has not been convicted because they could not find any evidence against her but at least, the two worst culprits have been put away for good! Can you believe it? After all these years!

You would never guess either who it was to have brought them to justice. It was Metin's cousin, Şenol. He is the one, maybe you remember hearing about him or Metin might have told you, who worked at the time at Metin's father's restaurant and he had always been close to Metin. The two of them were the same age group, him being two years older than Metin.

He had been aware that Metin was back in Manisa at the time, although not the full circumstances about why he had returned when he had not seen him for a long time and had been told lies about where he had gone. However, he had found it highly suspicious and finally took matters into his own hands. All by himself, with the help of a Private Investigator, he had started making enquiries about the events evolving around Metin's disappearance and after a long time, he was finally successful in finding out what had happened.

In the newspaper cuttings, I have enclosed, you can read about the conviction (Although it's in Turkish, I'm sure you can figure out what it says at least you get the gist). The picture I have enclosed is of Metin's cousin, as I believe you have never met him in person. He is a nice and honest young man and was a good friend to Metin, as well as his cousin. He was the only one from that family Metin had actually stayed in contact and I also heard from him from time to time. Needless to say, Şenol has now also left Manisa and works in Istanbul.

When the police had interrogated Metin's father, they had also asked him what he knew about your baby. Şenol had known from his cousin that you were expecting and he knew you must have given birth around the same time when

Metin disappeared. So, obviously, he was curious about what had happened to the baby.

And here comes the other bombshell; during the police questioning, Metin's father also confessed that he had bribed his cousin, who worked at Izmir hospital and was the midwife who had delivered your baby, into kidnapping your son and putting him up for adoption. This is how Şenay ended up with that adoption agency and at the orphanage!

So, you see, Yasmin, you were right all along! Your baby WAS alive, not stillborn as they had told you, and you DID hear him cry after you had given birth. To be honest, I have always believed you. And you know why? Because a mother KNOWS, deep in her heart, she KNOWS. Also, you had been unaware of the evil that had been done to you and you would not have been able to prevent the abduction.

So, you see, Yasmin, we have finally got justice for Metin. I am sure you are just like me, very relieved to hear this good news and that Metin can now rest in peace. It took a very long time to get justice for your loving husband and it will also help Şenay to learn more about his father and how much he would have loved him, as well as the circumstances around his adoption. Be gentle with him when you tell him the truth but he is a young man now himself, and I'm sure he will understand and deal with this knowledge in an adult way. Please let me know more about your new life in Morocco and how you are getting on, and I hope that your own business will materialise at some point. You have come very far in life, and you will succeed with this as well, I have no doubt in my mind.

With all my love and happiness for your future. Give my big hugs and regards to Tahiri and of course to Şenay!

Truly yours, Esma."

Yasmin dropped the letter into her lap. Her tears were now falling freely. *Finally, justice*, she thought, *thank you, Allah*. My beloved husband, my love Metin has indeed found peace in heaven and justice has finally been done for the horrible actions of your parents and your uncle. She felt an overwhelming sense of relief and thankful to Şenol for finding out the truth. She couldn't wait to tell Şenay.

Oh, if I could only tell Metin, she thought, *that our son he had never known is alive and well, and always has been. That Şenay has been living in Morocco all those years, was raised by a lovely couple and has grown into a handsome, kind young man. Just like you were, Metin. Or maybe you have already known this, and it was you who has guided me to this place and this country to find Şenay, just as you have guided his adoptive parents to Turkey to find him.*

She sat by the window for a long time, lost in deep thoughts, her coffee and breakfast getting cold, almost forgotten. The deep blue Moroccan sky that greeted her through the kitchen window soothed her mind. She said a silent prayer for her great first love and hoped Metin had been given a special and beautiful place in paradise. He truly deserved it. She was convinced that he would always protect her and their son Şenay from his place in heaven.

Glossary
Expressions from Turkey and Morocco

Turkey

Merhaba:	greeting "hello" in Turkish
Güvercinada:	Pigeon Island, which gives Kusadasi its name
Simit:	round bread, similar to a bagel
Kahve:	Turkish coffee (very strong, brewed with lots of sugar)
Seni seviyorum	I love you in Turkish language
Sokak:	the word for street in Turkish language
Baba:	the word for father in the Turkish language
Anne:	the word for mother in the Turkish language
Günaydin:	the word for good morning in the Turkish language
Bazaar:	Markets in the Middle East
Cami:	the word for mosque in the Turkish language
Zeytin:	the word for olive in the Turkish language
Locum:	Turkish Delight
Dolmats:	stuffed rice wrapped in vine leaves
Elma cay:	Apple Tea (a Turkish speciality)
Güzel:	the word for beautiful in Turkish language
Gül:	the word for to laugh as well as the word for rose in the Turkish language, as well as it is a female name
Sevgilim:	my darling

Morocco

Ummee:	"My mother" in the Arabic language
Abee:	"My father" in the Arabic language
Hijab	Headscarf that Muslim women wear
Tagine	a Moroccan speciality, usually made with chicken or lamb

Couscous	a Moroccan speciality
Medina/Kasbah:	Old town, in the Middle East
Masjid:	the word for mosque in the Arabic language
Adhan:	the call for prayer in Islamic countries
Atlas:	Mountain range in Morocco
Té de mente:	Mint tea with fresh mint leaves
Kareem:	generous, honourable, but also a name
Tanoura:	Dance of the whirling dervishes, originated in Egypt in the 13th century

Information

While this novel is mainly a work of fiction, it has elements of my own real-life experiences and travel adventures from Turkey and Morocco. All the places mentioned in the novel, historical buildings, towns and countries exist.

Kusadasi is a small town on the west coast of Turkey and approx. a 1 ½ hour drive south of the port city of Izmir. It is very popular with tourist and many cruise ships touring the Mediterranean Sea dock there. The Grand Hotel Ephesus in Kusadasi does not exist, and back in 1991, there were very few big hotels in the town. Also, the shops in the Bazaars were still small at the time and many have expanded since. The Kaleici Cami (Kaleici Mosque) does exist, as well as the Bahar Street (Bahar Sokak) where the author herself used to live during her time of working in Kusadasi.

Ephesus was an ancient Greek city, built in the 10th century BC, located three kilometres southwest of present-day Selçuk in the İzmir Province. It is a favourite tourist attraction and can easily be reached from the cruise ship ports of Kusadasi or Izmir.

The town of Manisa in Turkey, only a 2-hour drive inland from the international port city of Izmir, was a small town of approx. 170,000 inhabitants in 1991. It has grown to a large city with a population of nearly 1.5 million in the year 2020, and it is now a booming centre of industry and services in the area.

The city of Fez in north-eastern Morocco, the second-largest city in the country, has indeed the largest Medina in the world. The old walled city extends to 8 km and has a population of over 200,000 inhabitants. The backdrop of the city is the impressive Atlas Mountain range. Fez is also home to the oldest, still operating university in the world. It is called the University of Al-Qarawiyyin and was founded in the year 859 AD. What is remarkable about it is that it was founded by a Muslim woman (Fathima Al-Fihri).

Marrakesh, the fourth largest city in Morocco, is situated west of the foothills of the Atlas Mountains. In the early 16th century, Marrakesh became the capital of the old kingdom of Morocco. The red walls of the city and various buildings, constructed in red sandstone, have given the city the nickname Red City or Ochre City. The famous square, Jemaa-el- Fnaa, is the busiest square in Africa.

The attractive Koutoubia Mosque in Marrakesh, just off the Jemaa el-Fna Square dates back to the 12th century, and is the largest in Marrakesh. The mosque, as well as the square itself, is a popular tourist spot. The restaurant "Al-Kareem" is the author's invention but it is based on various authentic restaurants located in the Medina of Marrakesh. The Botanical Garden, Jardin Majorelle with its special cacti section, fountains and ponds, is also a very popular and interesting place to spend time not only for visitors but also for locals.

The Tanoura Dance, also called dance of the whirling dervishes or Sufi whirling, originated in Egypt in the 13th century. It is a folklore dance. Tanoura means colourful skirt. When Tanoura was first practised, it was performed by males as a form of gaining spiritualism and closeness to God by the Sufis.

Güvercinada – Pigeon Island Kusadasi, Turkey

Moroccan Countryside

Koutoubia Mosque, Marrakesh, Morocco